THE SHOFAR
And
The BOOK OF ENOCH

A Time Travel novel

By Joshua Kreithen MD

First paperback edition published 2020

ISBN: 978-0-578-76525-9 (Shofar & the Echoes of Time, The)

To Missy,
Skylar,
Ginger,
Madison
and Gavin

THE SHOFAR
AND
THE BOOK OF ENOCH

THE SHOFAR CHRONICLES
BOOK 2

CONTENTS

CHAPTER 1

THE KING'S FAREWELL

An old man is lying in a bed. It's not just an ordinary bed... it's the most ornately carved and elaborate wooden canopy bed you could ever imagine. His back is propped up with several pillows beautifully embroidered with a gold and silver decorative pattern. An immense, and lush purple velvet blanket covers his lower body and the rest of the massive bed. He is wearing fancy royal blue silk pajamas. The surrounding room is very dark.

Yeshua looks from his bed. Although his vision is poor, he sees many shadowy figures slowly moving towards him from the periphery of the room. He glances down at his hands. They are the hands of a frail elderly man, wrinkled and decrepit. His hands slowly move upwards and he strokes his long, white beard. He tries to take a deep breath, however he cannot. His breaths are shallow and labored. He feels as though he is slowly being suffocated.

Yeshua has an epiphany. This must be his deathbed. This is the end. He doesn't have many breaths left.

From the shadows, the royal court gathers closely around the edges of the lavish bed. They await the death of the King. They have been waiting a very long time. Some have an expression of empathy and love towards the old man. Others have the look of contempt and malice. Some are crying. Others are smiling.

Yeshua looks at the gathering. He sees his beautiful queen closest to him. She smiles, then she reaches out and gently holds his hand. Next to her are many of the princes, knights, princesses, jesters and aristocratic fools of his Kingdom. They have all come to watch him die. Now is the end of his long reign.

Although he recognizes almost everyone's face in the room, he can't seem to remember anyone's names. In fact, he doesn't even remember anything about his monarchy. He cannot remember the past. There are virtually no memories he can recall from days gone by. He can only focus on the present moment. That's all there is... the present moment.

He looks into the eyes of those surrounding him. He feels as though he can read their thoughts. They are all considering the same basic thought. They are all thinking to themselves "Who will be the next King?"

In his mind, Yeshua ponders everyone's question with his last few breaths. Who will be the next King? Who will be his heir?

"My son of course, he will be the King," thought Yeshua. He was drawing his last breath. He could feel his life slipping into the darkness as he glanced around the room looking for his son. Disappointedly, he didn't see anyone he recognized as his male descendant.

Then he remembered. He never had a son. He had no male offspring.

He whispered his last words as he closed his eyes for the last time.

"But I never had a son..."

Yeshua realized that in absence of a true heir... his Kingdom would fall into complete anarchy and chaos as all the rival royals would take up arms against each other and try to claim the throne for themself.

"But I never had a son…"

He took his final last breath. The room faded, the light faded, the pain faded, everything faded.

"But I never had a son…"

All blackness. Nothing. Then the gentle sounds of the ocean were audible in the distance.

"Yeshua. Wake up! What are you talking about?" said Mohammed.

"Huh? What?" said Yeshua as he opened his eyes. He was on a lounge chair on a sand beach overlooking a beautiful ocean with arid mountains in the distance. Behind them was the pool area of a luxurious resort hotel. Mohammed reclined in his bathing suit on the lounge chair next to him. The blazing hot sun started to set in the west.

"What the heck are you talking about? You never had a son?" asked Mohammed. "What were you possibly dreaming about my friend?"

"I never had a son, Mohammed," explained Yeshua. "In my dream, I was the King in some kind of medieval time. I was very old and on my deathbed and realized I never had a son to be my heir. Then I died."

"You died in your dream?" asked Mohammed.

"Yeah. I think so," said Yeshua.

"Dude. You are not supposed to die in your dreams. You really have some messed up dreams my friend," stated Mohammed. "We are supposed to relax here in Eilat. Our orders were to get some R&R here in this beautiful resort on the Gulf of Aqaba, and definitely not take your last breaths and kick the bucket. So what else did you dream about during your nap? You were out for about two hours."

"I remember a bit of two other dreams during my nap," explained Yeshua. "The first one, I was like a caveman on a beach. It seemed like the stone age as I was fishing with spears and wore some kind of furry animal skin as my clothes."

"Hmmm. Maybe these are past life dreams you were having," suggested Mohammed. "Very interesting. Tell me more."

"Okay Dr. Freud," joked Yeshua. "So, I remember there were really tall cliffs along the beach, as far as the eye could see. Down the beach I could see a few cloth tents and other cavemen looking people. There were people cooking fish on some campfires. I had caught some fish and started walking towards the camp."

"And then what?" asked Mohammed.

"Well, that's about it for that part of the dream," said Yeshua. "I think that all the other people on the beach were my family or clan. It seemed like such a simple life. All we basically needed were fish to survive."

"What happened after that?" asked Mohammed. "You said there was a second dream."

"Yeah. I think so. I can barely remember. Something about some boats," said Yeshua.

"Boats? Really? Try to remember," asked Mohammed.

"Ahhhh. I wish I could. It was there in my memory for like a second when I woke up and now it's gone. I hate when that happens."

"Hate is such a strong word. You should remove that from your vocabulary," declared Mohammed. "Okay. Here's the plan… we are going to try a past life regression. That might work."

"Past life regression? What the heck is that?" asked Yeshua.

"In the library of the orphanage in Beersheba I found a book called 'Many Lives Many Masters' written by Dr. Brian Weiss," explained Mohammed. "In this remarkable book, Dr. Weiss uses hypnosis to have his patients describe their past lives in uncanny detail. It's all about re-incarnation."

"So… you want me to try hypnosis so I can remember my dream which may have been a re-incarnation memory?" asked Yeshua.

"Yes. Exactly," said Mohammed as he smiled.

"Cool. How do we do it?" questioned Yeshua.

"Close your eyes and relax," instructed Mohammed. "Take some deep breaths and let your mind wander."

Yeshua closed his eyes and slowly took some deep breaths. He relaxed and calmed his mind. He could still hear the rhythmic and calming sounds of the waves coming onto the sandy shore. He could feel a gentle warm breeze on his face coming from the east.

Mohammed's voice faded and became more distant. Time seemed to slow down.

"What do you see?" whispered Mohammed.

"I'm on the beach. The same beach as the cavemen. The tall cliffs are all along the edge and go far into the distance," described Yeshua.

"Are the cavemen there? What else do you see?" asked Mohammed.

"No. The cavemen are gone," said Yeshua. "There are hundreds of huge wooden boats off the shore. And there's thousands of men swimming in the water and boarding the boats."

"Boats? What kind of boats?" questioned Mohammed.

"They are our boats. We are leaving. It's time to go," said Yeshua.

"Go where? Where are you going?" asked an astounded Mohammed.

"Well hello there gentlemen, drinks?" asked Corporal Miriam Taylor.

Yeshua opened his eyes. Corporal Taylor stood next to his lounge chair. She was tall, blonde and beautiful and she was wearing a turquoise two-piece bikini that didn't leave much up to the imagination. She held two margaritas.

"I'm sorry, was I interrupting something?" asked Taylor.

Yeshua thought Taylor looked like an Angel. The sun setting in the west seemed to make glowing lights dance around her body.

"I'm sorry, yes please I would love a drink," said Yeshua as he sat up on his lounge chair. Taylor handed Yeshua a drink and sat on a lounge chair next to him.

"Mohammed, you?" asked Taylor.

"No thank you, ma'am. I don't drink. That is not my path," explained Mohammed.

"No problem. More for us," said Taylor as she took a sip of the other margarita and one eyed winked at Yeshua. "And by the way, no need to call me ma'am. Taylor is just fine."

Yeshua looked at Taylor's necklace. He always loved looking at the pendant on her necklace. It was two interlocking figures of eight in the shape of a cross. It was like two infinity signs intersecting.

"You boys have come a long way since your Krav Maga training," said Taylor. "I mean seriously, you two are heroes… saving the world and all. I'm glad we are all back together again."

Yeshua wondered why Taylor was there at the resort with them. It had been a month since their spaceflight where they stopped the Israeli satellite from exploding. Was she there to be their bodyguard and protect them?

"I bet you are both wondering why I'm here you," said Taylor. She looked around and made sure no one was close enough to hear their discussion.

"Honestly, someone needed to look after you," said Taylor. "You know, keep you out of trouble. And secondly, I have been waiting to receive our next mission from my contact."

"Our next mission?" asked Mohammed.

"Yes. They have something big planned. We will find out soon," said Taylor. She sipped on her Margarita. "Until then, lets soak up some rays and relax."

Yeshua looked southwards down the blue waters of the Gulf of Aqaba. He remembered coming here to the resort town of Eilat at the southern most tip of Israel during a high school field trip. He had never stayed in a nice beach hotel like this before. It seemed like a dream come true.

"What is south of here, down that way?" asked Yeshua as he pointed towards the waters off the beach. He immediately got that déjà vu feeling like he had been here before.

"This is a very interesting place," responded Taylor. "We are literally at the confluence of four countries. Across the water to the east you can see the mountains of Jordan. About halfway from here north to the Dead Sea in Jordan is the famous site of Petra. Just to the west of us is the Egyptian Sinai. And just to the southeast across the waters is Saudi Arabia."

"Saudi Arabia?" asked Mohammed. "It's that close?"

"Yes. There's so much history here," explained Taylor. "Did you know that just to the south of here in Egypt, there is a place on the coast called Nuweibaa. A few years ago I was visiting there and someone told me that's where Moses and the Israelites crossed the Red Sea. There's even an ancient monument there called the Pillar of Solomon that commemorates the event."

"Wait a sec. Are you saying the Gulf of Aqaba is the Red Sea from the Torah? The Israelites crossed here?" asked a surprised Yeshua. "If that's true, that would mean that Mt. Sinai really is in..."

"Saudi Arabia!" exclaimed Mohammed.

"Well that makes a lot of sense, actually," said Yeshua. "I remember the Moses story in the Torah very well. In the book of Exodus, Moses killed an Egyptian who was beating a Hebrew slave. He then fled from Egypt and went into the land of Midian. Moses spent forty years in exile there. When I looked it up on Google recently, it said that the Midian Mountains are in northwestern Saudi Arabia."

"Okay, so what does that mean?" asked Taylor.

"The Bible story says that Moses was in the land of Midian when he saw the burning bush," explained Yeshua. "In the Torah is it written something like this, I memorized it years ago…

"Moses was tending the flock of sheep of his father-in-law Jethro, the priest of Midian. He drove them into the wilderness and came to Horeb, the Mountain of God. And an Angel of the Lord appeared to him in a blazing fire out of the bush."

"My goodness," said Mohammed. "That means that your Holy Book says the Mountain of God is in…"

"Saudi Arabia… right there, and not the Egyptian Sinai Peninsula," said Yeshua as he pointed with his finger southeast over the Gulf of Aqaba. "Mount Sinai must be in Saudi Arabia."

"Wow. Are you sure, Yeshua?" asked Taylor. "I've been to the Saint Catherine's Monastery in Egypt. That's where they say Mount Sinai is supposed to be."

"You know, my whole life… I've been trying to figure out who 'they' are," said Mohammed smiling. "They say this and they say that. Who the heck are 'they' anyway? I need to know. I have many questions for these 'they' people. Do either of you two know them?"

Taylor and Yeshua laughed at Mohammed's joke. Their serious conversation about the Hebrew Torah seemed to have opened some mystical doors into the past.

"Yeshua, I have a question for you," said Taylor. "When you recited your Torah passage about Moses, you said an Angel of the Lord appeared to him in the fire of the burning bush. I always thought it was God that appeared to Moses in the bush."

"Yes, that's a very good question," said Yeshua. "I've been trying to figure that out too. There's definitely a repeating pattern, just like everything else in life. It seems that most of the time in the Bible, when something 'physical' needs to happen on God's behalf... an Angel is sent to do what needs to be done."

"Oh... I see," said Taylor looking somewhat perplexed.

"Yes. That's exactly what happens," said Mohammed. "God sends Angels to our world from the Angelic Realm with specific directions about whatever task needs to be performed."

"So, there's like an Army of Angels awaiting God's orders? You are saying the Angels are sent here to Earth to do specific missions?" asked Taylor.

"Yes, that is precisely what the Holy Books says," said Mohammed.

"And are their good Angels and bad Angels... like the Angel of Death?" asked Taylor.

"Well, yes and no," said Yeshua. "The Angel of Death was actually called 'The Destroyer' in the Torah. God sent the Destroyer to kill all the first-born Egyptians in retribution for how the Hebrews were treated as slaves for over four hundred years. That's why we call the ritual 'Passover' as the Destroyer passed over the Jewish houses and spared them."

"So the Destroyer is a good Angel? The Angel of Death?" asked Taylor. "The killing the innocent first born sons of the Egyptians was a good thing?"

"That's an interesting point," said Yeshua. "We see this as a horrible thing, killing and destroying in any situation from our perspective. However, there are many other stories of Angels being sent to execute God's judgments in the Bible. Look at the destruction of Sodom and Gomorrah for example."

Yeshua had another one of those intense déjà vu moments. He immediately had some flashback memories from the times he blew the Shofar and being spiritually transported back into biblical history. He recalled the first time at Tel Be'er Sheba when he helped Hagar and Ishmael find water to help them survive in the desert. He recollected the second time was when he and Mohammed helped David defeat Goliath in the Valley of Elah. He then replayed in his mind the last time he blew the Shofar in Jerusalem when they went to bring the ram to Abraham on Mount Moriah to be sacrificed instead of Isaac.

"God sends Angels to help those that need help," said Yeshua. "God also sends Angels to punish those who need to be punished."

Taylor stared at Yeshua. She stood up and wrapped her towel around her tanned body. The sun was setting over the western horizon.

"How do you know this?" asked Taylor. She seemed unsettled. "How can you be so sure?"

"Trust us," said Mohammed. "We have some insider information."

"Mohammed. You are a funny man," said Taylor. "I can never be sure when you are joking and when you are being serious. But, listen up. I'm going to retire for the evening. We are heading up into the Negev Desert tomorrow morning to meet my contact. I will see you both outside the Hotel lobby at 0730. Be prepared for a long hike."

"Yes ma'am!" said Mohammed grinning. "I mean Taylor."

Taylor made a funny face and stuck her tongue out at Mohammed. She then turned around and walked toward the hotel.

"I think she likes me. I think she really, really likes me," said Mohammed with a starry look in his eyes.

"Oh Mohammed. You are such a fool sometimes," replied Yeshua.

CHAPTER 2

JEBEL AL LAWZ

Yeshua walked alone in the barren, hot desert. The bright sun blazed directly above. Hot wind blew strongly from the south and whistled through his wavy, long red hair and beard. Yeshua was so very thirsty and his lips were dry and cracked. He navigated up and down the large sand dunes towards the south. He lost his balance and fell down one of dunes and lay at the bottom of the valley in exhaustion. Above, dozens of vultures circled in the sky.

Yeshua once again had that déjà vu feeling. This had happened before. He knew it. This moment had happened before, perhaps many times.

Yeshua dug deep with all his might. He got on his knees and crawled slowly up the next sand dune to the top of its ridge. He looked to the south. The sky was completely blue and clear (except for the vultures); however far in the distance he could see a huge pillar of clouds billow up into the heavens

"Get up," an inner voice said in his mind. "Get up and fly…"

Yeshua stood up. He placed his two index fingers and thumbs together and made a triangular shape with his hands. He held his hands up into sky and centered his hands so the pillar of clouds was in the center of the triangle that his fingers formed.

Yeshua jumped into the air and leapt off the top of the sand dune, just as a cliff diver would jump fearlessly into the ocean. He lunged his entire body with his arms forward, his hands still together in the triangular pattern.

Instead of falling into the depths of the sand dune valley below, his body defied gravity and he starting flying forward and upwards, towards the south. Yeshua went up, up and away! He could see a range of mountains far in the distance. Even further away... he saw a huge Mountain that was burning intensely on its blackened peak, like a volcano.

From the fire on the Mountain, Yeshua saw the huge pillar of smoke that rose far into the sky. He was flying in the direction of the Mountain and the colossal column of smoke coming from it.

Yeshua spread his arms out to his sides as he seemed to accelerate faster towards the Mountain. He had seen this Mountain before. It was Jebel al Lawz, in northwestern Saudi Arabia. He remembered looking down at it when his diplomatic mission flew over it en route to the conference in the capital city of Riyadh, just a few months earlier. He also had seen it many times in his dreams and visions.

Something caught Yeshua's eye as he flew towards the Mountain. There was something else ahead in the sky also soaring towards the Mountain. He could see something moving; however, it was just out of his range of vision to discern exactly what it was. He tried to fly faster to catch up to the presence.

Suddenly, the sky darkened. Massive black clouds emanated from all around the Mountain and surrounded the peak in a nebulous expanding fog. The figure Yeshua was following seemed to disappear into the amorphous haze.

Dozens of lightning bolts erupted from the supercharged clouds. Yeshua was bewildered and immediately tried to slow himself down, as he was about to fly directly into the bolts of electricity that streaked all across the heavens. A moment later, he felt the intense vibrations of the thunder roll through the sky in waves of roaring reverberations.

BOOM…

BOOM…

BOOM…

The thunder was deafening. Yeshua lost his concentration and he starting falling from the sky. Gravity took over. During his descent downwards, he heard coming from the Mountain…

"YESHUA…"

"YESHUA!"

"WAKE UP!"

Yeshua opened his eyes. He was sleeping in a hotel room. He heard Mohammed pounding at the door.

"Wake up Yeshua! Wake up!" yelled Mohammed as he continued pounding the door.

Yeshua arose from bed. There was a strange noise coming from outside the window of the room. It sounded like rain. As Yeshua opened the door to his dark hotel room a massive bolt of lightning came down from the sky and hit just nearby outside the hotel.

The flash of light illuminated Mohammed's face. Yeshua was shocked to see that Mohammed's eyes were totally black. There was no pupil, iris or white sclera… just black.

The thunderclap from the lightning sounded like an explosion and shook the room vigorously. Yeshua immediately pushed the switch on the wall next to the door and turned on the room light. Mohammed still stood in the doorway. His eyes were thankfully back to normal although he looked terrified.

"Mohammed, please come and sit down," said Yeshua as he motioned with his hand. Mohammed looked like he had just seen a ghost. He walked into the room and sat down on the couch along the wall. Yeshua closed the door.

The sound of the rain became louder outside. There was more lighting and thunder in the distance.

"I thought it didn't rain here in the South Negev," said Yeshua. He was concerned about Mohammed. He looked almost catatonic.

"What's going on with you, Mohammed? You seem way off. And why did you come bursting in here?" asked Yeshua.

"I, I… had a nightmare," replied Mohammed. "I don't usually remember my dreams. But this one I did, after the storm woke me up."

Yeshua looked at the clock by the bed. It said 5:30AM. The heavy storm started to pass to the east as the thunder and lightning slowly abated.

"I thought I was the only one with the bizarre dreams," stated Yeshua. "As a matter of fact, I just had another auspicious dream about flying to Jebel al Lawz."

"Horeb. The Mountain of God. The real Mount Sinai," responded Mohammed. "We must go there."

"Yes. I suppose we do. And what of your dream? What happened to you?" asked Yeshua.

"It was horrible," said Mohammed. He looked like he was about to cry.

"We… I mean you and I, we were somewhere in a large city. I'm not sure which one. We drove up to a small house in a ghetto neighborhood in a broken-down old car. We got out of the car and walked up to the house. In the distance I could see the skyscrapers of the city."

"Was this some kind of past life regression dream?" asked Yeshua.

"I don't think so. In the dream, we were the same as we are now. The same age and all, we looked the same," explained Mohammed. "It felt so real. The dream was so vivid, and I thought it was really happening… it didn't seem like a dream."

"Okay, then what happened? Why was it a nightmare?" asked Yeshua.

"Yeah. Getting there," said Mohammed. "So, we went into the house that was full of people we didn't know. Mostly, younger people. I guess it felt like some kind of house party. Anyhow, we ended up walking downstairs to the basement. It was full of people, but they were all were in some kind of trance."

"Uh oh," said Yeshua. "I think I see where this is going."

"So you and I looked at each other with confused expressions. Like perhaps we were in the wrong place," said Mohammed. "But then, someone in the room took notice of us and looked very angry that we were there. Did you ever see the movie *Invasion of the Body Snatchers?*"

"No. I never saw that one," said Yeshua. "I don't like horror movies at all."

"Well, in that movie... these aliens make clones of real people and then they try to kill the originals. When the alien clones see real humans, they point at them and make a horrible scream," described Mohammed. "Anyhow, in my dream the disturbed dude in the basement started to freak out on us like the aliens in the body snatchers. Then something really messed up happened."

"Oh sheesh. I'm scared now. What happened next?" asked Yeshua.

"So, the disturbed guy in the basement morphed into some kind of demon or devil looking creature. He then starting to run towards us, as if he were going to kill us," said

Mohammed. "Meanwhile, everyone else in the room starting morphing into those grotesque looking monsters."

"What a nightmare!" exclaimed Yeshua. He then recalled a past dream where he had faced some dark Angels coming out of Abraham's well in Beersheba. He wondered if Mohammed's dream about these evil creatures was possibly related.

"Thankfully, we had guns to defend ourselves," proclaimed Mohammed. "We both pulled out our glocks and starting shooting them all. It felt like a zombie apocalypse scene."

"Hmmm. Are you sure we were just defending ourselves or perhaps we were there to kill them?" asked Yeshua.

"That's a good point," said Mohammed. "I didn't think about it that way. Although, maybe we were there to take them out, like spiritual bounty hunters on a mission from Allah."

"I like that," said Yeshua. "Spiritual bounty hunters. So what happened next?"

"We killed a bunch of them, but there were too many," said Mohammed. "We ran up the stairs and they chased us as we reloaded our guns. We then ran out of the house and towards our car. They came out of the house and we shot several more of them, then we got in the car and sped away. My heart was pounding in my chest."

"That wasn't so bad," said Yeshua. "Seems like we won the day against the evil monsters."

"Yeah, but there was one last part of the dream," said Mohammed. "As we were driving away, we saw dozens of massive disk-shaped UFOs in the sky beaming huge lights down into the city. They were invading from outer space. Then I woke up to the lightning and thunder and ran to your room."

"Whoaaaa," said Yeshua. "You know what?"

"What?" asked Mohammed.

"You watch way, way too many science fiction movies," joked Yeshua.

"Shut up!" responded Mohammed as he threw one of the pillows from the couch towards Yeshua.

The rain stopped as the storm passed. The sun was starting to rise in the east over the beautiful Gulf of Aqaba.

"I have a good idea," said Mohammed. "Why don't we go watch the sunrise on the beach, do our morning prayers and meditation, grab some food and be ready for Captain Taylor by 0730."

"Sounds perfect," said Yeshua. "I don't think either one of us will be able to fall back asleep."

CHAPTER 3

THE RED CANYON

Taylor arrived exactly at 7:30AM and drove up to the hotel's main entrance in a grey metallic Land Rover LR3. Yeshua and Mohammed were waiting patiently by the palm trees next to the round stone fountain that was in front of the ornately decorated lobby. Yeshua whispered "shotgun" as the vehicle stopped and he got into the front seat. A perturbed looking Mohammed opened the door to the back passenger compartment and got inside.

"There's been a slight change in plans," said Taylor as she drove out of the hotel complex. "We're meeting my contact in the Red Canyon. There was a flash flood there last night and apparently he and his team have discovered something significant."

"Discovered something?" asked Yeshua. "What does that mean?"

"You'll see," said Taylor. "How did you boys sleep last night? That was some storm. It's very rare for a rainstorm like that to come through here."

"I had a horrible nightmare," said Mohammed. "I was battling evil aliens invading Earth, I think. The lightning and thunder woke me up."

"Invading aliens?" asked Taylor. "Are you sure they weren't the Watchers?"

"The Watchers?" questioned Yeshua. "Who are they?"

"Have you heard of the Book of Enoch?" asked Taylor.

"You mean Enoch from the Old Testament?" said Yeshua. "The one that walked with God? Noah's great-grandfather Enoch?"

"Yes. That Enoch. The one that God 'took' to the Upper Realms as he apparently never died," said Taylor. "So, long story short… not far from here, they found a copy of the Book of Enoch amongst the Dead Sea Scrolls and it almost perfectly matches the ancient Ethiopian texts. In that book, it describes the fallen Angels called the "Watchers," who disobeyed their orders and came down to Earth in physical form and made babies with human women."

"Wait a sec!" said Mohammed. "That's what Yeshua's Bar Mitzvah Torah portion was about when he turned thirteen. Something about giants called Nephilim."

"Exactly," said Taylor. "That's what the Book of Enoch is all about. It describes in detail the two hundred fallen Angels and their lust for beautiful human women. Their main leader Samyaza defied God's orders and many other rebellious ones such as Azazel who taught humans forbidden technology."

"So, I remember that passage in the Book of Genesis very well," said Yeshua…

"The Nephilim were on the Earth in those days, and also afterward, when the Benei Elokim would come to the daughters of man, and they would bear for them. They were the mighty men, who were of old, the men of renown."

"Yes. Very good memory Yeshua," said Taylor. "That's exactly the same story as what's in the Book of Enoch. The Book just goes into more specifics. Once God saw the corruption of the Watchers and their offspring... they were all punished, which also led up to the act of the Great Flood which wiped out just about everything in order to erase all the damage that they caused."

"Wow," said Yeshua. "They must have really angered God."

"Yes," replied Taylor. "The Earth had become corrupt and full of lawlessness due to the rebellion of the Fallen Angels."

"Let me ask you a question, Taylor," said Mohammed. "What happened to the Watchers? Surely the flood didn't destroy them. They were Angels, correct?"

"That's correct," said Taylor. "I believe the Archangel Gabriel caused many of the Watchers to kill each other in a civil war. And then the Archangel Michael bound their leader Samyaza and the rest of the remaining Watchers in some kind of abyss of fire forever."

"Forever is a very long time," said Yeshua.

"So Taylor, are you suggesting that the Fallen Angels were not actually Angels at all but Aliens from outer space?" asked Mohammed.

"I don't know," said Taylor. "But that certainly would make a great movie, don't you think?"

"Indeed it would!" proclaimed Yeshua.

"Ah. Here we are," said Taylor. She turned off the main highway and onto a dirt road. She put the LR3 into four-wheel drive mode.

"This may get a little bumpy," said Taylor. The landscape looked like an otherworldly desert planet, totally devoid of life. They passed a large sign that said 'Closed to the Public' with two Israeli soldiers in full gear standing on either side.

Their LR3 continued past what looked like a parking area and down into a sloped valley. Finally, Taylor stopped the vehicle, and everyone got out.

"I should have brought my Shofar," whispered Yeshua to Mohammed. He nodded back.

"We walk from here," said Taylor as she started briskly walking down into the narrow valley. "It will take about thirty minutes to get there."

"Where is 'there' exactly?" asked Yeshua as he and Mohammed followed Taylor downwards along the gravel path.

"You'll see," replied Taylor. "This place is called the Red Canyon. It's a continuation of the Wadi Shani that originates in the Sinai Egyptian Desert. Due to the rain last night, there was a flash flood here in the deep gorge and we will need to take the upper trail to our destination."

"Wow. I feel like I'm on a different planet," said Mohammed.

"As you can see, over the centuries… the water and wind have done an incredible job sculpting the red sandstone into fantastic shapes and colors," explained Taylor.

After walking a few hundred yards, the landscape changed: the canyon became narrow, and the walls became higher. It looked like a mini Grand Canyon.

"I've never seen anything like this," said Yeshua. "It's absolutely spectacular. Are we going down there?"

"Actually, no. Not down to the bottom," answered Taylor. "We're going to take a side trail to a secret archeological site."

"Ohhh," said Mohammed. "This gets better and better."

"Everything else you see on this trip beyond here is for your eyes only," declared Taylor. "No one else needs to know. We don't want any unauthorized civilians coming here."

"Yes ma'am," Yeshua and Mohammed answered in unison.

Taylor smiled, turned her head and kept walking along the trail. After a few minutes, she turned right along a side trail away from the slot canyon gorge. Yeshua and Mohammed followed. They noticed some small green shrubs growing along the trail.

"I guess some things do live here in the desert," said Yeshua.

"Yes, certain plants have adapted to the dry climate," stated Taylor. "That's evolution. It's not the strongest that survive… it's those most adaptable to change."

"Ahh. Thank you, Professor Darwin," joked Mohammed.

"Very funny Mohammed. Perhaps you were a comedian in a previous lifetime?" responded Taylor as she winked at him. She turned and looked upwards. "Okay. We climb from here."

"Climb where?" asked Yeshua. He didn't see any trail or steps up the rocky cliff nearby.

"Here," said Taylor as she started scaling the sandstone hill next to them. Yeshua and Mohammed followed her slowly and carefully upwards. After a few minutes, they came upon another trail that led them into a secluded valley.

In the center of the valley stood a grove of seven large acacia trees, full of green leaves. A small pool of water from the recent rain was in the center of the grove. The pool of water gave an incredibly mesmerizing inverse reflection of the trees and canyon behind it. Beyond the grove of trees was a shear sandstone cliff, and at the bottom of the cliff was a dark void that looked like an opening of a cave. There were some boxes of supplies and what looked like surveying equipment near the cave opening. Also, next to the cave was a young Israeli solider holding a fully automatic Tavor X95 submachine gun.

Yeshua said…

"And you shall make upright boards for the tabernacle of acacia wood. Ten cubits shall be the length of a board, and a cubit and a half shall be the breath of one board."

"What? What are you saying, my friend," asked Mohammed.

"That's from the Hebrew Bible," said Yeshua. "God commanded the Ark of the Covenant to be made from acacia wood. From those kind of trees right there. I recognize them from growing up in Beersheba."

"Ah, yes. They do look familiar," said Mohammed. "They are the only trees that seem to grow well here in the desert."

All the sudden, two men appeared from out of the cave. One was a middle aged Israeli solider; the other was an older man with white hair wearing a white button-down short sleeve shirt and tan khaki pants.

The old man with white hair saw Taylor, Yeshua and Mohammed standing at the other side of the valley, and he smiled and waved at them. Taylor smiled and waved back.

"Let's go," said Taylor. "We have arrived at our destination." She walked quickly down into the grove of acacia trees and straight towards the two men standing by the cave opening. Yeshua and Mohammed did their best to follow her fast pace.

Yeshua and Mohammed were equally surprised when she seemed to leap into the older man's arms and give him a full hug with her entire body.

"Miriam!" exclaimed the older man.

"Daddy!" replied Taylor. "So good to see you."

"Daddy?" whispered Mohammed to Yeshua, both standing a few feet away. They seemed to be more at ease after Miriam's public display of affection was actually with her father. Taylor turned away from her father and looked at Yeshua and Mohammed.

"Daddy, these are the two boys… I mean young men I was telling you about," said Taylor.

"Yeshua, Mohammed… this is my father, Professor Noah Taylor and his right-hand man, Colonel Cohen."

Yeshua and Mohammed replied, "Hello Sir, Hello Sir," and everyone shook hands.

"So… Daddy, what have you found here?" asked Taylor.

"It's a miracle," replied Professor Taylor. "We found this cave this morning as the flash flood from the storm last night eroded the sandstone and debris covering the opening on this cliff. It's likely that it's been hundreds or even thousands of years since anyone has been in this cave. On our first inspection, we believe we have found some petroglyphs inside."

"Sir, what exactly are petroglyphs?" asked Mohammed. "Are they some form of hieroglyphics?"

"That's a very good question, young man," said Professor Taylor. "I actually wrote my PhD thesis on that exact subject while I was at the University of Geneva many years ago. And that's also where I met Miriam's mother. Anyhow, simply put... petroglyphs are pictorial drawings on rocks that typically only represent exactly what the image is, for example a bird is a bird and a fish is a fish. Hieroglyphics on the other hand are carvings in rock where the images have phonetic elements, like the written pictorial language of the Egyptians or Mayans."

"That is absolutely fascinating," replied Yeshua. "And have you found some petroglyphs inside this cave? Who made them?"

"We believe from analyzing the other sites in this area of the Negev, that they were called the Shasu tribes. They were nomads who were mentioned in Egyptian historical hieroglyphics. As a matter of fact, in the tomb of Ramses the Second it is inscribed that he conquered the Shasu lands. Over the years, we have found hundreds of petroglyphs they made here in the southern Negev. Well, what are we waiting for? Let's go inside and see what's in there! Oh, and by the way... when inside, don't touch or move anything."

Professor Taylor turned and went into the cave opening. It was about four feet tall, and he had to kneel down to get inside. Colonel Cohen grabbed three flashlights from a nearby supply box and handed them to Taylor, Yeshua and Mohammed. They then all entered the cave single file, one at a time.

The cave was fairly small and musty. Yeshua was expecting something much more awe-inspiring. It was just one chamber, ovular in shape and about the size of a small military barracks. The roof was about ten feet high. The floor, was smooth and somewhat slippery, from the recent rainfall.

Everyone roamed inside the room and searched the space with their flashlights.

"I found something over here," said Professor Taylor. He was shining his flashlight on the wall adjacent to the cave entrance. Everyone gathered around him to look at what he had found. On the darkly pigmented gray wall there were several places which had shapes carved into the stone.

Everyone shone their flashlights on the wall. Near the top of the wall were two large circles etched into the cave with six small lines radiating from each. The carvings were a light tan color compared to the surrounding gray color of the rest of the wall. Below the circles were etched twelve long lines.

"Ah. I've seen these symbols many times before out here in the Negev," said Professor Taylor. "One of the circles represents the sun, the other the moon. The longer lines represent the lunar calendar, or twelve months of the lunar year."

"Could that represent the twelve tribes of Israel," asked Yeshua.

"I don't think so, I think these petroglyphs are much older than the timeline of the Exodus story, possibly closer to 4000 years old," explained the Professor. "Hopefully we can find some organic material in here and carbon date the occupation of this cave."

"Oh, my... look below at those lines," said the Professor. "See that image there?" He moved his flashlight downwards revealing another petroglyph. There was a longer image that looking like a slightly curving line with multiple cross hatches. "What do you see there?"

"That looks like some kind of snake, but it seems like it has many legs," said Mohammed.

"Very good, close guess," said the Professor. "But it's not a snake. Count how many legs it has."

"I count twenty-eight," said Yeshua.

"Yes, exactly," said the Professor. "And the back of the tail equals twenty-nine. We call this symbol the centipede, and it represents the twenty-nine days of the lunar cycle. The Shasu tribe must have of used this cave to count time."

"Are you sure it was the Shasu tribe that was here?" said Taylor from the back of the cave. She was shining her flashlight at a large rock along the back wall. "I found something over here. What's this?"

All the cave explorers walked over to where Taylor stood and directed their flashlights on the large rock, about four feet in diameter with a flat top. The top of the stone looked like it had been burned. There were symbols etched into the sides of the rock.

"Amazing. This looks like some kind of ancient altar," said the Professor. "And look at that petroglyph! I've seen that one before."

He directed his flashlight to a rough image, mostly scratched out, of what looked like a man wearing a strange hat and sitting on a chair.

"That's the image of the Sumerian Moon god called Sin on his throne. Usually his hand is stretched out to greet the moon, but it looks someone purposefully defaced the image."

"And what are these images here?" asked Yeshua. He pointed the beam of his flashlight on the rock nearby. There were two carved images in the rock next to each other. The one on the left looked like an upside-down letter "Y" and the one on the right looked like a backwards letter "L."

"Oh my God," said the Professor with a stunned look on his face. "Literally."

"What do you mean?" asked Colonel Cohen. "I mean, what does it mean?"

"Those two symbols are actually letters," explained the Professor. "It's an early form of writing called Old Negev or Proto Sinaic. It's a precursor language to modern

Hebrew. The first letter that looks like a backwards 'L' is actually the letter *Yod* in Hebrew and the upside down 'Y' is the letter *Hey*."

"So it spells *Yod Hey*," said Yeshua. "That means God, doesn't it?"

The Professor continued, "Yes. We have seen many similar inscriptions in other places here in the Negev. It means *Yah*, the name of the Hebrew God. It's the short form of the word Yahweh. We think these Yod-Hey rock carvings are perhaps the oldest written forms of the original name of the Hebrew God in known existence."

"And what of the other petroglyph symbols?" asked Mohammed. "The graven image of the Sumerian god sitting on his throne. Why is that also here on this altar?"

"Well, this is just my expert opinion as a senior archeologist," prefaced the Professor. "Based on the scratched-out marks... I think someone deliberately crossed out the Sumerian deity in deference to Yah."

"What does that mean exactly, Sir?" asked Yeshua.

"It means at some point," explained the Professor. "The occupant or occupants of this cave rejected the Sumerian god or gods and chose to worship the God of the Hebrews. This became an altar to Yah."

Professor Taylor pulled out a small brush from his pocket which looked like something a painter would use to create fine details. He gently skimmed the top of the altar and then looked carefully at the tip of the brush using the light from his flashlight.

"Perfect," said the Professor. "This is ash from burning something organic, probably some kind of sacrifice. Let's go outside now and get the carbon dating kit. In a few weeks, God willing… we be able to date this cave and know how long ago it was last inhabited."

Everyone exited the cave. Yeshua was glad to be back in the sunlight. He wished he had brought his Shofar to the Red Canyon and used it to transport back in time to see the people who were worshiping God in this cave thousands of years ago.

Professor Taylor walked towards the grove of acacia trees and proceeded to open one of the supply boxes. He started tinkering with some fancy looking equipment in a large wooden crate. Mohammed sat against the cliff face, resting and drinking a bottle of water. Colonel Cohen walked over to Mohammed and started to quietly talk to him, just out of earshot of Yeshua.

Taylor stood next to Yeshua under the shade of one of the beautiful acacia trees. "I have some questions for you, Yeshua," she said.

"Sure, anything," replied Yeshua.

"When you were thirteen, do you remember me taking care of you in the hospital after the terrorists blew up the bus you and Mohammed were in?" asked Taylor.

"I'm sorry... I don't remember you taking care of me. I guess I was in a coma," answered Yeshua. "Although I do remember seeing you when I became conscious again. When I saw you, I thought you were the most beautiful Angel I had ever seen."

Taylor smiled. She put her hand on Yeshua's hand. "You are very sweet, and kind," she said. "You have a pure soul. I have always wondered though... how did you survive the explosion? I saw that bus on the news. It was completely annihilated. I found out later that you threw your body over Mohammed to protect him. How did you and Mohammed not have any physical injuries?"

"I suppose it was a miracle," replied Yeshua. "Maybe a guardian Angel was watching over us? I guess it just wasn't our time to walk with God."

"You know Yeshua," said Taylor as she stared deep into his eyes. "I think you are with God. And God is with you. And you know it."

"Excuse me," said Colonel Cohen. He stood next to Taylor and Yeshua under the acacia tree. Taylor pulled her hand off of Yeshua's. Behind them, Mohammed was doing his late morning prayers to Allah by the cave entrance. "I'm sorry if I am interrupting your discussion. I have a message for both of you, your new orders."

"Yes Sir," said Taylor.

"You will be going to Rome, Italy," stated Colonel Cohen. "In two days' time, you'll meet with your contact at the Arch of Titus in the Roman Forum at exactly noon. If anyone asks, you are there on vacation. Do you understand?"

"Yes Sir," said Yeshua. "But what about Mohammed? Will he be going with us?"

"No. He won't," replied Cohen. "He will be going to Saudi Arabia on a very important mission. Something very big is about to happen. You must leave now."

CHAPTER 4

EMPEROR TITUS

Two Days Later
Rome, Italy

Taylor and Yeshua walked along the Via Sacra path in the Roman Forum. Behind them loomed the nearly two-thousand-year-old gargantuan Coliseum. The bright sun shone overhead in the partly cloudy sky.

Yeshua glanced at his wrist and looked at the time. The watch read 11:52AM. Slung over his back was the spiral Shofar, his prize possession.

Yeshua marveled at the magnitude of the sprawling Roman Forum's ancient ruins. To his right lay the remnants of the once magnificent Temple of Venus and Rome, now the home of the Roman Catholic Church of Santa Francesca Romana. In the distance, to his left, were the foundations of the Elagabalium Temple and the Palatine Hill.

"This place is absolutely colossal. Where exactly are we going?" asked Yeshua.

"To the Arch of Titus," replied Taylor. "It's just ahead. And I know you all too well Yeshua... we'll be right on time. Don't stress out about being late. We got this, trust me."

"I do trust you Taylor," said Yeshua. "More than you know."

The Arch of Titus was now easily visible directly ahead as Taylor and Yeshua continued along the Via Sacra, also known as the Sacred Street. Yeshua was astonished at the size and scale of the rectangular monument. It was constructed of white limestone and stood at least fifty feet tall. Four decoratively carved columns rose upward flanking the giant semicircular inner arch. In the center on the top of the monument were large Latin words carved into the white stone façade.

"What do those words mean up at the top?" inquired a curious Yeshua.

"I'm not a hundred percent sure," replied Taylor. "However, I think it says something like... 'The Senate and the people of Rome dedicate this to the deified Titus Augustus.'"

"Deified?" asked Yeshua. "And what does that mean?"

"Titus was a Roman Emperor, like Caesar," responded Taylor. "They worshiped the Emperors as gods, holy divine beings."

Yeshua and Taylor stood at the base of the monument. The entire structure was roped off, preventing anyone from walking under it. Yeshua looked into the interior of the extravagantly carved construction. On either side of the inner portion of the arch, at least twelve feet above the ground level were two very large sculpted scenes with many people in various poses.

On the left image, he recognized something familiar: several men in robes holding up or perhaps carrying a giant seven-branched menorah. Yeshua realized it was the same exact image on the State of Israel's national emblem.

"Taylor, what's that menorah doing there in that sculpture? Why is it here in Rome?" asked Yeshua.

"This Arch glorifies the Roman destruction of Second Jewish Temple and the fall of Jerusalem orchestrated by Titus Flavius Augustus," said a man's deep and resonant voice behind Taylor and Yeshua.

They both turned about and saw that a young Roman Catholic priest with short blonde hair, wearing all black (except his white clergy collar), was standing there.

"That image shows the ransacking of the Jewish Temple by the Roman army and their troops stealing the sacred Hebrew ritual objects. The holy Menorah and all the spoils of their victory were then brought here to Rome in the year 70 AD," the man said.

Yeshua and Taylor both looked at the priest with mystified expressions.

"Oh, I'm terribly sorry… please let me introduce myself," said the priest. "I am Monsignor Matteo Giovanni, official diplomat of the Holy See. Welcome to Rome. And you must be Yeshua and Miriam."

"Yes," said Taylor. "We're honored to meet you. Please call me Taylor, though. I would prefer that."

"Ah. But Miriam is a much more meaningful name," said the Monsignor. "Miriam was sister of your Prophet Moses. However, I'm happy to call you Taylor."

"Actually, Father... I was raised a Catholic by my Mother," said Taylor. "My Father is Jewish... It's a long story."

"Monsignor, are you saying this monument was made to honor the man responsible for the destruction of Jerusalem?" asked a dishearten Yeshua. He felt sick in his stomach as a horrible feeling of dread came over his entire body. His right ear softly made a low pitch buzzing sound for just a moment, and then stopped.

"Yes, it was. That is its purpose," explained the priest. "Titus and the Roman legions laid siege to Jerusalem in response the Jewish rebellion against the Empire. The city fell; the Temple was destroyed and the Romans killed or took prisoner almost the entire Jewish population."

"Gosh. That sounds something right out of Star Wars," half-joked Yeshua. "The Empire. The Emperor. The Rebellion."

"Yes. Unfortunately, the dark side crushed the rebellion with an iron fist in that particular episode," stated the young priest. "With that being said, I want you to turn around. Tell me what you see."

Yeshua and Taylor turned around. The huge Coliseum and the Arch of Constantine stood just to the east of the Forum, still clearly visible in the distance.

"I see the Coliseum. Isn't that where they had the gladiators fight and where they fed the Christians to the lions for entertainment?" asked a curious Taylor.

"Yes, and here's a brief history lesson... it's thought that when the Romans defeated the Jews and destroyed their Temple in the year 70, they brought thousands of Hebrew slaves here to help construct the Coliseum," explained the priest. "Also, the Romans used the stolen wealth from the plundering of Judea to fund and finally finish building the Coliseum. The newly crowned Emperor Titus commemorated the inaugural games in the year 80 during a devastating plague outbreak here in Rome. Ironically, he died mysteriously less than year later."

Yeshua thought back to the vision he had after his Bar Mitzvah in the ancient fortress of Masada. He remembered seeing the Roman Legion finally break through the fortress and find that almost all the Jewish rebels had taken their own lives rather than becoming captives. Perhaps they knew it was better to die on their own terms instead of coming here to Rome and being forced to build the Coliseum as slaves.

Yeshua also remembered seeing a young boy with red hair being captured by the Romans during his vision at Masada. The boy (who looked just like Yeshua) gave the general of the Romans a message from the Hebrew zealot leader Elazar ben Yair, and then he was sent to Rome as a prisoner of war to confirm the Roman victory over the Jews at Masada.

"And what became of the slaves," asked Yeshua. "Did any of them survive?"

"I think so, at least some of them did," said the priest. "Also, we know that when the Romans brought the enslaved captives from Judea... a few of them were early Christians. And when they came here, they spread 'The Word.' A couple hundred of years later... around the year 300, Constantine became the first Emperor to convert to Christianity and favor the Christian Church over the pagan gods of his predecessors."

"So you are saying by bringing all the slaves here after the defeat of Judea, their influence eventually led to the shift of worship away from the Roman pantheon of many gods?" asked Yeshua.

"Well, the history is much deeper and more complex than that; however there are many historians who would agree with you," said the priest.

"This is all so fascinating," said Yeshua. "I had no idea. How do you know all this?"

"Let's just say I'm quite a history buff. There's also another recent speculation that the eruption of Mount Vesuvius was a major factor in the spread of monotheism in the Roman Empire," stated the priest.

"Mount Vesuvius... wasn't that the volcano that destroyed Pompeii?" asked Taylor.

"Yes, and also the city of Herculaneum next to Pompeii," stated the priest. "They were completely annihilated. The volcano exploded without any real warning in year 79, the same year Titus became Emperor and one year before the inaugural games of the Coliseum. Some historians think that many Romans viewed the obliteration of the two cities, like Sodom and Gomorrah... as a punishment from the Hebrew God in vengeance for the Romans destroying Jerusalem and enslaving the Hebrews."

"So, you're saying that some Romans started to covert to monotheism after the volcano erupted?" asked Yeshua.

"Yes. And likely more than just some. Perhaps many. That's what a few credible historians are now saying," responded the priest. "They even found ancient graffiti at an excavation in Pompeii that actually spelled the words Sodom and Gomorrah. It must have been an evil place, especially for the subjugated slaves forced to live there and serve their Roman masters. After the tragedy of Vesuvius, it is thought that many Romans started to reject the hedonistic and immoral ways of their culture and gravitate towards the more righteous Judeo-Christian ways.

Yeshua felt a powerful wave of awe come over him. He stood in the very place where the Romans celebrated the defeat and destruction of his own people. At that moment, he had an epiphany. The Jews had actually survived. In fact, they had survived all the destructions and enslavements throughout history.

There was a repeating pattern of recurrent events that Yeshua now clearly understood. All the ancient cultures and empires that tried to enslave and destroy the people of Israel were now gone, extinguished. Only some of their monuments and buildings survived, as well the written chapters in the history books describing the rise and fall of each empire. The Egyptians, the Assyrians, the Babylonians, the Greeks, the Romans and even the Nazis no longer existed. Yet the people of Israel were still here, still alive... they had survived all of it, every persecution and genocide. And now, Yeshua stood here in the heart of the ancient Roman Empire and he smiled. He was the survivor.

"We have about three hours before our meeting with the Cardinal," said the Monsignor. "Would you like a tour of the Church of Santa Francesca Romana and then I could also show you some of the Forum."

"I would love that," replied Taylor.

"Ummm… would you mind if I go check out the Coliseum while you are getting your tour? Something is calling me there," said Yeshua. "Is that okay?"

"Sure, no problem," responded Taylor. "You know what they say… when 'Rome, do as the Romans do.' "

"Well said indeed," responded the Monsignor. "Let's all rendezvous at the Arch of Constantine in exactly two hours. We have a driver who will then take us to the Vatican for our meeting at the Sistine Chapel. Oh, and Yeshua, take this… it a pass for the VIP entrance of the Coliseum. You can go right in. You won't have to wait in the long lines."

Monsignor Matteo handed Yeshua a laminated card with an image of a Roman Gladiator holding a sword.

"Thank you," said Yeshua. "I mean grazie."

"Prego!" replied Matteo. He nodded his head down slightly, closed his eyes and smiled.

Yeshua turned and walked briskly towards the Coliseum, his Shofar still slung over his back.

"Why does he have a ram's horn with him?" the priest asked Taylor as they walked towards the Church.

"I was wondering the same exact thing myself," she replied.

Yeshua again marveled at the Coliseum as he made his way along the Via Sacra. The left side of the giant building had three levels of arches and columns topped with an even more impressive taller fourth level wall. The right side of the building looked more like ruins, as it appeared to be missing most of the decorative exterior present on the other half of the building.

Yeshua bypassed hundreds of tourists waiting entry to the ancient arena, and then found the VIP entrance nearby with virtually no line. He showed his laminated gladiator card to the security guard; then he walked through one of the large exterior arches into the building's interior main curved hallway. The scale of the construction was breath taking.

He got that déjà vu feeling once again. It felt like he had been here before, as everything looked so familiar. Somehow, Yeshua knew exactly where he needed to go as something seemed to guide him along the main hallway and then down the stairs which led him outside, revealing the interior of the massive structure.

Rather than looking like a modern arena or soccer stadium, Yeshua was surprised to see that most of the floor was missing within the large oval of the lower level. He could see what looked like a catacomb or labyrinth in the basement of the Coliseum below where the floor should have been standing. Also, there was no seating in the entire multi-level building. Instead, there was just ruins of arches and walls. It looked much different on the inside than he was expecting.

Ahead, Yeshua saw a group of people with a tour guide on a platform above the edge of the huge oval that was the once the Coliseum floor. Just as their tour guide was about to talk, he opportunely joined the group of tourists in order to listen to their speaker.

"Here you see the vastness and greatness of the Coliseum, which is the most popular tourist attraction in the world," declared the tour guide in a heavy Italian-English accent. "Below you can see what remains of the hypogeum, beneath where the original floor existed. This underground area is known to have gone through twelve different stages of construction and included chambers for gladiators, wild animals and vertical shafts and pulley systems."

"The Coliseum was completed in the year 80 and could comfortably seat 65,000 spectators," the tour guide stated. "During the inaugural events hosted by the Emperor Titus, they filled the arena with water and staged huge naval battles called naumachia where the different fleets of boats were occupied by small armies of slaves on death row which represented conquered maritime powers such as the ancient Greeks, Egyptians and Persians. Each spectacle would usually be a "fight to the death" and famously the Emperor would give a thumbs up or a thumbs down to determine the final winners and losers. Any questions?"

"Yes, where did the Emperor sit?" asked an Asian man wearing thick black glasses.

"A very good question, Sir," responded the tour guide. "As you can see, or actually can't see... there are no seats visible here as most of the marble and limestone blocks were repurposed into other local buildings over the centuries.

The Emperor and the other important members of the Roman leadership sat in a raised platform section along the middle of the northern part of the lower level. We will actually go there now."

The tour group followed their guide as they all left the small platform overlooking the hypogeum. Yeshua stood alone and in awe. His left ear started to buzz slightly as it had done many times before. Instinctively, he carefully pulled his Shofar from the sling on his back and into hands. It seemed to faintly glow, as Yeshua knew it was time. It was time to sound his ram's horn.

Shofar in hand, Yeshua brought the mouthpiece up to his lips and he blew hard into it with all his might. The horn beamed out a really big, long blast.

Ba-ba-baaaaaaaaaaaaaaa...

He sounded the Shofar two more times.

Ba-ba-baaaaaaaaaaaaaaaa...

Ba-ba-baaaaaaaaaaaaaaaa...

Then, everything changed. Yeshua began to lose consciousness and everything faded to black. He felt nothing. There was only darkness. He was completely out of his body, like in a dream. It felt as if he was moving through the darkness, like floating. He could sense some movement forward; yet he was definitely not aware of his physical body. He couldn't feel his hands. Then, he saw something up ahead. Out of the darkness came an array of lights. First it was quite dim, and then as he got closer, he saw that he was flying through some kind of strange tunnel formed of repeating concentric circles. The lights got brighter, and he saw a magnificent display of multicolored circular patterns rotate around him, as he seemed to glide through a magical infinite space.

The kaleidoscopic patterns morphed and shifted around him, as he seemed to fly even faster and deeper into the tunnel. From the end of the tunnel he saw a bright light approaching rapidly. He was flying incredibly fast and literally he came out through the light at the end of the tunnel.

Suddenly, his spirit seemed to hover above the water that filled the Coliseum. A dozen wooden boats full of men floated in the huge space at the bottom of the arena. Thousands of yelling, cheering and screaming Roman spectators occupied the seats all the way up to the roof. Overhead, there was a massive umbrella like structure that shaded most of the interior from the strong sun above.

Each of the boats held about 30 men with half of them sitting and holding long oars. Each boat had a tall central mast with a large flag at the top. The flags had different symbolic emblems embroidered onto them. He saw one flag with the Eye of Horus that must have been an Egyptian boat. One flag had a thunderbolt on it representing the Greeks. Another flag looked like a man surrounded by the wings and a tail of a bird, representing the Persians.

Yeshua then saw a flag with a gold menorah on it... it was the Israelite boat. Yeshua, still in a spirit-like apparition form, levitated over the waters towards the boat of Hebrews. As he got closer, he saw the raised platform on the north side of the Coliseum where the Emperor sat on a throne-like seat. It was Titus Flavius. Yeshua knew it. Important generals, senators, and beautiful women in elegant, colorful robes surrounded him. Two boats protected the Emperor's seating platform with Eagle emblems on their flags, and they were occupied with dozens of heavily armed Roman soldiers.

As Yeshua reached the Jewish boat, an older man with a scar on the left side of his face stood next to Titus and made an announcement. The sound of his voice resonated loudly due the perfect acoustics of the oval stadium.

"Citizens of Rome, esteemed senators and guests, Emperor Titus Flavius Caesar Vespasianus Augustus welcomes you to the commencement of his inaugural festivities of this splendid and majestic amphitheater. We have something very special for your entertainment today, a grand naumachia featuring all the conquered peoples of our dominant and glorious Roman Empire!"

The entire stadium erupted with loud cheers from the tens of thousands of Roman onlookers. Yeshua then recognized the man with the scar on the left side of his face. He had seen him many times before. He was the Roman soldier from Masada, and he was the Nazi officer from Amsterdam. He was the dark Angel's from Abraham's well, and he was Goliath. He was the Iranian who kidnapped him in Saudi Arabia. He was Yeshua's arch-nemesis... his seemingly eternal evil antagonist.

"Here on this lake are our most despised and insurgent adversaries," said the Roman with the scar on his face, now a top general of the Roman legions. "Only one of these armies will win the day, by defeating all the others...

and those who triumph today will be granted their freedom by our merciful and honorable Emperor."

Yeshua was not in physical form; he was more like a nearly invisible ghost-like apparition. As the crowd intensely applauded again, Yeshua looked around the boat of Hebrews. About half of them sat on short wooden planks and held long oars directed down into the water; the other half wore padded leather armor and held short swords. All the men in the boat looked nervous, scared and bewildered.

Then Yeshua saw a man who looked very familiar. He wore a white tunic and stood in the back of the boat and held the rudder. He had long red hair and a beard and was thin and emaciated. It was the boy who was taken prisoner in Masada, now all grown up. He looked just like Yeshua.

"What is that down there in the water?" said one of the men in the boat. He spoke in a strange form of Hebrew; however, Yeshua understood him. There was a lot of movement in the waters below.

"Are they sea serpents?" another man asked, as a scaly head of one of the giant creatures came above the surface.

"No. They're Nile crocodiles," another man said. "There's dozens of them in the water. Don't fall in there."

"Today begins one hundred days of celebration of Emperor Titus and the Flavian's extraordinary victories and monumental achievements for our Empire," continued the Roman general with the scar on his face. "Every day we will see thrilling and compelling acts here in this Amphitheatre staged just for you... the people of Rome! Please stand and thank our Emperor Titus for his benevolent generosity."

All the Romans stood up from their finely polished marble seats and clapped and cheered their newly crowned God-Ruler.

"The generosity of Titus?" said the red bearded man in the back of the Hebrew boat near Yeshua. He spit into the water. "This pile of rocks was built by thousands of Jewish slaves and paid for by the blood of Judea."

All the men on the boat turned and looked at the red bearded man. "Listen up," he said loudly as all the Romans continued to salute Titus. "Do you hear what they said up there? The so-called champions of this disgusting and atrocious tournament will be given their freedom. Do you hear that my Israelite brothers? FREEDOM! By the will of God... we can do this together."

The red bearded man climbed up and stood on the railing of the back of the boat, just as the Romans sat back in their seats after applauding Titus.

The Hebrew man who looked liked Yeshua then loudly spoke the words of the Shema in Hebrew, the centerpiece of Jewish prayer.

"Hear, O Israel; the Lord our God, the LORD is ONE."

His words reverberated and echoed within the entire Coliseum as the Hebrew's boat floated near the center of the Coliseum. The now silent Romans who filled the stadium appeared confused and in disbelief after hearing the Hebrews' prayer to their God. On the Emperor's platform, the senators and generals looked out in disgust. How dare the slaves disrespect their Emperor! The general with the scarred face turned and looked at Titus. Titus nodded at him. The general walked over to the edge of the platform overlooking the boat armada in front of him.

"Let the games begin. May the best men win!" yelled the general.

Back on the Hebrew boat, the man who looked like Yeshua climbed back down from the edge of the boat and held the rudder. All his brothers in arms looked at him. Yeshua moved his spirit form towards the back of the boat and next to the man who was very likely him in a past life reincarnation.

"Here's the plan," the red haired-man said. "We will not fight just yet, for that is certain death. We will row towards the far end of the lake, for that is where we make our stand. Now, make it so my brothers… row! Row for your lives." He pointed towards the empty west side of the far edge of the Coliseum's lake.

Nearby, the Gaul ship with a horned boar symbol on its flag rammed directly into the Persian ship and split it into two. Several of the Persians fell into the water and were immediately gorged by hungry crocodiles swimming below.

The Romans spectators cheered and clapped at the bloody spectacle. Meanwhile, all of the Hebrews in their boat sat down and took their oars, two men to each one. Yeshua noticed that the Romans at the top of the Coliseum's upper gallery didn't seem to be as enthusiastic as the rest of the bloodthirsty spectators. They weren't cheering and clapping.

"Row, Row!" yelled the past life Yeshua as he turned the rudder to the left and the boat started moving to the west. The men rowed in near perfect unison as the small ship moved through the murky waters.

A few yards away, the Carthaginian boat with what looked like a pawn chess piece on its flag floated side by side with the Greek boat. The slaves on those boats were engaged in direct sword battle and hand to hand combat as they boarded each other's boats. The Romans continued to express their total delight and glee with their cheers.

Yeshua felt a sense of pride as he watched his people work together and attempt to survive this wicked blood sport of the Romans. As the Israeli boat moved away from the central crowd of ships and towards the western part of the lake, he saw the Egyptian boat turn and head straight towards their boat. It was on a direct collision course to ram their boat in half.

The red bearded man saw the Egyptian boat moving towards them and yelled, "Row faster! Row faster!" However, the weak and starved Jewish slaves could not row any faster. Years of mistreatment and the heavy labor of forced construction of the Coliseum had taken its toll on them. They could not row any faster.

The Egyptian boat was going to ram the Hebrew boat. It was getting closer and closer. The Egyptians congregated at the front of their ship with their swords, waiting to board the Hebrew boat and attack. It was inevitable.

Yeshua, still in spirit form and observing this epic battle as a non-participant, came up with an inspirational idea. He recalled the first time he blew the Shofar and was transported through the mystical tunnel back into biblical times. He helped Hagar and Ishmael by diving into the deep well and pushing the water up to them. He remembered telepathically lifting the water upwards in his spirit form and causing it to flow upwards and out of the well so Hagar and Ishmael could drink.

If he could do that, maybe he could help the Hebrews here in the Coliseum. He could see the Egyptian boat just yards away on a straight course towards them as it gained momentum. The leader of their boat held the rudder steady and screamed "Ramming speed!"

Yeshua focused hard and levitated his soul/spirit form out from the ship and down into the waters behind the their boat. The huge crocodiles swam around him, although they could not see him, thankfully. With all his might, he tried to push the boat forward without success. He couldn't seem to move the boat at all. The Egyptians were getting even closer. He tried to push the boat forward again without success.

"Row! Row!" screamed the red-haired man in the Hebrew boat. He could see that in just a few moments the Egyptians would slam into their ship and lead to certain disaster.

Yeshua remembered pushing the water upwards at the well at Beersheba, and at the beach at Ashkelon. He seemed have some power over the water, like telekinesis. He intensely focused again within the waters behind the boat. Instead of trying to move the boat directly, he channeled all of his energy into the swirling waters. He concentrated deeply and began to mentally push the water at the rear of the boat. In an energetic crescendo, he could feel water rush and flow strongly forwards, towards the rear wake of the ship. It started to work... the Hebrew boat's speed became faster.

From the Emperor's platform, Titus excitedly stood up to watch the Egyptian boat ram directly into the Hebrews. He thought it would be a fitting end for them, their conflicting adversarial history with the Egyptians ran throughout the centuries, all the way back to the time of Moses and the Pharaohs. This time, the Israelites would be the ones to drown in the waters.

Unexpectedly, Titus saw the Hebrew boat surprisingly accelerate away from the Egyptians as what appeared to be a substantial wave of water appear behind the Israelites and push them rapidly forwards. The Egyptian boat, which at first looked like it was going to certainly T-bone the Jews, now narrowly missed them. Titus sat back down on his throne with a disgusted look on his face. He was so fed up with these annoying and stubborn Jews, as they had always been a thorn in the side of his Empire.

Back on the Hebrew boat, a triumphant Yeshua came/flew up and out of the water and back onto the ship. He saw the Egyptian boat pass by just behind them, their armed men scowling and grimacing. The man with the red beard holding the rudder raised his right hand with his outstretched middle finger and pointed it towards the thwarted Egyptians.

Meanwhile, in the center of the Coliseum lake, there was mass carnage as several of the boats were all bunched up together. Hundreds of men were killing each other in mortal combat. Blood spilled from the boats and into the water below. The crocodiles feasted on their dismembered bodies as the Roman crowd continued to yell and applaud the massacre.

The Hebrew boat, near the far side of the western part of the Coliseum lake, headed straight for the tall retaining wall. The man who looked like Yeshua gave his crew new orders.

"Everyone on the left side of the ship stop rowing," he yelled. "We need to turn around."

His men followed his orders as he turned the rudder and steered the boat. The boat made a 180-degree sweeping turn and then faced into the direction of the center of the lake.

"Stop rowing men," said the red bearded man. "Catch your breath for a moment."

Their boat slowly came to a stop as they watched the havoc and brutal slaying that took place in the main armada battle a couple hundred of yards away. Meanwhile, the Egyptians were now engaged in a close battle with the Celtic boat, which had an image of a trinity knot on its flag. The

Celtic rowers used their oars like pikes and smashed the Egyptians men on their boat.

Yeshua then noticed small objects hitting the interior of the Hebrew boat. The Romans spectators were throwing small rocks, eggs and rotten vegetables from the first level of the Coliseum. Then, he saw a dozen or so Roman soldiers with bows and arrows sent from the Emperor's platform and towards the west side of the Coliseum, in the direction of the Hebrew boat.

The man with the red beard saw the armed soldiers coming their way. He gave his men new orders.

"It is time to row again my brothers!" he said. "Full speed ahead."

All the men started rowing again. The hail of pebbles and vegetables subsided as they made some distance from the edge of the retaining wall and the lunatic spectators. The red-haired man steered the boat towards the nearby Egyptian and Celtic boats nearby. Yeshua saw exactly what he was doing… he was about to ram their boat into the side of Egyptians.

In the meantime, the Egyptians and Celts were fighting each other savagely as their two boats were side to side. They were too occupied to take notice of the Hebrew boat coming towards them at full speed. In the midst of battle, one of the Egyptian men turned and saw the front of the Israelite boat surging towards them. He screamed; but it was too late… the pointed bow of the rapidly moving Jewish vessel plunged in deeply and then violently shattered the port side of the Egyptian Boat.

As the Egyptian boat broke apart and burst, the momentum from the powerful collision forced the adjacent Celtic ship to roll over and completely capsize into the water. The surviving Egyptians and Celts all fell into the water and perished.

The Roman spectators reacted to the Hebrew's two-birds-with-one-stone takeout of the Egyptians and Celts with massive cheers and applause. Emperor Titus, however, was not so pleased. None of the occupants of the Emperor's platform seemed entertained. They did not want to see the Jews win this competition.

Back in the center of the lake, the fierce Gauls had managed to become the sole survivors of the main battle. The rest of the ships were either sunk or full of dead bodies. The leader of the Gauls, a giant man with long black hair and a beard, saw the last remaining opponent still at play on the lake... the Hebrew's ship. He raised his bloodstained sword and he screamed at the top of his lungs as he pointed it towards the Israelites. His crew took to their seats and they all began rowing in the direction of the Jews.

The Israelite boat was still stuck into the hull of the split Egyptian Boat. The Hebrews were doing their best to push away its shattered wooden remnants using their oars, but to no avail. The red-bearded man who looked like Yeshua turned around to see the Gauls coming straight for them from the rear aft of his ship. There wasn't much time left. It was time to make their last stand.

"Men, to arms! Prepare to be boarded," he yelled. All the Israelites grabbed their swords and oars and headed towards the back of the boat, awaiting their adversaries. A moment later, the Gaul ship smashed into the Hebrews and the rampaging barbarians leapt into their vessel en masse.

The Gaul men were trained warriors, recently captured in battle by the Romans. They were savage fighting men, whereas the Hebrews were mostly exhausted civilian slaves who had toiled for years building the Coliseum. Now that the Coliseum was finished, the Roman's final solution for the expendable Hebrews slaves was as fodder for their macabre and grisly entertainment.

The Hebrews fought bravely on that opening day of the Coliseum against the Gauls. They did their best, yet they were far outmatched by the Gauls' expertise with their swords and their mortal combat skills. One by one, the Israelites were being methodically slayed by the much stronger and more powerful Gauls.

Most of the Roman spectators were in frenzy as they cheered and applauded; however, the upper level of Roman onlookers filled with woman and slaves remained silent. Some of the slaves cried at the sight of the grisly massacre.

Titus stood up again from his throne to triumphantly watch the final defeat of the Hebrews. He simultaneously reminisced about his siege and complete destruction of Jerusalem Temple ten years earlier. He smiled as he felt the verge of ultimate victory.

Yeshua, still in spirit form, watched in horror as his people were being slaughtered by the Gauls. More than anything he wanted to intercede, he wanted to stop the killing. Then, he recalled the time he and Mohammed used the Shofar together and they went back in time to help

David battle Goliath. He remembered that Mohammed actually moved his spirit into David and helped him throw the final stone to defeat the giant. He literally went into David to boost his aim and strength.

In an act of desperation, Yeshua focused all his energy and moved his ethereal spirit into the man with red hair. As their souls seemed to merge, Yeshua could actually see through the eyes of past-life self. He sensed the warm wind blowing on his face. He smelled the scent of death around him. He felt the cold steel of the sword handle in his right hand.

One of the Gauls immediately attacked him with his blade. Yeshua deftly moved out of the way and then kicked him hard in his chest. The off-guard barbarian fell from the side of the boat and into the crocodile-filled waters. Nearby, Yeshua saw one of the Gaul warriors about to kill one of the Hebrew oarsmen. He saved him by stabbing the swordsman through his arm.

The battle was coming to its finale. There were just a few Israelites and Gauls left alive. Two more Gauls attacked Yeshua simultaneously with their swords. Time seemed to slow down as Yeshua deflected each slash and jab methodically and skillfully. Then, with surgical precision, he mortally wounded both of the assaulting barbarians. They fell into the water. The huge crowd of Romans responded with heavy applause, including many of the women and slaves sitting in Coliseum's upper level.

Yeshua felt something painfully sting him on his right leg. He looked down, expecting to see a Gaul's blade piercing through his flesh. To his surprise, he saw several small, black mosquitoes swarming around him. One the pests had just plunged its sharp proboscis into his leg and was consuming his blood. He quickly smashed the mosquito with his left hand.

The behemoth leader of the Gauls saw Yeshua and last few remaining Hebrews towards the forward of the ship, all immersed in ferocious combat with the last few remaining Gauls. He screamed loudly and started running full speed towards the man in the red beard.

With seemingly superhuman strength and speed, Yeshua fought off and pushed back the three nearby marauding Gauls with his sword. Then, almost like a choreographed dance, the surviving Hebrew oarsman pushed the barbarians off the boat with their long paddles.

Yeshua turned just in time get a glimpse of the Gaul leader surging at him with his saber. As he ran at the red-headed Hebrew, he grasped his blade handle with both hands over his head and tried to slice the much smaller Jewish man in half. Like a seasoned fencer, Yeshua whirled around and perfectly parried the Gauls sword lunge. The two steel swords clanged together and caused a loud bell-like ringing sound that reverberated throughout the Coliseum.

"Touché!" yelled Yeshua in his mind as he fended off the Gaul's attack, but surprisingly the red bearded man also said the same word out loud. The Gaul leader grunted and said something in an explicative manner, which Yeshua thankfully could not understand.

The two men exchanged lunges and parries, attacks and counter attacks with their sharp swords, like two opposing combatants with light sabers from the Star Wars movies. The three surviving Israelite oarsman stood and watched from afar on the boat as the Roman spectators appeared to be cheering for the red-haired Hebrew man to win the fight.

In the Emperor's platform, across the other side of the Coliseum lake from the final battle, the Roman general with scar on the left side of his face approached Titus.

"And what if the Jews win?" he asked the Emperor. Titus was still standing on the edge of his podium overlooking the swordfight. Although he had the best view in the stadium, he did not look pleased. The Emperor whispered something into his general's ear and then the general walked towards the back of the platform and spoke to one of his soldiers. The legionnaire then left the platform and quickly started to run towards the opposite side of the Coliseum through the massive building's interior arched marble corridors. A troubled Titus returned back to his throne and sat down, almost pouting.

Yeshua continued to battle and combat the giant Gaul with his sword. He defended another lunge, and counter attacked with a riposte. The Gaul surprisingly jumped at him as he parried and shoved the red-bearded man down to the ground with his outstretched left arm. As Yeshua fell down, he lost grip of his sword and landed hard on the wooded floor. While Yeshua lay stunned below, the Gaul laughed loudly as he wound up his final thrust to definitively end the duel.

Miraculously, lying on the deck of the boat right beside Yeshua, was a broken oar. The end of it was sharp where it had snapped in half. He quickly grabbed the oar, and just as the huge Gaul leader bent down to pierce him with his sword, Yeshua stabbed him through the left side of his chest with the oar. Unable to reach Yeshua with his sword, he fell forward, impaling himself deeper onto the sharp pole. Just as his blade was about to cut into Yeshua's face, the three surviving Hebrew oarsmen pushed the impaled Gaul off the boat, and he landed into the water with a huge splash. The crocodiles swarmed his body as the entire Roman crowd, including the upper level, erupted in cheers. The Jews had won the day!

Yeshua, still in spirit inside the red-bearded man, stood up with the help of his three shipmates. As the victors of the Roman naval battle naumachia, they were widly celebrated and cheered by the Roman spectators. In response, the Hebrews raised their arms up to the sky and pumped their fists... They had gained their freedom with their hard fought triumph. Suddenly, Yeshua felt another sharp sting on his leg. He looked down to see another pesky mosquito sting him. There seemed to be another swarm of mosquitos flying around him.

As Yeshua swatted away the mosquito, the entire Roman crowd erupted in loud booing which didn't make sense to the Hebrews until Yeshua turned around to see the Emperor Titus standing at the edge of his podium with his right arm outstretched and his thumb pointing downwards. Yeshua tried to remember from his history lessons what it meant when the Emperor put his thumb down. Was that good or bad? Obviously, the crowd wasn't pleased about the thumbs down, so it didn't seem like favorable news at all.

Yeshua turned away from the Emperor and was dismayed to see 20 roman archers standing nearby on the retaining wall of the first level of the Coliseum. The arrows in their bows aimed directly at the Hebrews.

Behind Yeshua, the Emperor Titus made a hand gesture as he simulated a motion slicing though his neck. The archers immediately released their arrows towards the Yeshua and his three Israelites brothers. Time again seemed to shift as the arrows came raining down on the Hebrews, piercing through their flesh. As the four men fell to the ground as they died, the Roman crowd became silent.

Yeshua had never felt so much pain before. The arrows were sharp and plunged deeply inwards. As he lay on the boat's wooden planks, he felt the blood drain out from his ruptured arteries and veins as he prepared to die. The life force was bleeding out from the red-headed man's body. It was near the end.

Above, Yeshua could still see the golden menorah emblem on the boat's flag, still waving in the wind. Something strangely shifted, and he could feel his spirit slowly detach from his past life self as the red-bearded man took his last few breaths.

Instead of transmuting back into his ethereal soul form, his spirit seemed to miniaturize and merge directly into the bloodstream of man who looked just like him, his past self. Like floating down a tunnel, he seemed to circulate into the jugular vein flowing through his neck, then travel into the superior vena cava and then into his beating heart. He flowed through the vessels in the lungs, then through the pumping ventricle and out through the aorta. The red-bearded man's pulse was weak and thready as his intravascular blood volume was almost depleted from the fatal arrow injuries.

Yeshua's spirit energy continued to flow in the current of blood past the distal aortic bifurcation and then into the femoral vessels of the leg. Then he could feel a transference of the oxygenated blood back into the venous system. He entered a large vein and suddenly and strangely he felt like he was being abducted by an alien spaceship. He seemed to be sucked into a long, winding tubule out of the dying man's body.

The perspective shifted again. Everything was vibrating and buzzing. Yeshua was disoriented and confused. Where was he? What had happened? He looked outwards and saw the hazy image of Emperor Titus's platform ahead. The Emperor was still standing there, now smiling. The Roman spectators continued to boo loudly, like the displeased fans at a Philadelphia Eagles football game.

There were three strange lines in Yeshua field of vision. Two thicker lines went upwards into the sky on sharp angles and the other was in the middle of his view going downwards and looked like a sharp spear. There was something at the tip of the spear-like object that was red. It looked like blood.

"Wait a sec," said Yeshua to himself. "What is going on here?" he asked himself. He seemed to be rapidly flying towards the Emperor's platform. He looked to his left and right. Shockingly, there seemed to be translucent wings flapping up and down rapidly with black veins and spots on them connected to his body.

"I'm a freaking mosquito," yelled a flabbergasted Yeshua within his mind. He remembered all the mosquitoes biting him while he was fighting the Gauls on the boat. His spirit must have mystically transferred into one of the bloodsucker mosquitos as his past life reincarnation died from his arrow injuries.

"Okay, how do I steer this thing?" he thought himself. "How do I fly like a mosquito?" He saw his target ahead. It was Titus. Ha! He was going to have his revenge and sting Titus. Yeshua focused intently and controlled the mosquito's wings. It worked... he took over the insect's flight controls system and steered the bug right at the Emperor's face.

Titus heard the buzzing coming. He heard the high pitch vibrations of the mosquito in his right ear, then saw the small black bug flying near his head and tried to swat it away. He turned his head and starting walking back towards his throne. The mosquito, however, had different plans. The small flying bug flew up Titus's right nostril to sting him deep within his nasal cavity. It was payback time!

Yeshua steered the mosquito up the dark tunnel of Titus's nose. Then everything shifted again as everything went black.

CHAPTER 5

THE SISTINE CHAPEL

From the blackness, Yeshua saw a huge human-like form materialize ahead in the distance. An enormous man towered in front of him, hundreds of feet tall. At first Yeshua thought it was a giant... like the Nephilim from the Books of Moses; however, it didn't move at all. Appearing completely stationary and looking like an enormous statue, it stood in the middle of a green fertile meadow surrounded by a vast desert plain. On either side of the mammoth figure flowed two black, muddy rivers. Behind the statue, to the west, was an enormous mountain range.

As Yeshua's vision cleared, he saw that the head of the statue was made from pure, glowing gold. He wore a majestic king's crown and had long hair and a beard. His muscular arms were crossed in front of his armored, bulky chest, and his entire upper torso appeared to be made of bright, shiny silver. The plate armor of his mid-section appeared bronze, and his legs looked to be made from iron.

Standing in the vast valley, the gargantuan statue's sandaled feet looked quite strange. They were made from what looked like a mixture of iron and mud or clay.

Yeshua marveled at the wonder before him. In the distance, he heard a loud rumbling sound. From the titanic mountain range behind the statue, a massive landslide tumbled downward from the tallest mountain's peak. All the surrounding ground shook violently as an earthquake sent seismic waves in every direction. Huge amounts of stone and debris descended from the mountaintop. Yeshua watched in awe as a giant rock appeared to be cut out from the side of the mountain and separate itself from a tall, adjacent cliff.

Suddenly, there was an explosion. The huge rock, at least the size of a giant blue whale... shot out towards the direction of the immense statue. Yeshua panicked as he saw the colossal stone fly towards his direction. He ducked as it passed overhead and then watched it hit the massive human figure directly in his feet.

Like a meteorite, the rock smashed and burst the bottom of the statue. The entire figure slowly collapsed and broke into thousands of pieces of debris and dust as it came crashing down towards the ground. A large sediment cloud formed and expanded outwards from the implosion.

The dust enveloped Yeshua. He started choking, and just as he was about to suffocate, a breeze began to blow steadily from the west. The wind quickly swept away the smoke and grit from the air, and Yeshua could breath more easily.

Then something shifted. Time seemed to distort and speed up. Nearby, Yeshua saw a man who looked just like the statue staring at the rubble of his effigy. Tears rolled down his face. The wind became much stronger as the tiny shattered statue fragments blew away until they all disappeared.

The only thing left visible was the giant rock that came from the mountain, still lying on the ground where it had landed. Magically, it expanded and morphed as it rapidly grew larger. It transformed into a tall stony mound, then into a large hill, and then became a considerable mountain.

Yeshua's perspective suddenly changed, and he seemed to be looking from above, in the sky. The mountain looked very familiar. It kept growing larger, and then he clearly recognized its shape. It was definitely Mount Horeb, the mountain of God. It seemed to expand even more and fill the entire Earth.

"Yeshua, Yeshua... are you okay?" yelled Taylor as she shook him in the back of a stretch limousine.

"Yeah, I think I'm okay," responded a very groggy Yeshua. He slowly opened his eyes to see Taylor sitting next to him. As always, she looked like an Angel. Appearing very concerned, Monsignor Giovanni sat across from them.

"Gosh, I was so worried about you," exclaimed Taylor. "Apparently you passed out in the Coliseum. They said you blew your Shofar and then went unconscious. What happened?"

Yeshua looked at the Monsignor. He wasn't sure if he completely trusted him.

"It must have been the heat and jetlag, and maybe some dehydration," explained Yeshua. "I'm fine. Totally fine. Just a few bad mosquito bites here and there."

"We were about to take you to the hospital," said Giovanni. "Thank God you have revived."

The Monsignor said something in Italian to the limousine driver, and they made an immediate right hand turn along a side street. The car then drove onto a short bridge over the ancient Tiber River.

"I'm curious; what's our meeting about? Why are we here?" asked Yeshua.

The Monsignor pushed a button on the side panel of the door next to him and a black glass window rose upwards towards the roof, which then completely separated the driver compartment from the passenger compartment.

"Does he not know?" asked Giovanni as he looked towards Taylor in a perplexed way.

"Actually... he doesn't know anything. But we trust him, and so should you," replied Taylor.

"Wait a sec," interrupted an agitated Yeshua. "What do you mean we? Who exactly is 'we'?"

"Yeshua, calm down," said Taylor. "All will be revealed. I need you to be patient."

"And I am curious, Yeshua," said the Monsignor. "Why do you carry that old ram's horn with you? It looks like it came right out of the Bible."

"It's my good luck charm," responded Yeshua.

"Luck. That's an interesting concept," replied the Monsignor. "Honestly, I don't believe in luck. I think that everything happens for a reason. I think that people who believe in luck just don't have a firm understanding of how statistics works. And then, even what most people call luck just might be divine intervention."

"What do you know about divine intervention?" asked a curious Yeshua.

The limousine turned into the green and lush Vatican Gardens, just to the west of the immense dome of the St. Peter's Basilica.

"I know that luck did not bring the three of us together on this auspicious day," stated Giovanni. "We are here for a reason, for a purpose. And I don't really know much about you, although I am sure it was destiny that chose you to sit across from me in this car. That is what I call divine intervention."

"Honestly, I don't exactly know why I am here," replied Yeshua. "At least can you tell me who it is we're meeting in the Chapel?"

"We are meeting with the Vatican's Secretary of State Cardinal Marco Romano," answered the Monsignor. "He is the Holy See's second in command. He will take your message to the Bishop of Rome."

"Our message?" asked a very confused Yeshua.

"Yes. I, we... have a very important message for him," answered Taylor. "I was going to tell you everything earlier; however, you passed out in the Coliseum."

"Ah, we are here," said Giovanni. The limousine stopped along a narrow street next to the Vatican museum. A strangely dressed medieval looking Vatican guard opened the back door and Taylor, Yeshua and Giovanni exited the vehicle.

As Yeshua followed Giovanni and Taylor towards the museum entrance, he stared upwards and marveled at the enormous multiple tiered dome of the St. Peter's Basilica. He was completely speechless. He wished his best friend Mohammed could be here to see this amazing feat of architecture. He wondered how Mohammed's mission to Saudi Arabia was going and hoped that he was safe.

They entered through a guarded outside door, and then passed through a small chamber and through another door.

Yeshua thought he was in a dream as they entered into the Sistine Chapel. Incredible paintings with hundreds of human figures covered all the towering walls and the long, arced ceiling. He was overwhelmed with admiration at the masterpiece.

Except for one lone man standing in the middle of the room, the rest of the Chapel was entirely empty. He was an elderly white-haired man, dressed in black robes and had a red cap sitting on top his balding head.

The Monsignor quickly walked over to the old man, followed by Yeshua and Taylor, and then greeted him.

"Cardinal Romano, your Eminence... so good to see you," said Giovanni.

"As I am you," responded the Cardinal. "And who do you have here with you?"

"This is Taylor and Yeshua," replied the Monsignor. "They are here from the Holy Land. They have a message for you that we discussed earlier."

"Hello, your Eminence," said Taylor. Yeshua said "Hello," and smiled.

The Cardinal nodded at both of them and smiled back.

"Yeshua, hmmm," said the Cardinal. "Do you know that was the name of our lord and savior?"

"Excuse me? Sir," replied Yeshua.

"Your name. In your Hebrew language... it means Joshua, correct?" asked the Cardinal.

"Yes," responded Yeshua. "It translates to Joshua."

"Yes. Of course it does," said the Cardinal. "And where do you think the name Jesus comes from?"

Yeshua recalled overhearing the group of nun's conversation in Jerusalem about the origins of Jesus's name.

"I believe that Jesus's real name was Yehoshua, in Hebrew," replied Yeshua. "It was later translated to the name 'Lesous' in Greek, then to 'Issues' in Latin, then finally to 'Jesus' in English during the 1500s. So technically, all the Christians should be worshiping a man named Joshua, in English," responded Yeshua.

"Oh my," said the Cardinal. He grinned. "Impressive knowledge from such a young man. I believe you are technically correct."

Yeshua looked at Taylor and Giovanni. They both had shocked and bewildered looks on their faces.

"Tell me, Yeshua," said the Cardinal. "What do you see when you look up at this majestic ceiling here… what catches your eye?"

Yeshua looked directly upwards and scanned at the all hundreds of magnificent paintings of human figures created by Michelangelo approximately 500 years ago. In the center of the roof, he saw a reclining naked man nearly touching fingers with an older bearded man surrounded by several naked figures. He had seen this image before. It was the famous image painting of God creating Adam.

"That painting in the center, I see Adam," said Yeshua. "But there is something about the rest of the painting that I just don't understand."

"What is that, my son?" asked the Cardinal.

"Can I be completely honest with you and speak freely?" asked Yeshua.

"Yes, of course," responded the Cardinal.

"The painting… it clearly violates one of the Ten Commandments given to Moses by God on Mount Sinai," answered Yeshua. "The Third Commandment states… **Thou shalt not make unto thee any graven image**. That means in addition to outlawing of the worship of idols, it is also forbidden to create any physical images of God. God, or rather God the Father is transcendent, eternal, without physical form. And furthermore, to my knowledge, no where in the ancient scriptures does it describe God as an old bearded man wearing a robe."

"Very good and astute observations," said the Cardinal. "However, it also says in the book of Genesis that man was created in God's image, and therefore God must look like a man. Additionally, since the Son of God, Jesus... became incarnate and physical, a certain economy of images are permitted by the Church."

"Well... with all due respect, it seems as though the Church has no problem changing the Ten Commandments when it seems convenient," said Yeshua.

"Yeshua, please! We are not here to argue theology," interrupted Taylor.

"It is perfectly okay," said the Cardinal. "I am enjoying this discussion. It is rare to have someone be so forthright and candid with me. It is actually refreshing. Please, Yeshua... go on."

"So, as I was saying... for example, the Fifth Commandment states **Remember the Sabbath day, to keep it Holy**. For Jews, that is Saturday. Saturday is the Sabbath. It has always and forever been Saturday. It was the seventh day when God rested after creation of the Universe. But the Christians changed it to Sunday. They changed God's Commandant."

"Another exceptionally mindful observation, I am quite impressed with you," replied the Cardinal. "Well, I must say... aren't most of us glad that the Church made Sunday a second Holy day? Otherwise most of the world wouldn't have a two-day weekend."

The Cardinal smiled and Taylor, Yeshua and even Giovanni softly laughed at his humor.

"My young Jewish friend, do you have any other revelations or epiphanies about Michelangelo's masterpieces?" asked the Cardinal. "Then I want to hear your message."

"I think I'm fresh out of epiphanies for the moment. It's been a long day," replied Yeshua.

"Your Eminence," said Taylor. "We have a message for you of the utmost importance."

"And where did this message originate from?" asked the Cardinal.

"It's... as best I can describe, a prophetic vision," answered Taylor. "A plan to initiate world peace."

"And who, may I ask... had this exceptional vision?" questioned the Cardinal.

"I did," replied Taylor. "It came to me in a dream, not long after I met Yeshua, a few months ago."

"Please do share this dream with me," requested the Cardinal.

"I was at the Temple Mount, in Jerusalem; it was a sunny day," described Taylor. "I was like a silent observer, watching from high above. I saw a dozen or so figures walk towards the Dome of the Rock from different directions. I seemed to fly or hover downward to get a closer look; then I started to recognize some of the men. There was the Pope, the Dali Lama, a Hassidic Rabbi and a Muslim Imam and several other important religious looking men."

"How miraculous!" said the Cardinal. "What happened next?"

"They walked into the Dome of the Rock together," answered Taylor. "I then seemed to fly through the top of the golden dome to see within. All the religious leaders stood in a circle around the ancient foundation stone, in-between the tall columns holding up the golden dome. They all closed their eyes and seemed to be in deep thought or meditation. Then, after a few moments, they all raised their arms to the sky and started chanting a prayer in unison."

"How wonderful," said the Cardinal. "What did they say?"

"All is One. All is One. All is One... over and over again. Then I woke up," stated Taylor.

"And that is why you are here? To share with me your vision?" asked the Cardinal.

"Yes and no. There's more," replied Taylor.

"They are here to petition the Pope to fulfill the revelation," said the Monsignor. "They want the Pope to come to Jerusalem and walk onto the Temple mount. They want all the world religious leaders to go inside the Dome of the Rock."

Yeshua looked at Taylor with an expression of total reverence. Apparently he was not the only one with esoteric dreams and mystical premonitions. Everything began to make more sense now.

"We are currently requesting all the great religious leaders to be summoned to the Temple Mount, in the name of world peace," said Taylor. "That is why we are here."

"I will take your message to the Bishop of Rome, my child," replied the Cardinal. "You have my blessings. Now I must leave you. Giovanni will escort you back to your car in the Vatican Gardens when you are ready, and please do take some time to enjoy the beautiful artwork here in the Chapel before you leave."

The Cardinal slowly bowed his head and closed his eyes briefly, then turned and walked away. He left through one of the doors on the far side of the huge room. The closing door made unusual sounding echoes in the chamber.

As Yeshua looked around the room, one of the smaller paintings on the opposite wall seemed to stand out more that any of the others, even more than the epic Last Judgment. He walked over to large mural and examined it closely as it seemed to be calling to him. On the top of the wide painting appeared three winged angels holding spears and swords. They were attacking devil or demon-like creatures below. In the middle of the image was an old bearded man lying on a bed.

"What is this painting?" asked Yeshua. "What does it mean?"

Monsignor Giovanni and Taylor walked over and stood next to Yeshua below the painting.

"This is called *The Dispute over the body of Moses*, painted by Matteo da Lecce in 1574," said Giovanni. "It is based upon a verse in the Epistle of Jude, and describes the Archangel Michael quarreling over Moses's deceased body with the Devil. Apparently the original text describing the event has been lost and Jude just paraphrased the story in his writing."

"Why were they fighting over Moses's body?" asked Yeshua. He did not remember that story from any of his studies.

"There are many theories," explained the Monsignor. "My favorite one is that God did not want Moses's burial to be worshiped by the Jews, which was the Devil's plan. The Angels must have taken him. And to this day, no one knows where Moses is buried."

"I don't remember the Epistle of Jude," said Yeshua. "Is that in the New Testament?"

"Yes, it is," answered the Monsignor. "It's actually one of the shortest books in the Bible, just one chapter of 25 verses. Interestingly, Jude also quotes directly from the Book of Enoch. He describes that the Lord would come with thousands of his saints to render judgment on the wicked deeds of the entire world. Are you familiar with Enoch?"

"Yes, I know Enoch very well," said Yeshua. "His book describes the Watchers, 200 fallen Angels that came to Earth and made offspring with human women. Their children were called the Nephilim, the mighty men who were of old, the men of renown."

"Yes, exactly," said Giovanni. "The Watchers were supposed to do precisely that... watch. They betrayed God when then chose intervene in human matters and lustfully fornicate with women."

"The Book of Enoch absolutely fascinates me," said Yeshua. "It also describes the fallen Angels teaching mankind the art of war, and other technologies and sciences such as writing, agriculture and astrology."

"That reminds me of the story of Prometheus when he steals fire and gives it to humanity," replied Taylor.

"Yes, he was punished severely by Zeus for his betrayal. So many of the ancient myths from cultures around the world parallel the story of the Watchers and the Nephilim," responded the Monsignor. "Divine beings that came from the sky and mated with humans. The Greek Titans and demigods, the Sumerian Anunnaki, the Norse Legends, the Mayans and even many of the Indian Vedic and Hindu stories."

"It seems like there must be some kind of truth to all those epic historical legends if they existed in so many different times and cultures," said Taylor. "What if they describe the same actual events, just told in similar ways with different names and characters?"

"And what if they were some kind of colonizing space aliens, coming down to Earth from the sky to exploit our natural resources and have some fun with the natives?" asked Yeshua. "Is it possible that they would be described as deities or angels by our long distant ancestors?"

"That is certainly possible," said Giovanni. "As the story goes, the actions of the Watchers, be they bad angels or extraterrestrial aliens… angered God so much that the Earth was nearly destroyed by a great flood. Only Noah, his family and many pairs of different animals, were saved to start over and repopulate the world. God then gives Noah seven laws for all of humanity to follow."

"The flood story is also told in hundreds of ancient cultures all around the world," said Taylor. "My father is an archeologist who said that the Sumerians have a very similar flood story where a man named Ziusudra is told by their God Enki to build a huge boat to avoid being drown by a flood sent to destroy mankind."

"Yes, perhaps you are right, Taylor," said Giovanni. "The names are different; however, the characters and events are perhaps the same."

Yeshua looked up again at the painting of the flying Angels fighting the demonic creatures over Moses's body. He looked at the Angel Michael in the center, holding his sword and striking down evil as God's messenger. He looked so familiar.

"And the message is possibly the same in all the stories, across all the cultures and religions," said Yeshua. "Do good and good things will happen. Do bad and bad things will happen. That is the will of God, the law of Karma."

"I believe you are absolutely correct my friend, the golden rule," replied the Monsignor. "That reminds me of a quote from one of your famous Hebrew Rabbis… Hillel. He says 'What is hateful to you, do not do to your fellow. This is the whole Torah, the rest is explanation, now go and learn.'"

CHAPTER 6

THE BAHÁ'Í

Haifa, Israel
Military Headquarters
Two Days Later

Yeshua, Taylor, Mohammed and General Cohen sat patiently in a small, plain conference room with no windows. The door opened and General Geller walked inside. Everyone stood up in attention as the door closed behind him.

"At ease," said Geller and everyone quickly sat back down. The General walked to the head of the conference table and sat down in a chair. He opened a manila folder lying in front of him and went through some papers for a few moments. Mohammed and Yeshua looked at each other and smiled.

"I see phase one is going perfectly," said Geller. "You have all made contact with your initial assignments and delivered the messages. Is that correct?"

"Yes, Sir," said everyone in unison.

"Perfect," replied Geller. "And now I have new assignments for you. General Cohen... you will go to meet with the Sephardi Chief Rabbi, the Rishon Lezion, in Jerusalem. Mohammed and Yeshua, you will go to the Bahá'í Temple here in Haifa and find their religious leader. And Taylor, your father has requested your presence. I will deliver you a message later with his exact location and arrange for transportation. Any questions?"

"Yes Sir," replied Mohammed. "What do we do after we meet with our next assignments? Do we come back here?"

"No. You definitely will not come back here," answered the General. He reached into his pocket and pulled out four small, black cellphones. After looking at each one, he slid them across the table to Yeshua, Mohammed, Taylor and Cohen.

"After you deliver your messages, we will let you know your next assignment. Just text the word 'Zion' to let us know," explained Geller. "Otherwise, do not use these phones for normal communications."

"Yes Sir," said everyone in unison again.

Geller looked through the papers again in the manila folder. He looked surprised as he read through one of the reports.

"Yeshua?" said the General sternly. "It says here you passed out unconscious in the Coliseum while in Rome. That you almost jeopardized the mission. What happened exactly? Are you fit to continue?"

"Yes Sir," replied Yeshua. "I am 100% fine. I think I was just really dehydrated. I forgot to drink enough water as I was so excited to go to Rome. I promise that won't happen again."

"Are you sure you don't need a complete medical evaluation?" asked Geller. "Perhaps Mohammed should go on without you."

"I am absolutely good to proceed," pleaded Yeshua. "There will be no more setbacks. I am completely healthy and ready to deliver the messages. You have my word."

"It's not your word I'm concerned about," said General Geller as he stood up from his chair. He started to walk towards the door. "I sense there's some kind of secret you're hiding from us. You have some power or ability you aren't revealing."

The General opened the door, then turned back to look at everyone still sitting in their chairs. "You are dismissed. Good luck with your missions, Baruch Hashem."

Thirty minutes later, an Uber dropped Mohammed and Yeshua at the UNESCO Square at the base of the Bahá'í Gardens in Haifa. They left the car and walked towards the circular geometric plaza centered with a beautiful, flowing fountain. Directly to the west, a giant staircase cut up the middle of a steep green hill. Ten stone terraces surrounded by inspiring landscaping of elegant trees and flowers led up to a massive gold domed shrine which sat midway up the hill.

"That shrine, it reminds me of the dome of St. Peter's Basilica in Rome," said Yeshua as both he and Mohammed began their ascent up the stairs of the mountain. "I wish you could have seen it."

"Yeshua, it feels like it's been forever since we have spoken," said Mohammed. "So much has happened. Tell me all about your trip to Italy. What happened at the Coliseum?"

"You won't believe it," replied Yeshua. "I sounded the Shofar and went back in time to the opening day of the inaugural Coliseum games."

"Wow! You travelled back in time almost 2000 years? And you were a gladiator?" asked Mohammed.

"Yes and no," replied Yeshua. "At first, I was just in spirit form… like we were when we went back in time during the David and Goliath battle. The absolutely cool thing was, they had flooded the floor of the arena with water and staged a huge naval battle."

"Really, with boats?" asked Mohammed. "They made the whole thing into a lake?"

"Yes, there were a dozen or so small war vessels. It was a fight to the death," answered Yeshua. "I found a Hebrew ship… it even had a menorah on its flag. And another unbelievable thing was one of the men looked exactly like me. Just like David looked like me, and the child Isaac at Mount Moriah."

"So, this was another past life regression?" questioned Mohammed. "You went back and saw yourself again?"

"Yes!" replied Yeshua. "Incredibly, he was the same child all grown up who I saw captured in Masada by the Romans and who was taken as a slave. That's the vision I had on my Bar Mitzvah Day. However, when I went back in time after blowing the Shofar in the Coliseum, he was eight years older and the leader of the Hebrew slaves on their warship."

Yeshua and Mohammed reached the halfway point up the stairs. They were both slightly out of breath after walking hundreds of steps. They took a short break on one of the stone terraces and looked out onto the sprawling port city of Haifa.

"So, what happened during the battle?" asked Mohammed.

"At first, I was a silent observer," explained Yeshua. "But then, as the battle with the other boats raged on... I found a way to help them. I was able to go into the water and push the boat faster to avoid being rammed by the Egyptians. Later, I actually moved my spirit into the red-haired man who looked like me and helped him fight some much stronger barbarians."

"Ah. Just like I went into David and helped him defeat Goliath," replied Mohammed.

"Yes, exactly like that," said Yeshua. "My spirit, or soul completely merged with him. We became one, and I used my military training to win the day."

Yeshua and Mohammed continued up the long staircase towards the golden Shrine of Bab.

"What about you, Mohammed?" asked Yeshua. "Tell me about your trip."

"Well... it was not nearly exciting as yours," responded Mohammed. "I travelled to Mecca and met with the Imam of the Grand Mosque. I was given a wonderful tour of the al-Masjid al-Harām and prayed at the Kabaa. I delivered my message and completed my mission."

"How was your message received?" asked Yeshua. "Did the Imam agree to come to the Dome of the Rock and help declare world peace?"

"No. He did not," replied Mohammed. "He said he would take the request back to his council to discuss it. He also asked me which other world religious leaders were being asked to attend, and I told him I didn't know for sure."

"Oh, before I forget... there was something else from my trip," said Yeshua. "I had another one of those wild dreams."

"Please do tell, my friend," replied Mohammed. "You have the most fascinating dreams. What happened? More Nazis?"

"No. No more Nazis thank goodness," responded Yeshua. "In the dream, I saw a giant statue that looked like some kind of King. His head was made from gold, his chest silver, his mid-section bronze, his legs iron, and his feet a mixture of iron and clay. And then, a giant stone flew out of a mountain and smashed the whole thing to pieces."

"Did the stone turn into a giant mountain afterward that filled the Earth?" asked Mohammed.

"Wait... how do you know what my dream was?" answered a very surprised Yeshua. "That's impossible! But yes, it actually did turn into a mountain... it turned into Jebel al Lawz, the black mountain in Saudi Arabia."

"Ahhh... yet another reason we must go there. Your dream is a story from your Hebrew Prophet Daniel," said Mohammed. "I'm surprised you don't know it. It's from the book of Daniel, which takes place after the Babylonians destroyed the first Israelite Temple in Jerusalem in 587 BC. Daniel is taken captive and becomes an advisor and dream reader for the Babylonian King Nebuchadnezzar."

"Yes, I do remember some of stories of Daniel," replied Yeshua. "But I never read the book. He's the one who survived the Lion's den. I don't recall much about that dream though. What does it mean?"

"David interpreted the King's dream. Incredibly, that's the same dream you had," said Mohammed. "It was a prophecy of the future. He told Nebuchadnezzar that the gold head represented his Babylonian kingdom, which would be followed by another kingdom representing the silver chest, then a kingdom representing the bronze mid-section and another for the iron legs. Finally, the feet represented a fifth kingdom; then the entire statue was destroyed by a stone representing the power of the eternal Kingdom of God."

"Wow, Mohammed... how do you remember all that?" asked Yeshua. "And did the prophecies come true?"

"Let's just say I have a photographic memory," explained Mohammed. "I remember everything I read. And yes, apparently the prophecy did come true. The dream accurately predicted the subsequent major world empires after the Babylonians."

"Really? How so?" asked Yeshua.

"Not long after Nebuchadnezzar died, Babylon was conquered by Cyrus the Great and the Persians. Interestingly, it was Cyrus that let the captured Hebrews return to Israel to reclaim their homeland and build the second Temple in Jerusalem."

"And I assume the bronze empire was the Greeks?" said Yeshua.

"Yes, Alexander the Great and the Greeks defeated the Persians and the iron empire became the Romans, who conquered the Greeks," replied Mohammed.

"But who is the empire that represents the clay and iron feet?" asked Yeshua.

Before Mohammed could answer, they reached the top of the stairs at the base of the giant Shrine of Bab, 511 steps up from the UNESCO Square below. An older women with an olive complexion wearing a flowing floral robe and headdress was waiting for them at the black wrought iron gate at the lower entrance to the Shrine.

"You must be Mohammed and Yeshua," she said in an Arabic-English accent as she opened the gate. "I have been waiting for you."

Yeshua and Mohammed both slightly bowed their heads and entered through the gateway. They weren't sure if they should shake her hand.

"We are very pleased to meet you," said Mohammed.

"My name is Ashti Jafari," she said. "I am here as a representative of the Bahá'í faith. I understand you have a message for us."

"Yes, we have a very important request for you," responded Mohammed. "But first, would you mind telling us a little about this incredible Shrine and gardens here. I've never seen anything like it. It's so beautiful and serene."

"Of course," said Ashti. "This is a mausoleum for Báb, the founder of our faith. Do you know anything about our Bahá'í traditions?"

Yeshua and Mohammed both looked at each other and shook their heads.

"Sorry, we don't," said Yeshua.

"Our religion teaches the essential worth of all religions and the unity of all peoples. It was founded in 1844 in Iran, and our Prophet Bahá'u'lláh had a revelation that he was a messenger of God... like Moses, Christ and Muhammad. He saw himself as a divine educator, with a purpose and destiny to uplift mankind through love and unity. We are taught that all the great Prophets are sent by God, as part of an orderly progression of revelation during each historical era to help humanity progress with its spiritual evolution. At the heart of our teachings is the goal of a unified world order that ensures the well being of all nations, races and faiths."

"That is exactly why we're here," responded Yeshua. "We have a message for your leader. It's about world peace."

"I am sorry to disappoint you, young man," said Ashti. "We have no leader. There are no clergy. We have a nine-member spiritual assembly who govern the affairs of our faith."

"Umm... well, is there someone we can speak to that can deliver a message to the assembly?" asked Yeshua. "Are you a member?"

"Unfortunately, I am not part of the Universal House of Justice," she replied. "I recently escaped Iran after years of persecution and jail for my beliefs. However, I am happy to relay your message to the assembly. What do you wish to communicate?"

"We have a vision for world unity," stated Yeshua. "We request that all the leaders and appropriate representatives of the world's major religions come to Jerusalem and walk on the Temple Mount and go into the Dome of the Rock and declare world peace together."

"That is quite a vision, young man," said Ashti. "I am sure when I relay your message to the governing members it will be met with open arms. I will let them know as soon as we conclude here. Do you have anything more you would like them to know?"

"No. That is the entire message," responded Yeshua. "However, I have two questions for you. I am very curious about some of the things you said about Bahá'í"

"Please, you can ask anything, and I will answer to the best of my ability," she said.

"Why were you persecuted in Iran?" Yeshua asked. "Why were you jailed?"

"That is an easy question to answer, young man," replied Ashti. "Both the Sunni and Shia religious Muslim sects consider the Baha'i to be deserters and apostates from Islam. In my home country of Iran, this has led to brutal public attacks, arrests, executions and torture of Bahá'ís over the centuries."

"Oh my, I am so sorry," said Yeshua. "Thank God you escaped."

"It's similar to how we on the Sufi path are treated by traditional Islam," explained Mohammed. "I wish we could all just get along and accept each other as brothers and sisters."

"Yes, that is one of the main principles of our Bahá'í faith... universal acceptance, tolerance and unity," said Ashti. "And what was your second question, young man?"

"You said something to the effect that God's ultimate plan is revealed through each Great Prophet as religion and humanity evolve and progress through time. Is that correct?"

"In essence... yes," responded Ashti. "Our Prophet Bahá'u'lláh was one of a long line of true Manifestations of God who also include Muhammad, Christ, Buddha, Zoroaster, Krishna, Moses, Abraham and Adam. Each world teacher shared a divine message in each era to help shape society for the better."

"So, when will the next Prophet come?" asked Yeshua. "It seems that we are in desperate, shallow times and certainly need someone to help the world to become a better place."

"That may be true," answered Ashti. "However, the Bahá'u'lláh predicted it would be at least another 1000 years until another Messenger of God would appear."

"1000 years? That's a very long time," said Mohammed.

"However, the Bahá'u'lláh does describe that God sometimes choses ordinary people to act as a prophets, albeit what is considered a minor prophet, to inspire and endow them intentionally to intervene in human affairs when needed. Perhaps that is why the both of you are here."

"You think we are some kind of prophets?" asked Yeshua.

"Yes, isn't it obvious?" responded Ashti. "Your mission is world peace. You are messengers of God's will. I see the purity in your souls and the unconditional love in your hearts. I am certainly blessed and honored to be in your presence. I will now relay your request to our assembly. I hope and pray that your requests to all the world religious leaders are fulfilled. Goodbye, for now..."

Ashti slightly bowed her head, turned and walked away. Yeshua and Mohammed also bowed their heads as she left. They both looked at each other in silence for a few moments.

"Did you hear what she just said?" asked Mohammed. "She said we are some kind of prophets. That God chose us to bring about world peace."

"Well, Mohammed... I say this in the most humblest way possible," said Yeshua. "After everything that's happened, I think that makes total sense. For heaven's sake, we have a magical Shofar that sends us back into the past as Angels whose roles are to change the outcome of human history."

"Good point," replied Mohammed. "We definitely are on a mission from God."

Yeshua pulled out his little black phone given to him by General Geller. He texted the word 'Zion' to the one and only contact on the phone whose name was ironically Al Einstein. After a few moments, a message was sent back that said... **Go to Haifa military airport 0700. American flight to Baghdad. Destroy phone.**

CHAPTER 7

BABLYON

The United States Air Force C-130J Super Hercules military transport plane landed smoothly at the Camp Victory Army Base in Baghdad. Yeshua and Mohammed deboarded with Elijah Spencer, the American who was in charge of the United States Peace Delegation from their previous trip to Saudi Arabia. They climbed into the back of a beige Humvee parked nearby which then drove away from the airstrip. Two men in khaki colored US Army uniforms sat in the front of the vehicle; the older one was driving. As they left, Yeshua looked back and saw dozens of fully geared American troops boarding the giant transport airplane.

"Where are all those troops going?" Yeshua asked Elijah as he made sure his Shofar was okay in his large backpack next to him.

"They are heading back to the good ole' USA," he replied. "Those men have completed their tour of duty. We are slowly decreasing our presence here. It's time to go home."

"You Americans should have never come here in the first place," said Mohammed. "There was so much suffering and unnecessary bloodshed. As I recall, they never even found any weapons of mass destruction."

"Those decision were made a long time ago, for their own reasons and purposes," said Elijah. "Now, we are doing our best to restore some balance and autonomy here."

"So, where are we going?" asked Yeshua. "Honestly, we have no idea why we are here."

"No one told you?" asked Elijah. "We're headed to a small town called Hillah, just south of Baghdad. Ever heard of it?"

"Nope. Never heard of that place," responded Yeshua. Mohammed then shook his head. "Should we know anything about it?"

"It's where the ruins of ancient Babylon are located," replied Elijah. "We are going to meet with Corporal Taylor and her Father. Apparently they've discovered something important in the ancient ruins and we need to make sure they are protected while they do the excavations."

"Protect?" asked Yeshua. "From whom?"

"There's still some of these bad actors from the Islamic State roaming around," responded Elijah. "When some rumors got out that there's a few Israeli archeologists snooping around the ruins, we got concerned that some of the locals would call for all out Jihad. So that's why we are going there. As I recall, Yeshua... you have some kind of psychic gift that alerts you when danger is nearby. Correct?"

"Yes, that's correct," responded Yeshua. "I get a high pitch buzzing sound in my right ear when something potentially bad is about to happen."

The Humvee stopped at a military checkpoint. The driver showed the heavily armed guards some papers, and then started driving again. They left the base complex and drove south into a sparsely populated barren looking wasteland.

"Is you right ear buzzing now?" asked Elijah.

"No," replied Yeshua. "And I hope it never does again."

"I hope so too," said Elijah. "For all our sakes."

"Elijah, if you don't mind me asking... I have a question for you," said Mohammed.

"Sure, what's up?" he responded.

"Our mission to Saudi Arabia... do you have an update?" asked Mohammed. "Are the Israelis and Palestinians going to work on the peace plan we discussed? Are they going to vote for the Palestinian representative we met as their leader and start the final negotiations?"

"I can't really comment on much of that," replied Elijah. "All I can tell you is there's been an unexpected delay in the Palestinian general elections, and for now and the whole plan is currently in limbo."

The Humvee headed south on Highway Eight. They passed several small towns. Along the dusty road, a bunch of young children played soccer. Occasionally, they would drive past a burned-out pick-up truck or car. Yeshua wondered how much death and destruction this road had seen during the Gulf Wars.

"Yeshua, they told me... after our peace conference in Riyadh, were you kidnapped by the Iranians?" asked Elijah.

"Yes. Right after we left the meeting, our car was hijacked, and they kidnapped me. They took me on a boat heading towards Iran," replied Yeshua. "They wanted the identity of the Palestinian representative so they could assassinate him and derail the peace process."

"And I assume you didn't tell them. Did they torture you? How did you survive?" questioned Elijah.

"No. Of course I didn't tell them," replied Yeshua. "And yes, they were pretty brutal with their interrogation techniques."

Yeshua recalled that Mohammed telepathically mind controlled one of the terrorists on the boat and stopped him from being killed by the man with the scar on his face. Yeshua looked at his best friend and smiled in gratitude, then directed his attention back to Elijah.

"I luckily had a wristwatch with a GPS rescue signal, so was able to activate it," continued Yeshua. "Then the cavalry showed up to rescue me, thank God."

"Yes, I saw the report about the Navy Seals rescuing you," said Elijah. "It's a miracle you made it out alive."

"Indeed it was," said Mohammed. "The Universe works in mysterious ways."

"Indeed it does," replied Elijah.

After about twenty minutes, the Humvee turned off the main highway and took a side road. They passed the carcasses of two old half destroyed Russian tanks. Impact craters of various sizes still littered the ground.

They drove though some pastures, then made a left turn and parked near a landing pad full of antiquated helicopters. Everyone got out of the Humvee and Yeshua grabbed his olive-green pack and placed it on his back. To the west, he could see some really tall tan colored mud-brick walls beyond a large group of oak trees.

"And welcome to Babylon," said Elijah as he walked along the grove of green trees to the north. The two Army men from the Humvee flanked him on either side, and Yeshua and Mohammed followed behind.

"Your ears buzzing?" asked Elijah.

"No, nothing," replied Yeshua. Elijah made a thumbs up gesture.

"Oh, and by the way," said Elijah. "This is Army Specialist Reed and Jones. Sorry for the delay in introductions."

The group cleared the trees and approached a large multi-level tiered wall made from sand colored mud bricks. To the north, a long canal of water stretched off into the distance. Dozens of tall palm trees surrounded the perimeter of the wall.

"This was the main entrance to Babylon," said Elijah. "The famous blue Ishtar gate was just south of these walls, as well as the famous hanging gardens... one of the Seven Wonders of the ancient world."

They crossed next to the threshold of the outer walls. Directly in front of them stood a large grey statue of a lion on a stone pedestal, and under the lion's feet was the shape of a human figure. Beyond the statue was a vast, sprawling area of irregularly shaped brick ruins.

"What's that?" asked Mohammed. "There were lions here in Iraq?"

"Yes. Remember the story of Daniel and the lion's den? It's a statue of an Asiatic lion," replied Elijah. "They used to roam all the way from Turkey and the Middle East deep into Asia. Now, only a few hundred exist in small preserve in India. This lion statue is a national symbol of Iraq and they say it's over 2600 years old and was created during the time of King Nebuchadnezzar."

"Why is it trampling a man?" asked Yeshua.

"The lion statue was meant to create fear in the adversaries of the Babylonians," replied Elijah. "It's symbolic of the Babylonians crushing their enemies."

Yeshua saw some movement in the ruins to the west. There were several people partially hidden in depths of the mud brick pits. He recognized Taylor moving about the one of the section of the ancient remains.

"I see Taylor over there," said Yeshua.

"Yes, that's the archeological team," said Elijah. "We are here to protect them. Let's head that way."

They started walking toward into the dilapidated stone and mud-brick ruins. To the west in the distance was a large modern looking fortress on a hill.

"What is that place?" asked Mohammed. He pointed to the huge building.

"Oh. That Saddam's Hussein's Babylonian Palace," replied Elijah. "Back in the day, he was hell bent on making this a major tourist spot and a display of his power. Too bad he didn't care much for real archeology... most of the fancy walls you see here and that Palace are hasty reconstructions for his theme-park project plan, built without any regard for preserving the original structures."

"And these ruins we're walking in, what were they?" asked Yeshua.

"These are the remains of what was called the Northern Palace," said Professor Taylor, who had snuck up behind them.

"Ah, Professor Taylor... so good to see you," said Elijah. They shook hands. "I assume you already know Yeshua and Mohammed. This is Reed and Jones. We're here to protect your archeological mission."

"Thank goodness," said a relived Professor. "Ever since we found the cuneiform cylinder here at our dig a few days ago, we've attracted a lot of attention."

"The cuneiform cylinder? What is that?" asked Yeshua.

"It's a 2500-year-old clay inscription from the time of Cyrus the Great," said Taylor, who now joined the group.

"Taylor!" exclaimed Yeshua. He was smiling.

"Hello Yeshua, Mohammed, Mr. Spencer, gentlemen," she said as she nodded towards everyone.

"Please, call me Elijah. So nice to finally meet you," said Elijah.

"We think we found another version of the Cyrus cylinder, likely a duplicate copy," said Taylor. "It's in bad shape, but we could make out some of the more important passages."

"What is the Cyrus cylinder?" asked Yeshua.

"The original cylinder was found here in the ruins of Babylon, not far from this location in 1879," explained the Professor. "It dates back from the 6th century BCE and is a declaration from the Persian King Cyrus the Great who conquered Babylon. It's a clay tablet written in Akkadian cuneiform script and describes the events of his victory over the Babylonian King Nabdonidus."

"Oh, wow," said Yeshua. "I never heard of that artifact… it sounds really important, historically."

"Yes, the original cylinder is in the British Museum in London," replied the Professor. "And interestingly, the passage on the cylinder we found is perhaps the most important inscription pertaining to the biblical Hebrews."

"Really? What does it say?" asked Yeshua.

"It says, and I will do my best to paraphrase the writing," replied the Professor.

"Cyrus declared... **From many ancient places, and sacred centers on the other side of the river Tigris, whose sanctuaries had been abandoned for a long time, I returned the images of the Gods, who had resided there, to their places and I let them dwell in eternal abobes. I gathered all their inhabitants and returned to them their dwellings.**"

"And how does that relate to the ancient Israelites?" asked Mohammed.

"Very good question," responded the Professor. "After King Nebuchadnezzar and the Babylonians destroyed Jerusalem, they brought the surviving Hebrews here as captives. They spent 70 years here in exile. When King Cyrus captured the city, as the story goes... he freed the Jews and let them return back to Israel to rebuild their Temple."

"Ah... I see," said Mohammed. "That's what the passage on your cylinder implies. That Cyrus gathered all the captive foreigners here and he let them return to their homelands."

"Yes, that's exactly how we are interpreting King Cyrus's declaration."

"Professor! Professor! We found something," yelled one of the men digging in an adjacent excavation pit.

"Wonderful, how exciting," exclaimed the Professor. He and the entire group walked quickly over to see what was happening in the nearby ruins. There were several men uncovering a large white stone deep in a pit with the image of a winged human on it. They were using small shovels and brushes to separate it from surrounding clay and sand.

"Oh my, what a beautiful find," said the Professor. "Museum quality. Probably 7th century BCE. It's a winged Apkallu with a banduddu and mullilu."

"Apkallu, banduddu, mullilu?" asked Yeshua.

Yeshua looked carefully at the man on the stone tablet that the professor was calling an Apkallu. As the archeologists carefully brushed the sand from the carving, Yeshua was amazed to see that the figure's head looked exactly like the head of an eagle. The eagle-man had long braided hair and held something that looked like a pinecone in one hand. In the other hand he was carrying what looked like a women's pocketbook. He had two beautifully carved massive angel wings coming from his back. And surprisingly, he seemed to be wearing a fancy bracelet on his wrist that looked exactly like a modern-day wristwatch.

"Yes, he is called an Apkallu... one of seven Mesopotamian sages who brought knowledge and arts to humanity after a great cataclysm," said the Professor. "The banduddu is the bucket container he is holding and the mullilu is the object that looks like a pinecone in his other hand."

"What's the purpose of the bucket and cone?" asked Mohammed.

"As the story goes, the Apkallu were sent by the Creator to our Earth to serve as protectors, lawgivers and cleansers."

"Like the Archangel Michael?" asked Yeshua.

"Yes, just like the Archangels of the Judeo-Christian traditions," replied the Professor. "However, these divine beings pre-dated the biblical Angels by thousands of years. Now, where was I? Oh yes... back to the pinecone and the buckets."

"Sorry for interrupting," apologized Yeshua.

"There are many theories about the cone and the bucket that the winged Apkallu are holding," explained the Professor. "There are dozens of similar ancient carvings found all over what was once the vast lands of the Sumerians. The most common explanation is that the cone would be dipped into the bucket containing holy water and then used to purify objects. Another belief is perhaps the bucket was full of tree pollen, and the cone would be dipped into the pollen and then used to fertilize trees."

"Dad, come on... that's not what you really think," interjected Taylor. "Tell them your theory."

"Well, it's not really a theory," said the Professor. "It's more like the science fiction version."

"Oh, please do tell," asked Elijah.

"So, I'm not sure these creatures are just mythical metaphors," explained the Professor. "I think they were highly advanced beings from a different star system or dimension. They are represented with wings because they could fly through time and space."

"I knew it! Space Aliens," said Yeshua.

"They are perhaps those who are described as the race of Anunnaki by the Sumerians and later the Babylonians," said the Professor."

"Wait a sec," said Elijah. "I remember reading a book about the Anunnaki. They came to Earth hundreds of thousands of years ago from outer space to find gold. They made bases here and then created humans as a slave species to mine the gold for them."

"Yes, that book is called *The Twelfth Planet*, by Zecharia Sitchin," responded the Professor. "It's more or less a science fiction story without any real proof of archeological information."

"But Daddy, you said yourself that those stories might be true," said Taylor. "They are described in detail in the Epic of Gilgamesh. Tell them what you think the cone and bucket were actually used for by the Apkallu."

"Okay, Okay," responded the Professor. "So, I think the 'bucket' was some kind of advanced technology that produced high frequency sound waves, then they, the Apkallu or Anunnaki... used the cone to direct the sound waves into energy beams."

"Energy beams? Really... like Stars Wars?" asked Yeshua. "What did they do with the energy?"

The Professor smiled. "To cut stone, of course. They used the beams to cut through hard stone, like butter. And then they were able to levitate the stones and then move them. I think they used the dials on their wrists to tune the energy beams."

"Amazing. Why did they do that?" said Elijah. "To mine the gold?"

"Maybe," replied the Professor. "However, I think they also used their stone cutting technology all around the world at ancient sites like Peru, Egypt, Lebanon, Easter Island and Japan. If you look at the archeological foundations of those many of those sites, there are stones that are hundreds of tons or more created with laser precision."

"Like the stones that make the Pyramids in Egypt?" asked Mohammed.

"Possibly," said the Professor. "However, each pyramid stones weighs about three tons. That's not that much compared to other places in Egypt, Peru and Baalbek in Lebanon where there's over 1000-ton precision cut stones. There's just no way humans in those cultures could have quarried and moved them."

"So you really believe in the beings from other planets theory, Professor? Some kind of ancient aliens?" asked Elijah.

"I know it sounds crazy, but I do," replied the Professor. "And after years of archeological digs, I will explain why. I'll make a long story short for you and try not to bore you all. Any way, we need to get back to our digging soon, okay?"

"Okay, yes… perfect," said Elijah.

"Let's look at the ancient dynastic Egyptian technology for example," began the Professor. "We know they only had basic bronze tools and chisels 4 to 5 thousand years ago. And granite or basalt stone has a hardness scale of 7 to 8, with diamond being the hardest natural substance with a hardness level of 10. So, in order to cut and shape granite… the Egyptians would have needed a powerful cutting object or technology that was higher on the hardness scale. They just didn't have it."

"Hence your pine cone and bucket energy beam theory," said Elijah.

"Honestly, I don't have any other plausible explanations," replied the Professor. "There's just no way to perfectly and precisely cut and polish super hard granite thousands of years ago except with some type of highly advanced technology."

"Fascinating, Professor… I really like your angle on this," said Elijah. "I'm sure most of your contemporary archeologists would disagree with you."

"Yes, most of them do," responded the Professor. "However, there is a small group of us that believe there was a highly advance ancient culture that existed well before the Sumerians and dynastic Egyptians who were able to cut, move and perfectly place gigantic stones. The stones still exist in many places and we are just now revealing their secrets. And with all that being said, let's get back to our digging."

"Does anyone mind Mohammed and I take a look around?" asked Yeshua.

Elijah gave Yeshua an alarmed look. He quickly pointed to his right ear and asked, "Everything okay?"

"Yes, everything's just fine," replied Yeshua. "If you don't mind… we'd like to explore the place a bit. It seems safe enough. We will be very careful and return quickly. I mean, how often do you get to be in ancient Babylon?"

Taylor pulled out a black glock handgun from her side pack and handed it to Yeshua.

"We won't need that," Yeshua responded as he waved his hands. "We'll be totally okay."

"Be careful boys," said Taylor as she returned the gun back to her pack. "Just to the south of here along the outer walls is a reconstruction of the Ishtar Gate. It's impressive… check it out. And don't be too long… the locals aren't too fond of us Israelis."

"We won't," said Yeshua. Both he and Mohammed starting walking back towards the Lion Statue. Taylor, the Professor, and the others crawled down into the large archeological pit to help the dig team excavate the large white stone relief containing the mystical winged Apkallu.

"Do you think it's true?" asked Mohammed once they were out of earshot from the ruins.

"That what's true?" responded Yeshua.

"About those space aliens coming here and using their technology to cut the massive stones all over the Earth," said Mohammed. "That would explain so much, maybe even the lost city of Atlantis. Perhaps that's the ancient culture the space aliens helped which was destroyed by the great flood."

"I don't know," replied Yeshua. "Anything is possible. However, we have something that might help us to find out what really happened."

Yeshua opened his backpack and showed Mohammed his Shofar. He winked, and then closed the pack. They walked past the giant lion statue trampling a man, and then they turned south. The two young men then strolled down a dirt road in-between two giant ancient looking walls.

Ahead, in the distance they could see the brilliant blue Ishtar gate. The massive structure was decorated with images of dragons, bulls and flowers.

"This must have been to main entrance to city of Babylon," said Mohammed as they continued to walk towards the monumental gate. "Just think, almost 2600 hundred years ago... your Prophet Daniel and the surviving Israelite prisoners walked this very road into the city."

"Where they remained captives and suffered 70 long and painful years, until they were freed by King Cyrus," replied Yeshua.

They reached the base of the giant blue Ishtar Gate. A tall open arch led into the city ruins beyond. No one else around was roaming the ruins.

"I have an idea," said Yeshua as he slung his backpack around his body and opened it.

"You always scare me when you say that," half joked Mohammed.

Yeshua brought out his gleaming and smoothly polished Shofar. It sparkled in the sunlight. He closed his backpack and put it down on the ground near the Ishtar gate.

"Do you remember how we did this at the Golden Gate in Jerusalem?" asked Yeshua.

"Yes, of course I do," replied Mohammed. "It's perfect timing. Let's do this."

Yeshua stepped under the giant arch and placed his left hand on one of the large blue bricks along the inner wall and held the long, spiraled Shofar in his right hand. Mohammed stood next to Yeshua and placed his right hand onto an adjacent blue brick and his left hand on the Shofar.

Yeshua put the Shofar up to his lips and blew with all his might.

Ba-ba-baaaaaaaaaaaaaaa...

Ba-ba-baaaaaaaaaaaaaaaa...

Ba-ba-baaaaaaaaaaaaaaaa...

Everything went black.

Out of the darkness came a wonderful array of lights. First it was dim, and then a tunnel of repeating concentric circles formed in front of them. The glowing lights got much brighter, and Yeshua and Mohammed seemed to be flying through a streaming tunnel full of multicolored patterns and rotating circles.

"Mohammed, are you there?" asked a formless Yeshua.

"Yes my friend, I'm here… at least I think I am," said Mohammed. "Although, I can't see or feel my body, but I know I am here."

From the end of the tunnel they saw a rapidly approaching bright light. Then they came out through the light at the end of the tunnel.

Yeshua was back under the arch of the Ishtar Gate. However, there were dozens of strangely dressed people going in and out of through the city's entrance. Most of them had olive colored skin and wore long robes.

Suddenly, a donkey pulling a large white cart almost ran over Yeshua. He tried to jump out of the way from being hit, but he quickly realized that after sounding his Shofar, he was in a spirit form and not in his physical body. He looked around for Mohammed's apparition, but couldn't see any sign of his friend.

"Mohammed! Mohammed… are you here?" he telepathically yelled out as loud as he could. There was no response.

"Mohammed, where are you? Where did you go?" Yeshua screamed in his mind. A few quiet moments went by… again, no response. No one could hear him. He thought that his friend must have gone ahead into the city.

Yeshua concentrated and moved his spirit through the Ishtar Gate and into the sprawling, busy city. He passed by several Babylonian soldiers guarding the gate who were thankfully completely unaware of his presence.

Once through the outer walls, Yeshua beheld the most incredible view of his lifetime. Directly to his right stood the magnificent and fabled Hanging Gardens of Babylon. It was a giant complex of columned tiers, marble steps, ornate fountains and beautiful statues. Thousands of lush palm trees, exceptionally manicured topiary, and flowering shrubs decorated the entire structure. A massive waterfall flowed from the top of the gardens into a picturesque lake below, creating a wonderful mirrored image of the wonders above.

In the distance, a massive seven-leveled ziggurat pyramid shaped tower rose high into the sky, dwarfing the entire city. A large palatial temple building was next to the ziggurat. As far as the eye could see, thousands of brick buildings filled the entire landscape, all the way to the horizon.

Yeshua moved south down the main road of the city towards the palace. Perhaps that's where Mohammed would be, he thought. Along the very crowded street, dozens of vendors in wooden kiosks sold their items including fruits, vegetables, clothing and jewelry. They all spoke a strange language, yet Yeshua could understand them.

Finally, Yeshua arrived at the perimeter of the heavily guarded palace. Two massive stone statues of winged lions with a human head flanked the grand entrance. He recognized the head of the statue from his dream... it was King Nebuchadnezzar. Yeshua, still in his spirit form, passed through the Lions gate and into the palace. Again, the dozens of Babylonian guards didn't notice his presence.

Yeshua marveled at the architecture and monumental construction of the King's palace. Hundreds of white marble columns supported an incredible arched coffered ceiling. Dozens of the huge winged lion statues decorated the hallways of the buildings. A group of important looking Babylonians walked up a nearby stairway, and Yeshua decided to follow them. They all wore beautiful robes and fancy turbans on their heads.

At the top of the stairs was a huge golden door. Two muscular guards stood motionless in front of the entrance. When the group of the several important men reached the top of the stairs, the muscular guards pushed open the massive doors. They walked through into the wonderfully decorated chamber beyond, then guards slowly closed the doors behind them. Yeshua passed through just as the doors slammed close, again unnoticed.

Inside was the King's throne room. An immense chair made of gold and gems surrounded by golden winged lion statues occupied the entire back of the chamber. Scores of gold columns supported the black painted ceiling, decorated with images of golden stars in the shapes of the constellations.

Sitting on the throne was King Nebuchadnezzar. He wore a golden crown and gold robes. He looked just like the statue of the man from Yeshua's dream with the golden head. On either side of the King stood two important looking Babylonian soldiers in fancy armor. Both had large swords holstered in their scabbards hooked onto their belts.

The group of men that just had entered the room joined a larger gathering of men surrounding the King. Yeshua looked around the room hoping to see Mohammed's spirit aura. Sadly, he did not see or feel him nearby.

As Yeshua moved closer to the gathering of men surrounding the King, he was shocked to see a giant golden Menorah standing along the side of the room in a raised alcove. It looked exactly like the seven-branched Menorah that was on the relief statue on the Arch of Titus showing the Roman's carrying it off after they destroyed the second Temple in Jerusalem. It was the same Menorah on the modern coat of arms of the State of Israel.

"My God," Yeshua thought to himself. "That must be the original Menorah from the first Temple of Solomon. The Babylonians must have taken it from the Temple and brought it here after Nebuchadnezzar defeated and destroyed Jerusalem."

"I had a dream that bothers me," shouted the King loudly in front of the large gathering of men in fancy robes. His voice echoed powerfully in the chamber. Yeshua moved in closer towards the throne.

"I want to know what it means," he requested.

One of the more distinguished looking elders wearing fancy robes walked forward from the group towards the King and bowed down.

"King, live forever! Please tell your dream to us, your servants, and then we will tell you what it means," he said.

"No, you must tell me the dream, and then you must tell me what it means," replied the King sternly. "If you don't, I will give an order for you to be cut into pieces. And I will order your houses to be destroyed until they are nothing but piles of dust and ashes. But if you tell me my dream and explain its meanings, I will give you gifts, rewards, and great honor. So tell me about my dream and what it means."

Yeshua looked at the entire group of men standing around the King. They looked shocked, confused and uneasy.

"Please, Sir, tell us about the dream, and we will tell you what it means," said the elder looking man. He spoke nervously.

"I know that you are trying to get more time," yelled the King. "You know that you will be punished if you don't tell me about my dream. So you have all agreed to lie to me. Now tell me the dream. If you can tell me the dream, I will know that you can tell me what it really means."

The elder man paused for a moment. His face was pale white. A tear rolled down his cheek.

"There is not a man on Earth who can do what the King is asking," replied the flustered and visibly upset old man. "No King has ever asked the wise men, the men who do magic, or the Chaldeans to do something like this. Not even the greatest and most powerful King has ever asked his wise men to do such a thing. The King is asking something that is too hard to do. Only the gods could tell the King his dream and what it means. But the gods don't live with people."

When King Nebuchadnezzar heard that, he became very angry. "Leave me now, all of you… leave!" yelled the King.

The entire group of men in fancy robes and turbans quickly left the room after the guards at the golden door opened the portal. They all looked very disturbed. Yeshua, still in his spirit form, stayed in the room near the King.

"Arioch, what think you?" asked the King to the important looking solider next to him.

"I do not know, Sir," he replied. "How can they know your dream?"

"If they claim that they are mystics, psychics and sages, they should know," responded the King. "Otherwise they are just liars, charlatans and thieves."

"Well said, my King," said Arioch. "What do you wish to do?"

"I will not tolerate any disrespect or mockery," exclaimed Nebuchadnezzar. "I want all my so-called royal court wise men to be executed immediately for incompetence."

"Yes Sir… I will make it so, my King. Your wish is my command," said Arioch.

Arioch left the King's side and walked out of the royal chambers and down the huge marble staircase towards the main plaza of the palace, now filled with Babylonian soldiers. Yeshua carefully followed him. He continued to look around for Mohammed without success. To his surprise, he saw a lone red-bearded man in a decorative blue robe walk through the main entrance of palace and stop at the sight of Arioch standing on the lower platform of the stairs just above the guards.

"Men, by the exalted decree of the King," shouted Arioch to the group of soldiers below in the plaza. "We have been ordered to round up and execute all of the King's wise men for betrayal and treason. Gather your sharpest swords and strongest armor, we leave now."

The guards quickly dispersed to the garrison towards the far end of the plaza to retrieve their weapons.

Yeshua watched the red-bearded man quickly walk up to Arioch and address him. Surprising, the man appeared to look just like Yeshua, albeit an older version.

"Why did the King order such a severe punishment?" asked the puzzled man.

"Daniel, where were you?" asked Arioch. "The King called his entire court to request his dream to be interpreted."

"I'm sorry I was late," replied Daniel. "I was disposed by other important matters. What was his dream? I can interpret it for him. No one has to die."

"The King asked all his wise men to tell him what his dream was, then interpret it," explained Arioch. "When none of them responded, he decided to have all of you executed."

"What? Nebuchadnezzar demands that we tell him his dream?" asked Daniel. "That is preposterous. How can anyone know what he dreamed?"

"He says if you are all truly wise men, you would know," said Arioch. "Otherwise, you are imposters and liars and should be executed immediately."

"Arioch, please let me speak with the King," requested Daniel. "Let me have an audience with him. I will tell him his dream. Do not kill me or the others, spare us."

"I will bring you to the King," replied Arioch. Just then, dozens of guards in full armor returned to the center plaza with their swords and shields.

"Men, stand down for now!" yelled Arioch. "I will go back to the King now and address you all later. Return back to your posts."

Daniel and Arioch walked up the grand staircase to the golden doors. The two guards opened the doors and they went inside the royal chamber. Yeshua followed closely and the door closed behind them.

"What is this Arioch? Why is Daniel the Hebrew here?" questioned a very angry King Nebuchadnezzar, still sitting on the throne and being fed fruits by two beautiful women. "I have already ordered his death and that of his friends. All of my wise men have failed me and I've ordered them to be executed immediately."

"My King, Daniel claims he can tell you your dream," said Arioch.

"You can?" asked the King. "You know what I dreamed?"

"My liege, I can tell you your dream," replied Daniel. "As your humble servant, I will just need some more time to understand what it means. When I do, I will return and explain it all to you."

"I will trust what you say," said the King. "Every time I have asked you and your Judean friends about something important, you have always shown great wisdom and understanding. You have always been ten times better than all the magicians and other wise men in my kingdom. Come back when you know what my dream means, and I will spare your life and all the wise men in Babylon."

"Yes, my King… you have my word," replied Daniel. Yeshua saw that he was trembling. Daniel turned around and quickly left the room through the giant golden doors and almost fell running down the stairs. Yeshua followed him out of the palace and into the urban mud-brick maze of Babylon.

After approximately 15 minutes of walking through the narrow streets, Daniel entered a small house in a very poor, ghetto-looking area of the city. Yeshua followed him inside. In the tiny, barren house sat three men huddled over a fire and cooking some soup.

"My friends, I have some troubling news," said Daniel. "The King has ordered our death."

"What say you?" replied the eldest man sitting on the floor. "We are to be killed? Why?"

"King Nebuchadnezzar has demanded that all his magicians and wise men tell him and interpret his recent dream, or we all will be murdered," explained Daniel. "I bought us some time and told him I will let him know soon what his dream was and what it means."

"Wait just a moment, he didn't actually describe the events of him dream to then be interpreted... he actually wants someone to tell him exactly what happened in his dream?" asked the youngest man sitting on the floor, still cooking the soup.

"Yes, precisely... he is expecting someone to tell him what happened in his dream," replied Daniel.

"And if no one can, we will all die?" asked the third middle-aged man sitting on the floor.

"Unfortunately, that is his plan," said a sad looking Daniel. He sat on the floor next to his three friends.

"Let us pray to God, Adonai... my friends," said Daniel. "We pray that God would be kind to us and help us understand the King's secret."

The four men closed their eyes and meditated and prayed for some time. The sun was setting in the west, and the room was getting darker as the light gradually faded from the sky.

Yeshua, still in spirit form, replayed in his mind all the incredible events that had transpired since he sounded the Shofar at the Ishtar Gate of Babylon. He wondered where Mohammed was, and hoped he was safe. He also wished he had read the Book of Daniel from the Old Testament and knew what would happen next in this biblical story.

Yeshua remembered the dream he had about the giant statue of gold, silver, bronze and iron that got destroyed by a huge flying rock. Back in Haifa, Mohammed had said, "David interpreted the King's dream. It was a prophecy of the future. He told Nebuchadnezzar that the gold head represented his Babylonian kingdom, which would be followed by another kingdom representing the silver chest, then a kingdom representing the bronze mid-section and another for the iron legs. Finally, the feet represented a fifth kingdom, then the entire statue was destroyed by a stone representing the power of the eternal Kingdom of God."

The four men stopped praying. They silently drank their soup, then Daniel's three friends said goodbye and left the small mud brick house.

Daniel crawled over to a meager burlap and straw bed in the corner on the room and lay down. He started crying, and after some time, fell asleep.

Yeshua suddenly had a wonderful idea. He thought to himself, "What if I could go into Daniel's mind while he was sleeping and show him the dream? That would work, right?"

Yeshua moved his spirit aura over to Daniel's sleeping body. He focused all his energy towards his mind and merged his being into his. He became one with Daniel.

Everything turned dark, then Yeshua could sense Daniel's soul moving through the void. Yeshua then pulled up the memory of his dream and replayed it like a movie in front of Daniel's soul.

From the blackness, a huge human-like form materialized ahead in the distance. An enormous man towered ahead hundreds of feet tall. He stood in the middle of a green fertile meadow surrounded by a vast desert plain. On either side of the mammoth figure flowed two black, muddy rivers. Behind the statue, to the west, was an enormous mountain range.

The head of the statue was made from pure, glowing gold. He wore a majestic king's crown and had long hair and a beard. His muscular arms were crossed in front of his armored, bulky chest and his entire upper torso appeared to be made of bright, shiny silver. The plate armor of his midsection appeared bronze, and his legs looked to be made from iron. The gargantuan statue's sandaled feet were made from what looked like a mixture of iron and mud or clay.

In the distance, there was a loud rumbling sound. From the titanic mountain range behind the statue, a massive landslide tumbled downward from the tallest mountains peak. All the surrounding ground shook violently as an earthquake sent seismic waves in every direction. Huge amounts of stone and debris descended from the mountaintop. A giant rock appeared to be cut out from the side of the mountain and separate itself from a tall, adjacent cliff.

Suddenly, there was an explosion. The huge rock shot out towards the direction of the immense statue, then hit the massive human figure directly in his feet. The rock smashed and burst the bottom of the statue. The entire figure slowly collapsed and broke into thousands of pieces of debris and dust as it came crashing down towards the ground. A large sediment cloud formed and expanded outwards from the implosion.

Nearby, Yeshua saw Daniel staring at the rubble of the annihilated statue. Tears rolled down his face. The wind became much stronger as the tiny shattered statue fragments blew away until they all disappeared.

The only thing left visible was the giant rock that came from the mountain, still lying on the ground where it had landed. Magically, it expanded and morphed as it rapidly grew larger. It transformed into a tall stony mound, then into a large hill, and then became a considerable mountain. It seemed to expand even more and fill the entire Earth.

Yeshua's perspective suddenly changed, and he looked down at Daniel's sleeping body. Daniel woke up and was smiling. It was morning in Babylon. His three friends entered the room together as Daniel rolled out of bed and stood up, completely refreshed. They solemn faces quickly changed to elated expressions when they saw Daniel's bold and confident smile.

Daniel said, "Praise God's name forever and ever! Power and wisdom belong to Him. He changes the times and seasons. He gives power to Kings, and He takes their power away. He gives wisdom to people, so they become wise. He lets people learn things and become wise. He knows hidden secrets that are hard to understand. Light lives with Him, so He knows what is in the dark and secret places. God of my ancestors, I thank and praise You. You gave me wisdom and power. You told us what we asked for. You told us about the King's dream."

"That is wonderful!" said the eldest of the three men. "Let us go to the palace and tell the King immediately. Our lives will be spared."

The four men left Daniel's house, followed by Yeshua's spirit aura. They walked through the labyrinth of narrow roads that weaved through thousands of mud-brick houses. They finally reached the main procession street leading to the King's palace. The humungous ziggurat towered into the sky nearby. High above, dozens of birds flew in circular, spiral patterns.

Daniel's group reached the palace gates and Arioch, commander of the King's guards, greeted them.

Daniel said to Arioch, "Don't kill the wise men of Babylon. Take me to the King. I will tell him what his dream means."

Arioch led Daniel and his group of friends through the opulent gates of the palace entrance, then into the main plaza and up the stairs to the King's chambers. All the wise men of the Babylon stood around the King, their heads looking downwards in sadness and fear. Behind them were dozens of royal guards, brandishing their swords.

Arioch took Daniel's arm and brought him directly in front of the King. He announced to the entire room, "I have found a man among the captives from Judah who can tell the King what his dream means."

The King asked Daniel, "Are you able to tell me about my dream, and what it means?"

Daniel answered, "King Nebuchadnezzar, no wise man, no man who does magic, and no Chaldean could tell the King the secret things he has asked about. But there is a God in heaven who tells secret things. God has given King Nebuchadnezzar dreams to show him what will happen later. This was your dream, and this is what you saw while lying on your bed. You began thinking about what might happen in the future. God can tell people about secret things… He has shown you what will happen in the future. God also told this secret to me, not because I have greater wisdom than other men, but so you, King, many know what it means. In that way you will understand what was sent through your mind."

"King, in your dream you saw a large statue in front of you that was very large, shiny and very impressive. The head of the statue was made from pure gold. Its chest and the arms were made from silver. The belly and upper part of the legs were made from bronze. The lower part of the legs was made from iron. Its feet were made partly of iron and partly of clay. While you were looking at the statue, you saw a rock that was cut loose, but not by human hands. Then the rock hit the statue on its feet of iron and clay and smashed them. Then the iron, the clay, the bronze, the silver, and the gold broke to pieces all at the same time. And all the pieces became like chaff on a threshing floor in the summertime. The wind blew them away, and there was nothing left. No one could tell that a statue had ever been there. Then the rock that hit the statue became a very large mountain and filled up the whole earth."

Yeshua tried to smile as Daniel told the dream perfectly to the King. However, in spirit form... Yeshua had no physical mouth or face as he was still a ghost-like invisible apparition.

"That was your dream. Now we will tell the King what it means," said Daniel. "King, you are the most important King. The God of heaven has given you a kingdom, power, strength, and glory. He has given you control, and you rule over people and the wild animals and the birds. Wherever they live, God has made you ruler over them. King Nebuchadnezzar, you are that head of gold on the statue."

"Another kingdom will come after you, but it will not be as great as your kingdom. Next, a third kingdom will rule over the Earth… that is the bronze part. Then there will be a fourth kingdom. That kingdom will be strong like iron. Just as iron breaks things and smashes them to pieces, that fourth kingdom will break all the other kingdoms and smash them to pieces."

"You saw that the feet and toes of the statue were partly clay and partly iron. That means the fourth kingdom will be a divided kingdom. It will have some of the strength of iron in it just as you saw the iron mixed with clay. So the fourth kingdom will be partly strong like iron and partly weak like clay. You saw the iron mixed with clay, but iron and clay don't completely mix together. In the same way, the people of the fourth kingdom will be a mixture. They will not be united as one people."

"During the time of the kings of the fourth kingdom, the God of heaven will set up another kingdom that will continue forever. It will never be destroyed. And it will be the kind of kingdom that cannot be passed on to another group of people. This kingdom will crush all the other kingdoms. It will bring them to an end, but that kingdom itself will continue forever."

"King Nebuchadnezzar, you saw a rock cut from a mountain, but no one cut that rock. The rock broke the iron, the bronze, the clay, the silver, and the gold to pieces. In this way, God showed you what will happen in the future. The dream is true, and you can trust this is what it means."

Then King Nebuchadnezzar bowed down in front of Daniel to honor him. The King praised him. He gave an order that an offering and incense be given to honor Daniel. Then the King said to Daniel, "I know for sure your God is the God over all the gods and Lord over all Kings. He tells people about things they cannot know. I know this is true because you were able to tell these secret things to me."

As the incense burned near the King, it made a few popping sounds, like the sound of popcorn kernels bursting open. Yeshua also heard some high pitch buzzing noises coming from the incense as well. There were more popping sounds, now even louder.

"Yeshua, Yeshua… wake up!" yelled Mohammed. "I hear gunfire. Get up!" He was shaking Yeshua's flaccid body on the ground.

"Uhhhh… what happened to you?" Yeshua whispered as he slowly opened his eyes. His right ear had a loud high-pitched buzzing sound. There were more gunshots firing off in the distance, to the north. It sounded like automatic machine gun fire.

"We must leave now," exclaimed Mohammed. "I think our friends at the archeological team are in trouble."

Mohammed helped a very disoriented Yeshua up to a sitting position. Yeshua then put his Shofar into his backpack lying on the ground nearby and flipped it onto his back as he stood up.

"I'm ready, let's go," said Yeshua. He still felt dizzy and shaky. He had just time travelled back and forth over 2600 years. "Where were you, Mohammed? Did you go back to ancient Babylon with me?"

"There's no time to talk about that now," replied Mohammed. "Follow me, run!"

Mohammed and Yeshua ran as fast as they could through the ruins of Babylon towards the location of the archeological site near the lion statue. As they got closer, they heard more gunfire. Yeshua's right ear continued to buzz loudly. Then he saw from the corner of his eye, along the outer northern wall of the reconstructed city, five or six militiamen wearing black turbans and firing Kalashnikov rifles in the direction of the dig location.

Yeshua grabbed Mohammed's arm and they both stopped running and quickly hid in the shadows of a nearby brick wall. As they peaked around the corner, they saw the armed insurgents about 50 yards away. The black turbaned men ducked down and took cover as they received return gunfire from the Americans and Israelis hiding in the ruins.

"What should we do?" Yeshua asked Mohammed. "I hope our friends are okay."

"It looks like they're pinned down in the dig pit across the ruins," whispered Mohammed. "At this point, I wish that you'd taken that gun from Taylor. It would have come in handy right now."

"Coulda, shoulda, woulda," replied Yeshua. "What's the plan now? How can we help them?"

"I have an idea," said Mohammed. "I'm going to go into meditation."

"What? Right in the middle of a freaking gun battle you're going to meditate?" yelled Yeshua.

"Yes… trust me, I have a plan," said Mohammed. "Just don't interrupt me, please. I need total silence, minus the gunfire."

Mohammed sat down on the stone floor and leaned up against the brick wall behind him. He crossed his legs and closed his eyes. He inhaled deeply through his nose and exhaled through his mouth.

A few moments later, Yeshua noticed that the gunfire stopped from the armed men with the AK-47s. He peaked around the wall, and to his surprise… one of men wearing a black turban along the exterior wall was hitting the other men violently with the butt of his rifle. He knocked them all unconscious; then climbed over the wall and jumped to the ground twenty feet below and out of sight.

Just as Yeshua's right ear stopped buzzing loudly, Mohammed opened his eyes. He was smiling. He said, "Well, how did I do?"

"What, ummm… what do you mean how did you do?" replied Yeshua. Then he remembered how Mohammed had mind-controlled one of the Iranian terrorists on the boat after he was kidnapped and saved him from being killed.

"Oh… you did that?" replied Yeshua. "You made that one bad guy beat up the others then jump off the wall."

"Yes I did," responded Mohammed. "It was the best option of all the possibilities."

"Yes. Very well done my friend, well done," said Yeshua. "You saved the day."

Chapter 8

Beta Israel

Ramat David Israeli Air Force Base
24 hours later

Yeshua and Mohammed sat in a large, plush conference room overlooking the vast runway of the Air Force Base. Three enormous Lockheed Martin C-130J Super Hercules transport planes sat on the tarmac.

The door opened, and a large entourage of military personal walked into the room, including General Geller, Colonel Cohen, Lieutenant Colonel Eliora, Sergeant Berg and Private Avraham. Yeshua and Mohammed immediately stood up in attention. Everyone walked over to the plush swivel chairs surrounding the oval wooden conference table and sat down.

"At ease, gentlemen," said the General. Yeshua and Mohammed sat down. "I read the report about the incident in Babylon. I am very impressed with the outcome. You two took out six Islamic State insurgents with heavy weapons and saved the entire archeological team. Only minor wounds to our side and no serious injuries."

"Thank you, Sir," replied Mohammed. "We are grateful for the opportunity to serve our country."

Yeshua looked closely at Private Avraham. He remembered Avraham very well from their Sayeret Matkal IDF training course a few months earlier. Avraham's family was rescued from Ethiopia during the Operation Moses airlift in 1984.

"I'm sure both of you are wondering why we're all meeting here," said General Geller. "Besides congratulating the two of you again for being superheroes and saving the day."

"Are you going to send us to Disney World for real this time?" asked Mohammed.

Under the table, Yeshua kicked Mohammed's leg fairly hard with his foot. Mohammed shot Yeshua a stern look.

"We assume this is a debriefing for our next mission," replied Yeshua.

"Exactly," responded Geller. "And there's a time and place for humor, young men... and this is not one of them. Colonel Eliora, please go over the plan."

Eliora stood up and walked over to the wall by the entrance of the room. She had a slight limp to her gait. Yeshua and Mohammed hadn't seen her since she took a bullet from an Iranian kidnapper in Saudi Arabia.

She pushed some buttons on a control panel, and the large glass windows overlooking the tarmac turned almost black. As the room dimmed, a video panel slowly lowered from the ceiling along the far wall of the conference room. The words "OPERATION ENOCH" were on the screen in large blue letters behind a white background. The "O" of the word Enoch was in the shape of a Jewish Star.

"Everything I say during this presentation is the highest-level top secret," declared Eliora. "This is for your eyes only."

She grabbed a remote control from the conference room table and said, "Operation Enoch is a planned humanitarian rescue mission to…"

Eliora pushed the forward button on her remote control and the image on the screen changed to a large map of Africa.

"Ethiopia," she said. She turned on her red laser pointer and placed a big red dot on a spot near the most northern part of Ethiopia on the map.

"We are going to airlift approximately 6,000 Ethiopian Falash Mura from the Aksum Airport in northern Ethiopia over the next six days," continued Eliora. She forwarded to the next slide, which was a close-up map of Ethiopia. There was a blue Jewish Star placed over the city of Aksum near the border of Eritrea.

"Excuse me, Lieutenant Colonel," said Mohammed. "May I interrupt with a question?"

"Yes, go ahead," replied Eliora.

"I know that thousands of Ethiopians Jews were airlifted from Africa to Israel… but who are the Falash Mura?" asked Mohammed.

"Yes, that's correct," answered Eliora. "Approximately 81,000 Ethiopians of Jewish descent, also know as 'Beta Israel' have been rescued since the 1970's during Operations Brothers, Moses, Joshua and Solomon. Operation Enoch will rescue the Falash Mura community, who were once Jewish and forcefully coerced into

Christianity by missionaries during the 19th and 20th centuries."

"Okay, thank you for explaining," said Mohammed.

Eliora forwarded to the next slide. It was a detailed map showing the flight patterns from Israel to the Aksum Airport in Ethiopia.

"We are beyond appreciative of Private Avraham's assistance in securing airport security with his family contacts in Aksum," stated Eliora. "We couldn't have done this without him. The three C-130J Super Hercules transports on the tarmac are fueled and ready to go."

Eliora forwarded to the next slide. It was a schematic diagram of the Super Hercules airplane. The interior was full of seating.

"We have retrofitted each airplane's cargo bay with approximately 100 passenger seats and a medic bay," stated Eliora. "We expect many of the Falash Mura to be in bad shape after trekking through hostile conditions in northern Ethiopia and nearby Sudan and Eritrea. We have activated dozens of medical personal and humanitarian support staff for the mission. Once back in Israel, we will start the repatriation and integration process."

"Great!" said Mohammed. "When do we roll?"

"This afternoon," replied Eliora. "We have three fully trained teams in place and ready to go. Colonel Cohen will lead team A, Sergeant Berg will lead team B and I will lead team C. Yeshua, Mohammed and Private Avraham will come with me."

"Yes ma'am," said Yeshua and Mohammed in near unison.

"There's another very important part of the mission to inform you about," said General Geller. "Thanks again to Private Avraham, we have sent a direct message to the Ethiopian Orthodox Tewahedo Church to request their participation in the Temple Mount Peace Initiative. We understand that the Archbishop of their Church will be travelling from Addis Ababa to Aksum today. We want Mohammed and Yeshua to deliver the message to him personally, understood?"

"Yes Sir," replied the two young men instantaneously.

"Now let's get this show on the road," said General Geller as he stood up. Everyone else in the room stood immediately. "Good luck and Godspeed, Baruch Hashem."

General Geller left the room quickly. Eliora placed the remote control back down on the table, then walked over and pushed a few buttons on the control panel next to the door. The video screen rose back up into the ceiling and the light pour back into the room as the windows became translucent again.

Out the window, Yeshua saw soldiers and medical personal boarding the three huge airplanes on the runway. On one of the planes, a small Jeep drove up a ramp into the cargo bay. Several soldiers were loading large wooden crates into the back of another plane.

"What's in those boxes?" Yeshua asked Eliora as he pointed out towards the runway.

"Food, medical supplies and blankets," responded Eliora. "And some weapons, in case we need them."

"I hope we don't need any weapons; however, it's always good to be prepared for any situation," said Sergeant Berg as he joined in on the conversation.

"Mohammed, Yeshua... it's so good to see both of you," said Berg. He shook both of their hands. "Lieutenant Colonel Eliora has been keeping me updated on your many adventures. We are all very proud of both of you. I am honored to have been part of your training."

"And we are as well for you to have instructed us," replied Mohammed. "I'm sorry that we didn't finish our training with Sayeret Matkal."

"No worries, Agent Mohammed," said Berg as he one-eye winked at him. "Your talents and skills are much better utilized with your new assignment."

"Isn't it time to go?" asked Private Avraham. "The planes are ready."

"Yes, it's time to commence phase two of Operation Enoch," said Eliora. "Gather your personal gear from the barracks and see you in exactly 30 minutes on the tarmac. Oh, and by the way... Yeshua and Mohammed, it's very nice to see you both again. You've come a long way since you walked into my office as newbie conscripts at the Hatzerim Air Base in the Negev."

Eliora smiled and left the conference room with Sergeant Berg and Private Avraham. Yeshua and Mohammed still stood in the conference room looking out at the three planes on the airstrip.

"So, here we go again... changing the world, one mission at a time," said Mohammed.

"I wonder, do you think I should bring the Shofar on this trip? To Ethiopia?" asked Yeshua.

"My intuition says to leave it here in Israel this time," replied Mohammed. "We will take it on our next adventure. Let's just focus on the mission at hand."

"Agreed," replied Yeshua.

The two best friends left the conference room and started walking towards the barracks.

"Mohammed, you never did tell me what happened to you after I sounded the Shofar at the Ishtar Gate in Babylon. Where did you go?" questioned Yeshua.

"Well, we both travelled into the vortex tunnel and came out through the light. I remember telepathically communicating with you," replied Mohammed. "Then I was in ancient Babylon, just like you were. I was in a spiritual apparition form, floating around as ghost-like aura, just like we were when we travelled back in time to help David defeat Goliath. However, you weren't anywhere to be found. I looked all around for you."

"I did the same," said Yeshua. "I looked for you everywhere."

"I passed through the incredible Hanging Gardens of Babylon, and then went to the top of the great ziggurat and looked out at the vast city," described Mohammed. "Then I saw some heavy smoke coming from a large open plaza near the temple palace."

"Yes, that was the King's palace, next to the ziggurat," replied Yeshua.

"There was a giant gold statute of a man that looked like a King in the middle of the plaza," described Mohammed. There were literally tens of thousands of people bowing down to the statue. I heard resonate and beautiful sounds of musical instruments including horns, flutes, harps and I think even bag pipes."

Yeshua and Mohammed entered their room in the barracks. They both grabbed their toiletries and put them in their backpacks. Yeshua carefully placed his Shofar under the frame of his bed and covered it with a military blanket. They left the room and locked the door behind them.

"What happened next?" asked Yeshua.

"I travelled down the ziggurat as fast as I could and towards the massive plaza," answered Mohammed. "When I finally got to the plaza, I saw three men being pushed into a burning furnace which was making the huge plume of smoke that I saw from the top of the temple."

"Wait a sec, this all sounds familiar," said Yeshua. "Isn't what you are describing a story from the Book of Daniel?"

"Yes, exactly," replied Mohammed. "What happened to you during your Babylon experience was exactly what happened as described in Chapter Two of the Book of Daniel. My experience was precisely what occurred in Chapter Three."

"Phenomenal. So, the Shofar sent us back to re-enact different chapters from the same biblical book?" asked Yeshua.

"It appears that way, yes," responded Mohammed.

"So what happened next after you saw the three men being thrown into the fire?" questioned Yeshua.

"I saved them, of course," answered Mohammed. "They were Judeans who refused to bow down to the golden idol of the King. Before they were completely incinerated, I jumped into the fire and pulled them out. However, something else incredible happened... I couldn't reach them in time as they were pushed into the fire. Their hands and legs were tightly bound with rope. Then somehow, I telepathically made a force field around them so the flames wouldn't burn them. Then as I got into the furnace, I unbound them and helped them all out of the fire. They weren't burned at all."

"Wow. It seems like you have the ability to control fire in your spirit form, just like I can control water," said Yeshua.

"Yes, I think you are absolutely correct," said Mohammed. "We have been given a wonderful gifts by Allah. And there's one more thing I can remember before I came back to my body in modern time Babylon."

"What was that?" asked Yeshua.

"When I came out of the furnace with the three men, the King and a large group of important looking men were standing there, looking in amazement," described Mohammed. "I could have sworn they were gazing right at me. They definitely saw me, my spiritual form... in the flames of the fire. As I brought the three men out of harm's way and away from the heat of the furnace, I heard loud popping sounds from fire... which were actually the sounds of the guns shooting from the Islamic State terrorists in our timeline. I then travelled back to our reality and woke up next to you, still passed out."

Yeshua and Mohammed left the barracks building and started walking towards the three giant airplanes sitting on the tarmac. The sunny Mediterranean sky was vibrant blue above without a single cloud visible.

"What do you think is really going on here, Mohammed?" asked Yeshua. "Why do you think we were chosen to receive Shofar? And when we go back in time, why are we reliving biblical stories?"

"All very good questions, my friend," responded Mohammed. "I think I have figured it out."

"Really, how so?" questioned Yeshua.

"Ever since we sounded the Shofar together in the Valley of Elah, I've been thoroughly researching the mystical time travel phenomenon produced by the ram's horn vibrations."

"Researching? How?" asked Yeshua.

"Using the magic of the internet," said Mohammed as he smiled. "It's a miracle that you can actually find the entire knowledge and history of the human race at the tip of your fingers using a computer."

"I know, right?" said Yeshua. "Please do tell. What did you find out?"

"It's like a series of breadcrumbs that we were meant to follow, and this last trip back to the biblical story of Daniel confirms everything I suspected," said Mohammed. "When I looked up Chapter Three of the Book of Daniel, it describes exactly what happened with the three men being rescued from the furnace. King Nebuchadnezzar saw a fourth man in the fire. That fourth man was me, in spirit form. In the book, it is written **'I see four men loose, walking in the midst of the fire, unbound and unharmed, and the appearance of the fourth is like a son of God.'** "

"Wait a sec, a son of God?" interjected Yeshua. "You were a son of God? I thought Jesus was God's only begotten son? At least that's what the New Testament says."

"Apparently God had plenty of Sons in the Hebrew Bible," replied Mohammed. "Remember the story about the Nephilim in Genesis Six? It's your Torah portion you read at

Masada. Absolutely fascinating. It says exactly... **'There were giants in the earth in those days, and also after that, when the sons of God came unto the daughters of men.'** So here we have another biblical scripture that describes a son of God."

"Yes, those sons of God were the Watchers, from the Book of Enoch. The 200 fallen ones," replied Yeshua.

"Yes. It makes sense now. The sons of God mean Angels. They were Angels," said Mohammed. "In the Book of Enoch, it describes seven holy angels, also called Archangels. They include Michael, Raphael, Gabriel, Uriel, Saraqael, Raguel and Remiel. After sounding the Shofar, we must be travelling through space-time in reverse as one of the Angels. Perhaps we are being trained as Angels for something that we're supposed to do in the future."

They were getting close to the massive transport airplane on the runway. Standing near the rear of the place, Eliora saw them and waved.

"Which Angel do you think I am?" asked Yeshua.

"I think you are the Angel Gabriel," answered Mohammed.

"Wow. Really? Are you sure... how do you know?" questioned Yeshua.

"Again, the magic of the Internet," responded Mohammed. "I looked it up. In the Book of Daniel, Gabriel appears to the Prophet Daniel to explain his visions. And that's what you did when you went back in time to ancient

Babylon. You dreamed exactly King Nebuchadnezzar's dream a few days ago, then went back in time and somehow showed the dream to Daniel while he slept and explained to him what it meant."

"Yes. I believe you are right. I must be Gabriel," said Yeshua. "And which Angel are you?"

"I'm not sure yet, I'm still trying to figure it out for sure. I think I might be the Archangel Michael," replied Mohammed.

"Why do you think that? How would you know?" asked Yeshua.

"The Archangels Gabriel and Michael are described as the guardian Angels of Israel, defending the Jewish people," explained Mohammed.

"So, we are like the dynamic duo of Angels?" said Yeshua. He recalled the painting of the Archangel Michael and two other Angels battling the demons over Moses's body in the Sistine Chapel. Perhaps Mohammed was right, he thought… perhaps they were here as protectors of Israel.

"What about Taylor?" asked Yeshua. "Do you think she's an Angel too?"

"Yes. I do," responded Mohammed. "I think she might be the Archangel Phanuel, the Angel of repentance and hope."

They reached the loading ramp at the rear of the C-130J Super Hercules and walked up. Private Avraham was putting some supplies into the army Jeep secured in the back of the plane. As soon as Yeshua and Mohammed were completely inside, the ramp closed behind them.

"Hello my friends," said Avraham. "We are ready to go, please secure yourselves other there on the seating platform. I will join you there in a moment." He pointed to dozens of empty passenger seats towards the front of the cargo hull.

The heavy-duty Rolls Royce engines turned on, and the four giant propellers on the plane's enormous wings started spinning rapidly. Yeshua and Mohammed felt the heavy vibrations of the airplane as it started to taxi along the runway. They both sat down in a couple of empty seats and put on their seatbelts. Avraham sat down next to them.

"Where is Eliora?" asked Yeshua.

"The Lieutenant Colonel? She's flying the plane," said Avraham. "We will be in Ethiopia in about four hours."

The C-130J reached its maximal ground speed and lifted off the runway and headed south, following the two other giant aircraft in tandem.

"Avraham, this whole mission is because of you, thank you," said Yeshua. "I remember the hike during our IDF training to the Valley of Elah very well. Didn't you say that your people were descended from King Solomon and the Queen of Sheba? And that you come for a royal bloodline of Kings?"

"Your memory is impressive," said Avraham. "Yes, that is the historical legend of our people. The Biblical King Solomon of Jerusalem had a child with the Ethiopian Queen of Sheba named Menelik. He became the first emperor of Ethiopia, and my family are supposedly his descendants, at least what my parents told me."

"And you still have some family there?" asked Mohammed. "They helped arrange this mission?"

"Yes, my grandparents have ancestors and relatives from several Falash Mura families who were forced to convert to Christianity generations ago," explained Avraham. "Due to a higher acceptance and tolerance of religious practices in Ethiopia, they now have changed back to practicing Judaism."

"So once we get to Ethiopia, what is our plan?" questioned Yeshua. "Are we going to meet with the leader of the Ethiopian Church?"

"Yes, that's the plan," said Avraham. "Once we land, we'll take the Jeep to the Cathedral of Our Lady Mary of Zion. The Archbishop will meet us there, and you will deliver your message to him. Meanwhile, the planes will be loaded with the Falash Mura and make the first return flight back to Israel."

"Do you know all about the message?" asked Yeshua.

"Yes. Eliora told me about the message," replied Avraham. "She said Colonel Taylor had a vision about all the world religious leaders coming together on the Temple Mount in Jerusalem and declaring world peace together.

You are going to ask the Archbishop of the Ethiopian Orthodox Tewahedo Church to participate, correct?"

"Yes, that is correct," replied Yeshua. "We want representation from every major culture and religion to participate. Thank you for arranging the Archbishop to meet with us. I hope he will agree to our request."

"I hope so too," declared Avraham. "I'm sure he will be honored to go to such a meaningful ceremony."

"Avraham, I remember you saying something else remarkable when you introduced yourself during our IDF training hike," said Mohammed. "You said the Ark of the Covenant was in the Church in Aksum. Is that the Church we are going to?"

"Yes. That is correct," replied Avraham. "And although I've never met him... my great Uncle is apparently a Guardian Monk who guards the Ark at the Chapel of the Tablet, right next to the Cathedral of Our Lady Mary of Zion."

"Whoa. Seriously? Are you saying we are going to be able to see the lost Ark of the Covenant in Ethiopia?" asked Yeshua.

"I don't think so," responded Avraham. "My understanding is that no one is allowed to see the Ark except for the Guardian Monks."

"But the Guardian Monk is your Uncle?" asked Mohammed. "Maybe he would make an exception for us."

"Maybe," replied Avraham. "Anything is possible."

"Hey guys, I'm pretty wiped out," said Yeshua. "I'm going to shut my eyes for a few and catch some zzz's before we get to Africa."

"That sounds like an excellent plan, my friend," responded Mohammed as he closed his eyes. "Some rest sounds very good right now."

Yeshua was exhausted. As soon as he closed his eyes, he immediately went into a deep sleep. Everything went black, like a complete void. There was nothing. After a few minutes, his neural pathways and eye movements changed, and he started dreaming. He found himself flying through the air, high above the Earth. The sun was setting in the distance and projected a wonderful spectrum of colorful rays in perfect tangential patterns as he flew above a series of canyons and mountains. Below, a fast river surged towards the orange and red glowing sunset, the colors reflecting off the water like shimmering diamonds of light. His body effortlessly glided through the wind amongst the scattered cream puff clouds.

Yeshua felt a presence far away, beyond the horizon and towards the source of the river flowing beneath him. He could feel someone or something calling out to him, like a telepathic whisper pulling him forward. Time seemed to speed up rapidly as the sunset quickly turned into dusk and then into night. Thousands of stars shone brightly above Yeshua as he continued to fly towards the source of the presence.

Ahead, Yeshua saw a familiar sight. At first, he saw a glowing and radiant amber light at the top of the tall mountain range. Then, from the highest peak, he saw a massive burning fire, almost like a volcano. A plume of dark smoke billowed into the night air. It was Mount Horeb... the mountain of God, in Saudi Arabia.

As Yeshua got closer to the fire, a voice softly spoke to him. It was the voice of a man.

"We have been waiting for you to join us," said the voice.

Yeshua sensed that the voice came from what looked like a cave opening within the valley of the burning mountain. The dark cave was nestled high up in a tall rocky slope across from Mount Horeb.

"We have been waiting for you to join us," said the voice, again.

Yeshua concentrated intensely and willed his spirit to fly towards the direction of the cave entrance. He saw that there was a faint light coming from the inside of the opening. As he turned himself and changed his trajectory, he felt the heat of the intense fire burning from the top of Jebel al Lawz... the real Mount Sinai. Below, he thought he saw hundreds of small lights and fires on the floor of the valley below.

"We have been waiting for you to join us," said the voice, again.

As, Yeshua entered the cave, his feet touched the ground and he stopped flying. The cave was large, but not deep. Sitting in the middle of the cave has a man wearing a dark, hooded robe. He could not see his face in the shadows. A lone flame from a small brass oil lamp in front of the mysterious man softly illuminated the cave.

"We have been waiting for you to join us," said the man, as he removed his hood and revealed his face. He was a very old man, exceptionally wrinkled with white hair and a long mustache and beard.

Yeshua instantly recognized him... he was Yohanan, the Rabbi who Bar Mitzvah'd him on Masada when he was 13. He was also the same man who had given him the Shofar when he was in a coma after the terror attack on his bus in the Negev. The last time Yeshua had seen the Rabbi was when he was praying at the Western Wall in Jerusalem.

"Pardon me for asking, but why are you saying 'we' when there is only you?" asked Yeshua. "And where are we? What is this place?"

"We are in the Cave of Elijah," the old man said. "The great Prophet sought shelter and refuge here after travelling 40 days and nights in the wilderness. This is place where Elijah spoke with God."

"And is that Mount Sinai across the valley?" asked Yeshua. "Where Moses received the 10 Commandments?"

"Yes, that is the Holy Mountain," replied the Rabbi. "And we have been waiting for you to join us."

"But I just see one of you," responded Yeshua.

"I am one, but I am many," said the old man. "You know me as Rabbi Yohanan in this earthly incarnation. As you may have realized, I have been guiding you along your path and keeping you out of harm's way. I am also known as Enoch. When I was taken to the upper realms, I became known as Metatron. I have many other names and forms... Yahoel, Zerah, Sebar, and Atatyah just to name a few."

"Out of harm's way?" questioned Yeshua. "I've been blown up, shot at, tortured and attacked more times than I can count. And you say you've been protecting me?"

"And yet aren't you still alive?" replied Enoch. "Let me ask you a question, young man... can you truly know the full value of something without knowing its opposite?"

"What do you mean?" questioned Yeshua. "I don't understand. Why have all these terrible things happened to me?"

"Can you know what hot is without knowing cold?" asked Enoch. "Can you know what true happiness is without knowing sadness? Can you understand light without also experiencing the darkness?"

"So, you are describing duality," responded Yeshua. "I see what you are saying. Yin and Yang. Day and night. Love and hate. You can't truly know and appreciate something without really knowing and experiencing its complementary opposite value."

"You have learned well, young man," stated Enoch. "Everything happens for a reason. You have come a long way in this lifetime."

"I have so many questions for you," said Yeshua. "Why do I keep dreaming about this place? Is there something I'm supposed to do? And why did you give me the Shofar? Am I training to be an Angel?"

"All your questions will be answered in time," said the old man. He stood up and walked past Yeshua towards the opening of the cave. The fire on Mount Sinai burned brightly. A huge, glowing comet was visible above in the dark sky centered by the faint outline of the Milky Way Galaxy. Yeshua followed him out of the cave and stood next to Enoch. The wind began to blow strongly.

"You must come here, with your friend Mohammed, and sound the Shofar," said the old man.

"And how are we supposed to get here? It's in Saudi Arabia," asked Yeshua as he looked out into the dark valley and towards the fire on the mountain.

Enoch did not respond. After a few moments, Yeshua turned his head and realized that Enoch was gone. He had disappeared, again. The small brass oil lamp still burned on the floor of cavern; the shadows flickered and danced on the walls of the cave.

Yeshua walked back into the cave to grab the oil lamp; however… just as he went to pick it up, the ground began to rumble and shake violently. Rocks and dust fell from the ceiling. It was an earthquake!

"Yeshua, wake up my friend," said Mohammed. "We are here. Wake up."

The giant Super Hercules airplane made a rough touch down on the battered landing strip at the Aksum Airport in Ethiopia. The entire plane shook powerfully as it quickly decelerated and then came to a full stop. The engines turned off, and the rotary blades came to a stop.

The giant cargo ramp in the back of the airplane started to lower downwards to the asphalt tarmac below. Yeshua, Mohammed and Avraham unbuckled their seatbelts, stood up and walked past the Jeep in the cargo bay.

As they got closer to the cargo ramp and exited the plane, they stopped and stood in complete awe at what was happening on the runway. As far as the eye could see, thousands of African men, women and children filled the entire airfield around the three Israeli transports. All the men wore colorful skullcaps. They were all here to be rescued and taken to the Promised Land.

Standing closest to the cargo ramp was an Ethiopian Rabbi. He was wearing a white yarmulke, tallis and held an ancient Torah wrapped in decorative gold linen.

"Allahu Akbar," said Mohammed. "There's so many of them."

Avraham walked down the ramp and spoke with the rabbi in Amharic, the native Ethiopian language. After a few minutes, the rabbi turned around and spoke loudly to the entire crowd of the Falash Mura. He motioned with his right hand as he held the Torah tightly tucked in his left arm. The entire crowd parted and made a wide gap of space from the back of the airplane into the distance towards the main airport road.

"What did he say?" asked Yeshua. "What did you tell him?"

"He thanked us and expressed his gratitude for delivering his people to the Holy Land," replied Avraham. "I told him we can only take about 300 people at a time on the planes and that it would take many trips to get everyone safely to their new homes."

"And why did they all move away and part like the Red Sea?" asked Mohammed.

"Oh, I asked him to make some space for us," said Avraham. "We're are going to hop on the Jeep and head into town to meet with the Archbishop."

"Well done, my friend. Very well done," said Mohammed.

Yeshua, Mohammed and Avraham released the restraining straps from the green army Jeep and got inside. Avraham turned on the ignition and drove it slowly down the ramp and in-between the vast crowd of very happy Africans. As they passed through, all the Falash Mura clapped and cheered enthusiastically.

"Lieutenant Colonel Eliora and the others will help load up the first round of the Falash and fly back with them to Israeli after the planes are refueled," said Avraham. "A small contingent of IDF soldiers and medics will stay behind with the rest of the people."

The Jeep drove past the huge gathering of the Beta Israelis on the airstrip to the south and then turned west onto the main two-lane airport road toward Aksum. The surrounding hilly rural country was dotted with farmland and pastures.

"This is a very beautiful country," said Yeshua. "Your family is from here?" asked Yeshua.

"Yes, from a nearby town called Gondar," replied Avraham. "That's where my parents are from. They were recused from a Sudanese refugee camp during Operation Moses in 1984. I was born in Israel… I've never been here before, to Ethiopia"

"It must feel very strange, to be here. The home of your ancestors," said Mohammed.

"Yes, it does feel that way. I've always dreamed of coming back here ever since I was a young child," replied Avraham.

The Jeep turned right at a fork in the road and entered the outskirts of the city. Simple white buildings lined the streets, and a few dozen villagers shopped along an area containing an outdoor farmers' market. Avraham slammed on the brakes when a young boy herded some stray goats as he crossed the road. The boy said something in a strange language, and then Avraham yelled at him and contined driving towards the west.

"What did he say?" asked a curious Mohammed.

"He said, drive more carefully... the pedestrians have the right of way here," replied Avraham.

"And what did you say back?" questioned Mohammed.

"I said, hey kid...be more careful with your goats," responded Avraham.

"Oh, I get it. Kid. Goats. Bahhhhhhhhh," joked Mohammed. All three of them laughed really hard for a bit. It was a much-needed moment of comic relief, which they all very much enjoyed in the middle of such serious and important events.

The Jeep made another right-hand turn and headed north within the sprawling town of Aksum. A large barren hill appeared to the north. They passed a town square with another busy farmers' market. Dozens of sitting camels rested in the shade nearby.

As the Jeep slowed down due to the heavy traffic around the farmers market, some young boys approached them holding some colorful trinkets in attempts to make a tourist sale. One of them had a gold painted lion wearing a crown and holding a staff in its paw. Avraham yelled at them to go away, and they continued driving north on the main road.

"That lion figurine, what was that?" asked Yeshua. "It looks so familiar."

"Ah, yes. That is the Lion of Judah," answered Avraham. "It is both the Ethiopian and Israeli national symbol. That Lion used to be on the Ethiopian flag and was the Royal Insignia of the Ethiopian Empire."

"Tell me again, how did the Ethiopian Jews get here? And why is the Lion of Judah the symbol of both countries?" asked Yeshua.

"There's an ancient book here in Ethiopia called the *Kebre Negest*," explained Avraham. "It says that around 3000 years ago the beautiful Ethiopian Queen of Sheba travelled to Israel and met with King Solomon in Jerusalem. They had a child who later became the first King in a long dynasty of Ethiopian Emperors. King Solomon was from the tribe of Judah, and it is written that many sons of the tribes of Judah and Dan accompanied the Queen of Sheba back here to Ethiopia. Those Judeans are supposedly my ancestors, as well as the over 85,000 Beta Israelites who were rescued by our predecessors."

"Wow. That is one amazing story," said Yeshua. "It's a miracle."

Ahead, a large gold domed building appeared above tree line, across from the hilly outcrop to the east. A fantastic starburst sculpture rose from the top of the dome.

"What's that building?" asked Yeshua.

"That is the new Cathedral of Our Lady Mary of Zion," answered Avraham. "We are almost at our final destination."

They passed the large church, and Avraham parked the Jeep under a shaded area along the street. Yeshua, Mohammed and Avraham got out of the vehicle. They were at the bottom of a small valley surrounded by rocky hills. Just to the north, stood eight massive stone pillars and several smaller pillars of varying heights reaching up into the sky. On the ground were also several huge fallen and broken monuments.

"Whoa. What are those giant obelisks doing there?" asked Yeshua.

"This is called the Northern Stelae Park," answered Avraham. "The largest one in the middle of the platform is called King Ezana's Stela. It is also called the Obelisk of Aksum. I have been waiting my entire life to come and visit this place. We will be meeting the Archbishop here, so you can deliver your message."

Avraham walked towards the Stelae Park, and Yeshua and Mohammed followed. They marveled at the enormity and construction of the largest obelisks. The off-white towers had false doors at their bases and were ornamented with dozens of inlays all the way to the top resembling windows.

"These were ancient royal burial sites of the Kingdom of Aksum... one of the greatest civilizations in African History. They are at least 1600 years old and older," said Avraham. "Interestingly, the Italians stole King Ezana's Stela in 1937 and erected it in Rome. It was eventually returned and finally reinstalled to its original location in 2008."

"They moved that whole thing to Rome? Then brought it back? It's gigantic," exclaimed Mohammed.

"Yes, I think it's about 80 feet tall and weighs around 160 tons," said Avraham. "It was quite a feat of engineering to reconstruct it. Amazingly, the large one that is broken on the ground over there was over 100 feet tall and weighed over 500 tons."

At the base of the largest obelisk on the platform stood two old African men wearing black robes. They both had long white beards, and on their heads they wore wide black rounded headpieces that resembled the shape of a top of an acorn.

Yeshua, Mohammed and Avraham walked up to the two men who stood in the shadow of the great obelisk.

"We have been waiting for you to join us," said the older looking man. Yeshua immediately had a strong déjà vu feeling.

"We are honored to be in your presence, your Holiness," replied Avraham. "This is Yeshua, Mohammed and I am Avraham. We have come from Israel on a mission of the greatest importance."

"We are the co-Patriarchs and Catholicos of Ethiopia, the Archbishops of Aksum and Ichege of the See of Saint Taklehaimanot," said the older man. "You have travelled a long way, what is the important message you have for us?"

"It's a message for world unity," stated Yeshua. "We request that all the leaders and appropriate representatives of the world's major religions come to Jerusalem and walk on the Temple Mount and go into the Dome of the Rock and declare world peace together."

"That is quite an impressive request," said the shorter and younger looking Archbishop. "And when is this event supposed to happen?"

"On the second day of summer, 2020... June 21rst," explained Mohammed. "There will be a total solar eclipse over most of Africa, the Middle East and Southern Asia. As the maximal shadow of the eclipse passes over Israel, that is the planned moment of the declaration of world peace."

"And why did you choose to ask us to participate?" asked the older man. "We are just a small church, much smaller than most."

"We want inclusion from all cultures, creeds and races," said Avraham. "We want representation of your congregation as well as others from Africa."

"The Ethiopian Orthodox Tewahedo Church is honored to join your peace project," said the younger man. "Who else will be included from Africa?"

"Our team will also be contacting the Coptic Orthodox Church in Alexandria, Egypt and the Dogon tribe from Mali to participate during the peace ceremony," replied Yeshua.

The older man closed his eyes, and raised his arms up to the sky. He chanted in the ancient Semitic Ethiopian language of Ge'ez, "**Qāla barakat za-Hēnōk za-kama**

bāraka ḫərūyāna wa-ṣādəqāna 'əlla hallawu yəkūnū ba-
'əlata məndābē la-'asassəlō kʷəllū 'əkūyān wa-rasī'ān."

"Wow. What did he just say?" asked Yeshua. The older Archbishop brought his arms down and held them together in prayer.

"He is quoting scripture from our Holy Book of Enoch," said the younger Archbishop. "It is the first verse from the first chapter. It says, '**The words of the blessing of Enoch, whereas he has blessed the chosen and righteous, who will be living in the Day of Tribulation, when all the wicked are to be destroyed.**'"

"The Book of Enoch. I am very familiar. Enoch was Noah's great grandfather. He walked with God," said Yeshua. "I'm just curious, though… what exactly is the Day of Tribulation?"

The older man opened his eyes and looked intensely at Yeshua. He smiled and said, "Do you know Enoch?"

"Yes. I know the Prophet Enoch," he replied. Yeshua thought about his recent dream in Elijah's cave where Rabbi Yohanan revealed himself as Enoch.

"Follow me, I have something wonderful to show you, my young Israeli friends," instructed the Archbishop. He started walking south from the Stelae Park towards the large domed Church across the open plaza. Yeshua, Mohammed, Avraham and the younger Archbishop followed. They passed the parking area where their Jeep was located and continued along a tree-lined path that led to the new Church of St. Mary of Zion.

As they travelled through the large Church campus, they walked past a few small groups of Askumites... everyone would pause, smile and nod towards the Archbishops and their guests. Curiously, the old man led them past the entrance of the huge domed Cathedral and continued along the tree-lined path to the south.

"See that building there," whispered Avraham as he nudged his head to his left. There was a small square stone building surrounded a fence. "That is the Chapel of the Tablet. That's where the Ark of the Covenant is kept."

Yeshua and Mohammed made silent 'wow' expressions with their faces. The Archbishop walked past the Chapel of the Tablet and led the group to another old stone building with a large dome on its top. An ornate giant Christian cross rose from the top of the dome.

The old Priest paused at the entrance of the ancient building and turned to address his group of followers.

"This is the Old Church of St. Mary of Zion," said the Archbishop. "This is the traditional place where Ethiopian Emperors have been crowned since the 4th century. It has been destroyed and rebuilt many times. Come, let us enter."

The Archbishop pulled out a circular key ring from his robe containing dozens of old looking metallic keys. He inserted one of the larger keys into the keyhole of the tall wooden door at the front of the church. He turned the key, then opened the door and went inside. Everyone followed him into St. Mary of Zion.

The vestibule of the Church was remarkable. A massive glass chandelier hung from the tall ceiling and brightly illuminated the rectangular room. Dozens of colorful old byzantine looking murals of biblical scenes decorated the walls, and several huge gold and red drapes hung through out the space. The place was empty... no one else was in the building.

The Archbishop walked into the large interior nave of the Church through the vestibule room. An even more impressive huge and elegant antique chandelier hung from the ceiling suspended by thick iron chains fastened to four giant arched columns under the main dome of the building. Small wooden pews were scattered along the walls of the large square room. Just like the vestibule, large decorate gold and red drapes adorned the many of the walls, with much larger ones covering the entire back wall of the main sanctuary along the back of the Church.

Above the curtains, high up on the back wall was a huge colorful multi-tiered biblical mural. The lowest tier of the mural contained pictorial images of the Adam and Eve story. The painting depicted the taking of the fruit of the Tree of Knowledge and the expulsion from the Garden of Eden. The large image at the top of the mural's centerpiece showed three old holy men with white hair, beards and mustaches. Each man held his right hand up, with two fingers gently raised in a benediction sign. In their left hands it looked like they were holding a small golden disk-shaped UFO object.

"For many years, as long as anyone can remember, the Holy Ark of the Covenant was kept here," said the Archbishop. Both the Ethiopian Archbishops walked to the back of the Church and pulled the center curtain to the right, revealing two huge doors behind it. They fastened and secured the curtain to a side fixture, which held them in place.

Yeshua recognized the very familiar images on the giant doors. Painted on the two panels of the ten-foot doors were two tall men wearing beautifully decorated multicolored robes. They both had golden halos behind their heads. They were Angels! One held a sword, and the other held a spear.

"Who are they?" asked Yeshua. "The Angels on those doors."

"They are the Archangels Michael and Raphael, from the Book of Enoch," replied the younger Archbishop. Mohammed and Yeshua looked at each other with bewildered expressions. "For centuries, behind these doors contained the Holy Ark. It was brought to Ethiopia during the time of King Solomon. However, the divine heat of the tablets began to crack the foundation of this building, so it was relocated next door within the Church of the Tablet."

"We have something very special to share with you," said the older Archbishop. He opened the two giant doors and exposed a small room beyond. Another gold and red curtain covered something large in the back of the space. The old Priest pulled out his key ring again from his robe, and then chose one of the larger antique-looking keys. He walked over to the curtain and pulled it to the side, exposing a wonderfully carved dark wooden bookcase along the back of the wall.

Hundreds of old books were visible through the mesh frame of an intricately designed glass and black iron wrought doorframe of the bookcase. The Priest placed his key into the lock of door and turned the key. He opened the door, and then pulled out a very large book from the bookcase. The cover of the book was deep blue and decorated with yellow stars. With the book nestled under his arm, he closed the bookcase and walked over to a small wooden altar along a nearby column in the sanctuary. He carefully placed the book on the altar and opened it to one of the first pages.

"This is the Book of Enoch," said the Archbishop. Everyone gathered around him to look more closely. It was written in a strange language, and the pages were adorned with a beautifully decorated green and yellow patterned border.

"This book is one of our oldest copies, dating back to the 15th century," said the Priest. "It was transcribed identically from a much older version and written in our traditional Ge'ez Ethiopian language. Our distant ancestors likely brought the original book here during the time of King Solomon and Queen Sheba. We now know that our Book of Enoch is authentic because many verbatim-translated fragments of the same book were found amongst the Dead Sea Scroll dating back to over 2000 years ago. The book tells the epic story of the biblical Enoch and the Watchers... the fallen Angels who betrayed God and interfered with humanity and mated with women, who then birthed evil offspring, called the Nephilim. God's wrath as a result of their corrupt actions later caused the Great Flood."

"I will translate a passage from the first chapter," continued the Archbishop. "And I then I would like to hear your thoughts on what you think it means."

He pointed his finger to the text and spoke the words...

"Enoch, a righteous man, whose eyes were opened by God, was shown a vision of the Holy One in the heavens by the Angels. And Enoch said 'From them I heard all things, and understood what I saw... that which will not take place in this generation, but for a remote one which is to come. The Holy Great One will come forth from His dwelling, and the eternal God will tread upon the earth, even on Mount Sinai, and appear in the strength of His might from the heaven of heavens.'"

The Priest stopped reading the book, then looked at Yeshua.

"That must describe the prophecy about the Day of Tribulation you mentioned earlier," said Yeshua. "When God returns in physical form and purges all the darkness from the world."

"Yes, that is correct," said the Priest. "And I will tell you that all the signs from the prophecies are telling us that it will be our generation who experiences the Tribulation... and I am now convinced that it will be triggered by your planned peace declaration event on the Temple Mount."

"What? You are saying that God is going to appear on Earth and smite all the evil doers next year?" asked a surprised Mohammed.

"It appears you are being guided by the hand of God," said the Archbishop. "But you already know that. We know the real reason why you are here."

"Let me ask you a question," said Avraham. "My great uncle is a monk in the Chapel of the Tablet. Do you think we would be allowed to see the Ark? Would that be permissible?"

"No one is allowed to see the Ark," said the younger Archbishop. "Once a year, we have a holy ceremony where the Ark is taken on a procession around the city. However, during the rest of the year... no one is allowed to be in its presence."

"Can you make an exception, just once?" asked Mohammed.

"Under most circumstances, I would say absolutely not," said the older Archbishop. "However, due to current circumstances and your auspicious visit... we will take your request to our council this evening and have an answer for you tomorrow morning."

"Okay, great. Thank you, your Highness," said Avraham. "Are there some accommodations nearby where we can stay?"

"Yes. There is the Yeha Hotel on top of the hill just to the east," said the younger Archbishop. "Just take the road up from the obelisks, then turn right at the Queen of Sheba's Bath. The Hotel is just up the road from there. It's not fancy, but will serve the purpose and has beautiful views of the valley."

"Queen Sheba's Bath... what is that?" asked Mohammed.

"Oh, it's a large cistern of water nearby, supposedly the swimming pool of Queen Sheba that's now thousands of years old," explained the younger Archbishop. "Feel free to jump in and cool off from this hot weather if you desire. We must leave now."

The older Archbishop returned the Book of Enoch back to the bookcase, locked the door, then closed the interior curtain. Both Archbishops unfastened the large curtain in the main sanctuary and pulled it back into place, completely covering the door paintings of the Archangels Michael and Raphael. They all left the ancient Cathedral through the vestibule and out the main door and past the outer gate.

"Will see you all in the morning, at 9AM inside the New Cathedral of St. Mary of Zion," said the older Archbishop.

"Perfect, we look forward to seeing you again," said Avraham. "Thank you for your time and hospitality."

"It is we that thank you," said the younger Archbishop. "We are honored to have you as our guests. Enjoy Aksum for the rest of today, as there are many sights to see. Just be very careful at night here, please be safe."

The two Archbishops turned away and walked north along the tree-lined pathway towards the main Church campus. Yeshua, Mohammed and Avraham stood at the edge of the blue fence surrounding the small Church of the Tablet.

"So right in there is the Ark of the Covenant?" asked Yeshua. "The most powerful and holy ancient artifact in the history of the entire world."

"That is what they are saying, but I'm not sure I believe them," replied Mohammed. "I've seen videos on YouTube of them carrying around the medium sized wooden box that is supposed to contain the Ark during the holy procession festival. If it were made of gold as it's described in Torah, there's no way it could be the authentic one."

Maybe the one they carry around isn't the real one," said Avraham. "Perhaps the wooden box just contains a replica. Maybe they keep the original one inside. I hope they let us see it tomorrow. My great Uncle is one of the monks who protects the Ark, I would also like to meet him."

"I wonder how Eliora, Sergeant Berg the others are doing with loading up the first round of the Falash at the airport," said Yeshua.

"They should be close to finishing refueling and heading back to Israel soon," said Avraham. "I say let's head back to the Jeep and find our hotel. I'm getting hungry for some real food."

"Good plan my friend, me too," said Yeshua.

"Me three!" said Mohammed. "Let's get some well-deserved rest and relaxation."

The three Israelis walked back through the Church campus and found their Jeep parked in the plaza across from the Obelisks. They got inside and Avraham turned on the ignition. He drove the Jeep out of the parking lot and north on the main road along the base of the large hill overlooking the city.

After a few hundred yards, they came to the large reflective pool of water called the Queen of Sheba's Bath. A small group of African cattle were along the far side of the rectangular cistern drinking some water. The main road forked, and Avraham turned the Jeep sharply to the right and drove up a steep slope.

At the top of the hill, they came to a complex of brick buildings nestled in a grove of dense trees. A large white sign along the road said 'YEHA HOTEL' next to a small parking area. Avraham pulled the Jeep into the parking lot and turned off the ignition.

They got out of the Jeep and were all amazed at the incredible views of the obelisks and the Church campus down in the valley below. The sun was setting in the west, and the entire panorama looked quite magical. Then, the three huge super Hercules transport planes interrupted the placid and peaceful moment as they flew convoy style overhead and towards the north in the direction of Israel.

"And so it is…" said Yeshua.

Suddenly, there was some loud noises coming from the dense shrubs nearby, and Avraham instinctively unholstered and quickly drew his Glock semi-automatic pistol with his right hand. He pointed the gun towards the location of the noise.

Mohammed and Yeshua both wildly started laughing as three cute monkeys came out of the shrubs and held up their hands like bank robbers who had just been caught by the local sheriff. The monkeys were small with white, brown and grey bodies, long tails and black faces with brown on the top of their heads.

"Very funny," said Avraham as he re-holstered his gun. "That's enough excitement for one day. Let's find the hotel reception and check in, then find some food... I'm getting really hangry."

They walked from the parking area to the main hotel building in the center of the grove. The monkeys followed them to the front door. They made some strange high pitch sounds that seemed like they were begging for food. Avraham 'shooed' them away as the three young men entered the building.

The lobby was dark and had a musty smell. The hotel was decorated with red wallpaper and antique looking wood panels. The check-in area had an interesting white stone wall around the main reception desk. A beautiful young Ethiopian woman stood behind the desk.

"Welcome to the Yeha hotel. I am Aida. Can I help you gentlemen?" she asked.

"Yes, we are looking for three rooms," said Avraham. "Just for tonight. And we'd like some dinner reservations, as soon as possible."

"Yes, of course," said the receptionist. She checked her computer on the desk briefly and said, "We only have two rooms available. We have a king bed suite and a double with two queens. I'm sorry, however, we had a large group of South African tourists arrive today."

"We'll take them," said Mohammed. "Avraham, you take the king suite and Yeshua and I will take the double."

"Are you sure?" questioned Avraham.

"Yes, absolutely," said Yeshua. "Mohammed and I used to live in an orphanage together and share the same room. It will be just like old times."

"And how is the food here?" asked Avraham. "Do you have a restaurant?"

"Yes, Sir," said Aida. "The food is very good. Authentic Ethiopian cuisine. They are serving dinner now at our restaurant. There is indoor and outdoor seating, and no reservations are needed. The rooms will cost 4,000 Birr, which includes all taxes and a buffet breakfast, and the three dinners will cost 1500 Birr. That is approximately $160 American dollars total."

"Oh wonderful, that sounds perfect," said Avraham. "Although, we are from Israel and not America."

"You are Israeli?" said the receptionist. Her eyes lit up. "My ancestors are Beta Israel. My grandparents were converted to Christianity. I've always wanted to move there, but my parents won't let me."

"We are here on a mission to fly the Falash Mura back to Israel right now," said Mohammed. "You could come with us tomorrow if you want too."

"I cannot," she said. "Thank you for your kind offer, however, my parents would never allow it."

Avraham handed Aida his credit card which she made a copy of it with her credit card imprinter. She handed the card back, as well as two large keys. One key had the number '18' written on it and the other key had a number '10'.

"The king suite is room 10, and the double is room 18," Aida said. She showed them the location of the rooms on the hotel map. "Enjoy your stay here. Check out is 11AM. If there is anything you need, please ask."

"Thank you very much," said Mohammed. "We will need a wake calls at 7:30AM please. Oh, and what kind of monkeys are outside? They seem very comfortable with humans."

Aida smiled and nodded. "They are called grivets, exceptionally clever ones they are. They are also called African green monkeys or savannah monkeys. Don't keep your eyes off your food or they will run off with it. So, it was very nice to meet you and let me recommend a very nice cup of khat tea after your dinners. That is one of our specialties."

Yeshua, Mohammed and Avraham left the reception area and walked through the lobby and towards their rooms.

"I'm going to take a quick shower," said Avraham as he got to the entrance of his room. "Then it's chow time. Let's all meet at the restaurant in about 30 minutes." He looked at his wristwatch. "See you at 8:30."

"Sounds like a plan," responded Yeshua. Avraham opened his door and went inside. Mohammed and Yeshua continued down the hallway towards their room.

"Did you catch it?" asked Mohammed.

"Catch what?" replied Yeshua.

"You know, the fireworks between Avraham and Aida, the receptionist," said Mohammed.

"What the heck are you talking about?" questioned Yeshua. "What fireworks?"

"I'm talking about the attraction between the two of them," said Mohammed. "It was like fireworks. Kinda like the energy between you and Taylor."

They reached their room and Mohammed opened the door with his key. They both went inside. It was a simple, clean room with two queen beds and a bathroom. The window overlooked the valley below and the Obelisk Park.

It was getting dark outside. The bright light of the planet Venus shone intensely in the western sky above the horizon.

"Whoaaaa. Wait a second," said Yeshua as he lay down on one of the queen beds. "What do you mean, the fireworks between me and Taylor? We have a strictly professional relationship. And she is my superior officer."

"You can try to justify and make excuses all day long, but it's obvious there's a strong attraction between the two of you," said Mohammed. He lay down on the other queen bed and rested his head on the pillow. "I can see it all over both of your faces when you look at each other."

"We are just friends," replied Yeshua. "Nothing more, just platonic."

"Don't kid yourself, buddy," said Mohammed. "Men and women can't just be close platonic friends. It doesn't work that way. Someone always gets 'feelings' at some point, and I'm not just talking about happy feelings... I'm talking about the romantic stuff."

"Well, gosh... I guess you might have a point there," replied Yeshua. "I think she is so beautiful, like an Angel... and every time I see her, I get this funny feeling in my chest. But she's way older than me...at least five years or more. And, I certainly wouldn't want to ruin our friendship by doing something stupid."

"That's your head talking there, brother, and not your heart," said Mohammed. "In life, you need to go with your heart. Otherwise, you'll become an old man with many regrets. You need to tell Taylor you love her."

"What? Excuse me... I love her?" replied Yeshua. "Do you even know what love is?"

"Yes, of course I know what love is," responded Mohammed. "Love is when you would take a bullet for someone. You would sacrifice yourself for them."

"Well... I guess I love you, Mohammed," said Yeshua. "I'd take a bullet for you any-day"

"Awwww, shut-up," replied Mohammed. "I mean, thank you. And I would take a bullet for you. I guess I used a bad metaphor for explaining love. I meant to say something witty about romantic love."

"Listen, let's talk about this some other time... the whole Taylor thing," stated Yeshua. "We have way more pressing things on our agenda."

"Okay, my friend," said Mohammed. "Deal. We will table it for another time. So, while we still have a few free moments... I'm going to find a quiet place outside to do my evening prayers. I'll meet you at the restaurant in 15 minutes."

"Sounds good," replied Yeshua. "Just watch out for those monkeys."

Mohammed left the room and walked down the hallway towards the hotel exit. Still lying in bed, Yeshua thought about Taylor for a few moments. He realized Mohammed was completely right in his assessment... he did love Taylor. He felt very happy feelings inside when he thought about her. Yeshua couldn't wait to be with her again, and hoped they would be seeing each other soon. He thought about sending her a text from his phone and check up on her to see how she was doing; however, he changed his mind. He was so very tired, and then closed his eyes and decided to take short nap.

Yeshua went quickly into a dream state. From a black void, he saw the image of the Archangel Raphael materialize in front of him which he had just seen on the sanctuary door inside the old St. Mary's Church of Zion. Rather than just the inanimate painting, Raphael was moving and alive. He held his long spear in his hands and walked through a vast desert. It was nighttime and very dark. Thousands of stars looked like the tiny flames of candles as they flickered in the black background. To the west, the spiral light of Venus shone the brightest and best in the sky. And from the northwest, just above the horizon, was a giant brand-new crescent moon. Crickets and cicadas sung their beautiful tunes in the dreamscape.

In the shadow of the moon, Raphael came upon an oasis of tall palm trees surrounding a small lake. The stars, Venus and the moon reflected perfectly along the surface of the water. As he walked towards the oasis... Yeshua saw two figures lying together by the waterside. Then Yeshua realized he was Raphael. He was no longer a silent observer in his dream; he was actually seeing through the Archangel Raphael's eyes.

There was a man and a naked women lying along the edge of the pool. As he got closer, Yeshua realized that the man was no man... he was much larger than a human and looked like some kind of demon. Even in the dark, he could see his skin was rough like leather, and his huge muscles abnormally bulged as he shared an intimate embrace with the woman below.

Yeshua silently stepped even closer to the couple and clearly recognized the woman's face as she kissed the demon man's lips. It was Taylor… she was entwined passionately with the beast. Yeshua felt some strong emotions he had never felt before. He felt intense jealousy and disappointment. He stood just a few feet away from of them and felt his breath taken away. His disappointment turned into a different emotion… he now felt anger. Then, the anger transformed into hate.

The woman that looked just like Taylor made a moaning sound of pleasure, and then she opened her eyes. Her eyes met Yeshua's eyes in the darkness. She quietly stared at him for a moment, and then formed a very surprised expression on her face. The demon sensed her change of focus and began to stand up and turn around to see what was happening behind them.

Yeshua heard a booming resonant voice inside his head…

"BIND AZAZEL BY HIS HANDS AND HIS FEET AND THROW HIM INTO THE DARKNESS. AND SPLIT OPEN THE DESERT WHICH IS IN DUDAEL AND THROW HIM THERE."

Yeshua saw the Demon lunge forward towards him, angrily. The naked women scurried away into the bushes nearby. Yeshua looked down at his hands. He held the long spear, the same one in the painting at the St. Mary's of Zion Church.

As Azazel the Demon was about to jump and surely gorge Raphael's body, Yeshua reacted and wildly swung his spear in the air like a baseball bat. The spear solidly hit Azazel in his chest who immediately fell over from the hard blow and landed on the ground. As he was writhing in pain, Yeshua quickly pulled a thick twine of rope from inside his robe and tied Azazel's hands and feet together.

Then, something even more mystifying happened. Yeshua turned and looked at the pool of water in the center of the oasis. When he held his right hand out towards the pool, then the water began to split apart in the center, and the entire lake washed away into the surrounding sand... revealing a dark pit below. Yeshua, still in Raphael's body, picked up the huge giant Azazel and threw him into the deep pit below.

The loud voice once again reverberated in Yeshua's mind...

"AND THROW ON HIM JAGGED AND SHARP STONES AND COVER HIM WITH DARKNESS. AND LET HIM STAY THERE FOREVER. AND COVER HIS FACE SO THAT HE MAY NOT SEE THE LIGHT. AND SO THAT, ON THE GREAT DAY OF JUDGEMENT, HE MAY BE HURLED INTO THE FIRE."

Yeshua saw dozens of large rocks and stones around the edge of the pit. Next, he pulled many of them from the ground and threw them into the newly created dark void in the center of the oasis. When Azazel's body was completely covered over, Yeshua motioned with his hand, and all the water swirled and flowed and returned from the surrounding sands and reformed the pool of water in the middle the palm trees.

The voice came one more time to Yeshua…

"AND RESTORE THE EARTH WHICH THE ANGELS HAVE RUINED. AND ANNOUCE THE RESTORATION OF THE EARTH. FOR I SHALL RESTORE THE EARTH SO THAT NOT ALL THE SONS OF MEN SHALL BE DESTROYED BECAUSE OF THE KNOWLEDGE WHICH THE WATCHERS MADE KNOWN AND TAUGHT TO THEIR SONS. AND THE WHOLE EARTH HAS BEEN RUINED BY THE TEACHINGS OF THE WORKS OF AZAZEL, AND AGAINST HIM WRITE: ALL SIN."

Yeshua stood by the reflective water in the center of the oasis and looked down. He saw himself as Raphael, the mighty divine Archangel. But, then he remembered… Mohammed said he transformed into the Archangel Gabriel when he went back to biblical times in Babylon and helped revealed Daniel's dream to King Nebuchadnezzar. How was it possible that he could be experiencing different events as both Angels?

Yeshua heard something rustling in the bushes nearby. He could see someone in the darkness. It was the woman who looked just like Taylor. She came out of the dense foliage and held some large palm fronds that covered her private areas. She had tears streaming down her face.

A loud vibrational sound rattled the entire oasis, and then Yeshua stirred and woke up. His phone was vibrating on the nightstand next to him. It was a text from Taylor! It read…

Hey there! How is your mission going? We are wrapping up things in America and heading back to home base soon. Can't wait to catch up!

Yeshua looked at the time. It was 9:30PM. He had totally overslept and was late for dinner. He greatly disliked being late for anything and decided to reply to Taylor's text later. He quickly jumped out of bed, left the room and hurried down the hallway towards the hotel restaurant.

Avraham and Mohammed were dining outside. Many of the surrounding tables were full of the South African tourists. Surprisingly, a plump older man with white hair wearing a khaki outfit sat next to them at their table.

"So nice of you to join us," said Mohammed as Yeshua approached. "Please say hello to our new friend…"

The old man stood up from his chair and reached out his hand towards Yeshua.

"Brian Forest, from South Africa," he said with a heavy accent as Yeshua shook his hand. They both sat down at the table, which was already full of interesting looking dishes of food. Avraham was stuffing his face with some yummy looking flatbread.

"I'm the leader of this bloody tour group," said Brian. "We travel all around the world and visit megalithic sites. We are visiting the Obelisk Park tomorrow and then off to the nearby town of Lalibela to explore the solid rock-hewn ancient churches carved right down into the volcanic tuff."

"That sounds absolutely fascinating," said Yeshua. He grabbed some of the food from the table and placed it onto his plate. "And what exactly are megaliths?"

"Ah yes, it's a strange and mysterious word... megalith," said Brian. "It means giant historical or pre-historical stone or stones that were used to construct massive structures or monuments, just like the huge obelisks down yonder road."

"Why do you find them so intriguing?" asked Mohammed. "What makes them so interesting?"

Yeshua dipped his flatbread in some kind of thickened sauce on his plate and started eating it. The combination was quite tasty and delicious.

"Because we believe that the true history of humanity is written into the megalithic stones created by our distant ancestors," explained Brian. "There's much more to our human story than what is being told to us by our so-called traditional historians and archeologists."

A couple of the cute grivet monkey walked over to a nearby table and one of the tourists threw them a few scraps of food. The monkeys seemed to smile as they picked up the morsels off the floor and started eating them.

"I love what you are saying," said Yeshua. "Tell me more. What is your favorite megalithic site and what does it tell us about our history?"

"Ahh... yes, yeeebo!" exclaimed Brian in approval with his South African slang. "You brus are kif. Thank you for inviting me to your table. This is my favorite dinner conversation. By the way, where are you chaps from and why are you here, anyway?"

"If we told you, we'd have to kill you," joked Mohammed as he winked one of his eyes. He paused for a moment and then said, "We are from Israel."

"Okayyy... well anyway, there's so many incredible places. It would be hard to pick just one," stated Brian. "I could go on and on about sites in Peru, Egypt, and Lebanon just to name a few. But I guess if I had to choose... my favorite megalithic site is in Turkey. It's called Gobekli Tepe. It's a huge archeological site they are just starting to uncover and it's full of carved T shaped pillars organized into circles full of masterfully crafted Neolithic artwork. And the unbelievable thing it's carbon dated to be at least 12,000 years old, which is a full 6,000 or so years before the history books claim organized structured civilization began. Its discovery has led to a complete redefinition of human history as we know it."

Yeshua recalled the conversation they recently had with Professor Taylor in Babylon about the stone cutting technology of the ancients.

"Brian, how do you think they cut all those giant stones, the megaliths... so many thousands of years ago with just simple bronze tools?" asked Yeshua.

Brian looked at Yeshua with an inquisitive expression. He gently stroked his chin with his right hand as he formulated a response.

"So glad you asked, my young friend," said Brian. "That's the 18-billion-dollar question. I think there was an ancient highly advanced worldwide culture that mastered the technology to cut and move stones that we don't even know how to do today with our modern tools."

"Are you talking about the lost civilization of Atlantis?" asked Avraham.

"Very possibly," replied Brian. "However, the myth of Atlantis described by Plato during the Greek era is about a highly advanced city that attacks Athens and is later destroyed as it submerged into the sea. In modern times, the term Atlantis has become an overused metaphor for any and all advanced lost civilizations that existed before known history. I believe as an archeologist... that many of the megalithic sites all around the world were skillfully created over 12,000 years ago by a lost global civilization. There was a cataclysmic event that destroyed almost everything, and it took almost 6000 years for humanity to recover and restructure into an organized civilization."

"So wait a sec," said Mohammed. "Are you talking about the great flood from the biblical stories?"

"No, this clearly was a different kind of apocalyptic event," explained Brian. "It was not a catastrophe from water and flooding... it was a devastating eradication by heat and fire."

"How does that relate to the megaliths?" asked Yeshua.

"Where did you find this kid?" jested Brian to Mohammed and Avraham as they ate more of the food from the table. "That's exactly the right question to ask. The proof is all in archeology. Many, many of the huge megalithic sites show evidence of tremendous damage from some kind of impact and melting from high heat. We see that at the super hard granite stonework at the places like Karnak Temple and Tanis in Egypt and around Lake Titicaca in Bolivia. There's clear evidence of some kind of explosion from either a comet blast of massive solar flare. Hey, maybe even that huge 500-ton 100 plus foot crumbled tower down there at the Obelisk Park was destroyed by the cataclysmic event."

"So what happened after the cataclysm?" asked Yeshua.

"Again, another good question. There's a historical consensus about a period called the Younger Dryas from about 13,000 to 12,000 years ago during the end of the last great ice age. Instead of a gradual warming of the earth and melting of the glacial ice… there was a 1,000ish years of a sharp decline in temperatures. Everything got mysteriously colder all around the Earth. We think whatever huge explosion damaged most of the global megalithic sites and led to the demise of their advanced civilization also caused a huge climatic change. Probably heavy smoke and debris from whatever happened darkened the skies for years and prevented sunlight from heating the earth. Think of it as a mini-version of what happened during the dinosaur extinction event 66 million years ago when a 9-mile-wide comet or asteroid hit the Earth in the Gulf of Mexico."

"So, do you think that Younger Dryas event was intentional?" asked Yeshua.

"What? How do you mean?" asked Brian.

"Well, do you think the cataclysmic event that wiped out the highly advanced human global civilization that could precision cut granite and make huge monumental structures was purposefully destroyed?" questioned Yeshua. "Or do you think that destruction event was just bad luck and bad timing for those people?"

"You know, I never thought about it like that," responded Brian. "However, you have an excellent point there. You are saying that... and let's just use the term Atlantis for lack of a better description of the ancient high technology society, that somehow they blew themselves up or were destroyed by either some kind of extra-worldly beings or divine intervention. That Atlantis culture fell not by a random interstellar explosion, but by a purposeful annihilation event."

"Yes, that's what I'm asking about," said Yeshua. "Is it possible?"

"I supposed anything is possible," replied Brian. "But you would have to go back in time to know for sure what happened. We would have to find some conclusive evidence in the archeological megalithic sites that proved purposeful destruction. Until then it's anyone's guess. I mean who knows, maybe space aliens came down in their flying saucers and blew everything up. One thing is for sure in my opinion... many, many of the oldest megalithic sites were later reoccupied by known cultures like the dynastic Egyptians and the Incas. For example, in Egypt... there's so many locations with super hard granite monuments that would not have been able to be made by the dynastic Egyptians 4,500 years ago with just basic bronze tools. And in Lebanon, there's no way the Romans could have cut, moved and placed the 1000 ton stones at the base of the Baalbek temple."

"Yes. They would have at least needed diamond cutting technology, correct?" replied Yeshua.

"Holy moly, son," said Brian. "Have you been secretly watching my YouTube videos? How would you know that?"

"We've had a similar conversation with Professor Noah Taylor recently," responded Yeshua. "He seems quite the expert on the subject we are discussing."

"You really know THE Professor Noah Taylor?" asked a very surprised Brian. "The archeologist? He's totally my hero and inspiration. I've been following his discoveries my entire life. Did he say anything about his theory of the real source of the stone cutting technology of the ancients?"

"Well, we were recently at a dig at ancient Babylon," said Yeshua. Brian's eyes immediately opened wider than seemed possible. "We found a relief statue of a eagle-headed winged man holding a cone and some kind of..."

"Bucket!" said Brian. "You actually found a stone carving of a winged mythical Apkallu holding a pinecone in one hand and what looks like a handbag in another, yes?"

"Yes, that's exactly what we saw there, buried in the sand," replied Mohammed.

The dishes on their dinner table were mostly empty, as the majority of the delicious Ethiopian food had been consumed. A young Ethiopian waiter came over to the table and removed most of the plates.

"Did the Professor say anything about the function of the cone and bucket?" asked Brian. "I believe they are called banduddu and mullilu in ancient Sumerian. No one knows for sure their actual purpose."

"Yes. He said they, the Apkallu… were multidimensional beings," said Mohammed. "And they used some kind of vibrational energetic sound wave technology using the cones and buckets to cut, lift and place the giant megalithic stones you are talking about."

"I knew it!" said Brian as he slammed his fist on the table. "That's what I think too! There's no way humans could have done it with just simple tools. I know there's way more to the story than we know."

Aida, the hotel lobby receptionist walked towards the table. Many of the other South African tourists had finished their dinners and retired for the evening. Avraham's eyes instantly lit up when he saw the beautiful Ethiopian woman standing next to him.

"I hope you gentlemen enjoyed your meals," she said. "Would you be interested in some dessert and khat tea?"

"Absolutely yes," said Brian. "We would love some. And what kind of dessert do you have?"

"Tonight, we have injera bread pudding topped with vanilla ice cream," she said.

"That sounds wickedly wonderful, thank you. And the food tonight was unbelievably delectable this evening," replied Brian.

Aida smiled, then turned around and walked back towards the hotel kitchen. Yeshua looked up at the night sky and he had powerful déjà vu feeling. To the west, the bright light of the planet Venus shined intensely. And to the northwest, just above the horizon was an enormous brand-new crescent moon. There was the serene sound of crickets singing in the darkness. Yeshua recalled seeing this same exact sky configuration in his recent dream just before dinner when he became the Archangel Raphael and banished the fallen Angel Azazel into a deep abyss.

"Ah my new friends, we are in for quite a treat," said Brian. "Have you ever had khat tea before?"

"Khat, that sounds familiar," responded Avraham. "Isn't that some kind of leaf? I remember my parents talking about it... it's from here in Ethiopia and has some kind of stimulant caffeine effect."

"Yes, that's correct... kind of," replied Brian. "The ancient Egyptians used the khat plant as a sacred substance.

They consumed the plant in ceremonies to help awaken and realize their divinity. Often, they would go into a mysterious transcendental state of consciousness. It would elicit a dream-like trance state that could be absolutely life changing and transformational."

"Wow. All that from a cup of tea?" asked Avraham.

Aida returned from the kitchen holding a large silver platter which contained four teacups, a fancy porcelain teapot, spoons, plates, napkins and a huge bowl with an incredible looking huge portion of bread pudding covered with white ice cream. She placed the tray on the table, and then poured tea into the four teacups from the teapot.

"Gentlemen, thank you for your patronage at the Hotel Yeha," she said. "Enjoy the rest of the evening to the fullest."

"And thank you so much for your hospitality," replied Brian. "We are completely blessed and honored to be here."

Aida nodded and smiled again. Her eyes seemed to glow in the dark Ethiopian night. Then she walked back towards the hotel and disappeared.

"Cheers, my esteemed Israeli friends," said Brian as he raised his teacup in the air. Yeshua, Mohammed and Avraham all took his cue and a held up their teacups. "Cheers!" they all said in said in unison as they clanked their cups together. Everyone took a big sip of their tea.

"Not bad," said Yeshua. "Not bad at all." He took another big sip as Avraham started digging into the bread pudding with his oversized spoon.

"This has been a most interesting evening so far," said Brian. "And it's only getting better. You know, they say... when you are on an adventure, you can never be lost."

"Well said," replied Mohammed after he finished a huge mouthful of the bread pudding and ice cream. He held up his spoon and before he dunked it back into the dessert bowl he said, "And there is no spoon."

Brian had finished his cup of tea and poured another one. He then topped off Yeshua's teacup.

"I've also heard about this khat plant," said Mohammed after finishing another mouthful of bread pudding. Some melted ice dream dripped down the side of chin. He was slightly slurring his words, as he seemed already somewhat intoxicated. "It is said that the Sufis use it to intensify their mystical experience and connect closer to Allah."

"Nice," replied Avraham. "I'll have another, please." Brian then refilled his teacup from the teapot.

After they finished the entire teapot and all the bread pudding, Yeshua noticed that he felt very hot and began sweating profusely. He looked at his friends and they all looked uncomfortable as well. Their faces seemed flush, and they were sweating profusely as well.

"Excuse me," said Avraham. He stood up, stumbled over to some nearby bushes and started loudly vomiting. Thankfully, there was no one left at any of the other tables to view him regurgitate most of his dinner into the shrubs.

Yeshua, Mohammed and Brian all started to uncontrollably laugh. They laughed so hard, tears streamed down their faces.

After a few moments, Avraham stopped throwing up and he stumbled back to the table. He said loudly, "not funny!"

"Listen guys, I'm freaking burning up," said Mohammed. "Does anyone want to go for a swim?"

"A swim?" replied Yeshua. "You're tripping. There's no freaking swimming pool here at the hotel to go swimming."

"Oh yes there is," said Avraham. "Just down the road… at the Queen of Sheba's Bath. Let's go jump in."

"I think that's a marvelous idea," said Brian. "I'm all in!" He stood up, and then almost fell over.

"Are you sure, is it safe to go there in the middle of the night?" asked Yeshua.

"Well, my friend… do you hear anything strange in your ears?" asked Mohammed as he slowly got up from his chair. He seemed to be somewhat unsteady on his feet.

"Huh?" asked Yeshua, as time seemed to shift and distort. Waves of color and sound danced around his body. He pondered Mohammed's question for what felt like an eternity. Then he remembered that he would always hear a high pitch buzzing sound in his right ear when something dangerous was about to happen. It took him quite a while to formulate an appropriate response in his brain and direct his mouth to speak the correct words.

"No," said Yeshua. "I don't hear anything." He felt like a thousand pounds in his chair. He couldn't move.

"Cool. Then let's roll!" said Mohammed. They all grabbed Yeshua by his shoulders and pulled him up to a standing position.

"What exactly was in that tea?" asked Yeshua. "I don't feel quite myself. Everything is kinda spinning."

"It's the khat in the tea," said Brian as he put Yeshua's right arm over his shoulder and helped him walk down the hill from the Hotel parking lot. "It's a mild hallucinogenic stimulant. No worries, all totally legal here in Ethiopia."

"Ahhh. Good, so we won't end up in jail?" asked Yeshua.

"I hope not," said Mohammed. "I don't think we are really jail material."

All four men started laughing hysterically as they stumbled down the steep hill towards the Queen of Sheba's Bath. Once at the bottom, although it was quite dark… the long rectangular pool of water glistened and sparkled in the night. There was some strong wind blowing through the valley, which caused some waves and ripples on the surface of the pond. Thousands of stars from above reflected in incredible swirling patterns along the moving waters of the small lake.

"I've never seen such an incredible sight," said Avraham as he stood at the edge of the bath. "It's like the entire universe is right there in the water."

"Last one in is a rotten egg," said Brian. He quickly removed all his clothes except for his britches, then ran and did a perfect cannonball into the water. The splash caused by his plump pale-white body colliding with the surface of the water looked almost like atomic bomb explosion.

As the thousands of water droplets from Brian's cannonball surged into the air, similar to all the galaxies expanding into the universe after the big bang... Yeshua saw a familiar sight. The droplets of water began to glow and sparkle, like fireflies on an early summer evening. Some of the orbs were yellow, some orange and others white. Rather than falling back into the water, they floated and levitated and slowly moved towards Yeshua as he stood along the side of the lake.

Mohammed and Avraham joined Brian in the water with much less fanfare as they walked down some steps and submerged themselves up to their necks.

"It's much colder than I thought," said Avraham.

"Hey Yeshua, are you coming in?" said Mohammed. "You okay?"

Yeshua stared blankly forward, still in a deep trance. The thousands of orbs gathered and flew around him in circular spinning patterns. He lifted his arms above his head as he took his shirt off. Many of the little orbs spiraled and flew around his hands and past his fingertips. He removed his sandals and his pants and began walking down the nearby steps that led to the lake.

Suddenly the orbs seemed to telepathically speak to him.

"We've been waiting for you to join us." The orbs seemed to all speak together in unison in high pitch voices; similar to the frequency of the buzzing sounds he would often hear in his ears.

"We've been waiting for you to join us," they said again. "Follow us. Follow us this way."

It was very dark outside, and the orbs illuminated the way as Yeshua walked slowly into the ancient Bath of Sheba. Above, the clear black sky was full of millions of sparkling stars. The orbs hovered all around him as he submerged his body into the cold water.

"Yeshua, I have a question for you," said Brian loudly, now treading water closer to the pool's edge. Yeshua immediately came out of his trance, and the orbs faded and disappeared.

"Sure, what's up?" replied Yeshua.

"What do you think of the khat tea?" asked Brian. "You look like you've seen a ghost or something."

"No, no ghosts," responded Yeshua as he treaded the deep water near Brian. "Although, it's like I'm dreaming. I feel like I'm in some kind of strange dream, rather than being awake."

"Yes, the khat will do that," said Brian. "It will open your third eye."

"Third eye?" asked Yeshua. "What is that? That sounds very intriguing."

"The third eye is the portal that leads to the deeper realms of existence and higher states of consciousness," replied Brian. "The mystics believe that by activating the pineal gland in your brain… also called the third eye, the soul will begin an ascension path of spiritual enlightenment."

"And the khat can open this so called third eye?" asked Yeshua.

"Yes, that what they used it for… all the way back to the dynastic Egyptians, and beyond," said Brian.

On the other side of the lake, Mohammed and Avraham seemed to be swimming across the bath and racing each other in the dark.

"To infinity and beyond," said Yeshua jokingly. "Let me ask you a question. Can this third eye open spontaneously? Like without taking drugs?"

"Oh yes, most definitely," said Brian. "That's the main focus of why many religious traditions… like the Hindus and the Buddhists, do years of meditation. They are trying to open their third eye."

"And other than drugs or meditation, any other reasons why someone's eye would open?" asked Yeshua.

"I suppose so," answered Brian. "Perhaps from lots of praying, or fasting, or sensory deprivation like being in a dark cave or such. There are many biblical stories about stuff like that."

"Got another question for you, my new South African friend... if you could ask God one question, what would you ask?" said Yeshua.

"What? Ask God a question?" replied Brian. "I like that thought. A question for God, hmm... let me think about that for a moment."

Still mostly submerged in the water, Brian gently stroked his chin with the index finger and thumb of his right hand. Avraham and Mohammed began swimming towards Yeshua and Brian from the far side of the lake.

"Oh... I got it," said Brian. He yelled, "GOD... WHAT IS THE MEANING OF LIFE?" His head pointing up towards the sky and his arms reached upwards. His words echoed into the valley several times, then there was total silence... except for the chirping of the crickets.

"THE MEANING OF LIFE... IS THE DIFFERENCE BETWEEN ONE AND ZERO," said a very loud, booming voice from the center of the lake. Again, the loud words echoed into the Ethiopian night.

"What the, huh..." said a very surprised Brian as he turned around towards the middle of the pool. Mohammed was treading water there, laughing hysterically. His big smile was faintly visible in the darkness.

"The meaning of life is the difference between one and zero?" repeated Brian. "What does that mean? Who told you that?"

"God told Yeshua that," said Mohammed, now much closer to them in the water. "When he was 13, while he was in a coma."

"God spoke to you in a coma?" asked Avraham. "Are you sure?"

"Wait a second… you had a near death experience and spoke with God?" asked Brian. "Is that why you were asking about how someone's third eye can open?"

"Yes, I suppose so," answered Yeshua. "When I was 13… a Palestinian terrorist blew up the bus Mohammed and I were riding while we were coming home from Masada in Israel. I was in a coma for seven days. While I was unconscious, God came to me in the form of a giant floating orb and told me that the meaning of life is the difference between one and zero."

"That is absolutely incredible," stated Brian. "And what a wonderful answer, in so many ways. What do you think it means?" Brian started to walk out of the Bath of Sheba, and the others followed him to the water's edge and also got out.

"Well, there are several ways to interpret it," said Yeshua.

"Actually, wow! There's like an infinite amount of ways to look at it," replied an obviously very excited Brian. "I mean, just mathematically speaking... the difference between one and zero is one. Everything is one!"

"Yes, all is one. **Here oh Israel, the Lord our God... the Lord is One**," said Yeshua by reciting the English translation of the Hebrew Shema prayer.

"And then consider what the value of zero really means... it's absolutely nothing. A total void," said Brian. Everyone grabbed their clothes off the ground and began to walk up the hill back towards the hotel.

"So the meaning of life is found within the difference of everything, which is 'One' and nothing, which is zero," stated Brian. "That is where we exist, in the physical plane of reality... between the experience of duality."

"Duality, what do you mean?" asked Avraham. "I'm not really fully understanding this conversation. Maybe I need some more of that khat tea."

"Look at this way," said Brian. "We find meaning by experiencing the full value of two opposites. For example... take war and peace. How can you truly know and appreciate the full value of peace without experience the horror of war? It's similar to a binary programming system, like in a computer. As you go into a digital system... you only have two values. One and Zero. The integer is either 'on,' representing a 'one' or 'off,' representing a 'zero.' The computer then creates a virtual reality as it interprets the differences between the ones and the zeros as a coded language."

"Are you saying we live in some kind of computer simulation, like the Matrix?" asked Mohammed. "I knew it... there is no spoon."

They approached the crest of the hill along the dirt road; the Hotel Yeha was just ahead in the distance. Above in the sky, the crescent moon appeared to slowly move across the heavens.

"Yes, the Creator... or who you call God, in my opinion, made this Universe like some kind science experiment." said Brian. "Why exactly, I don't know. Maybe he or really IT... was quite lonely and wanted to make something (One) out of nothing (Zero). The Creator purposefully made the exact physical conditions for galaxies, stars and planets to form... which then became the birthplace for life given just the right circumstances. And those special planets that were just the right distance from their suns, and rotated just the right way and were just the right temperature... the seeds of life would evolve into highly conscious beings who would look out into the vastness of space and thank their Creator for creating them."

"Wow. That's some heavy stuff," said Avraham. They all reached the main building of the hotel. Now mostly dried off, they all put their clothes back on and entered the empty lobby.

"It's been quite an enlightening evening, my new Israeli friends," said Brian. "However, it's time for me to retire for the evening. I have a big day tomorrow with my tour group and all."
"Yes, it's been very nice to get to know you, and thank you for sharing your insightful perspectives on so many

things," replied Yeshua.

"Enjoy the rest of your time here in Ethiopia," said Brian. "I'm sure we will cross paths again. And check out the videos my on the YouTube channel about megalithic archaeology and the origins of humanity. If you have some free time next year, sign up for one of my tours. We have trips to Peru and Egypt coming up."

"We will certainly look into it. It's been a pleasure to meet you," said Avraham.

"Oh, and by the way... they say the lost Ark of the Covenant is just down the valley here at the Church of the Tablet next to the Church of St. Mary of Zion," said Brian. "You should go try to check it out."

"Yes, we know. Thank you," said Avraham. "We might get to see it tomorrow. My great uncle is one of the guardian monks there."

"Well good luck with that," said Brian. He winked, shook everyone's hands, then turned and left the lobby as he walked toward his room.

"Interesting dude," said Mohammed. "And I really enjoyed that tea. I wonder if they have that back in Israel?"

"Ok guys, I'm totally wiped," said Avraham. "I'm going to shower this stanky water off me and then get some shut eye. Let's plan to meet at the jeep at 0800."

"Sounds perfect," said Yeshua as they walked from the lobby towards their rooms. "Good night and see you in the morning."

Avraham went into his room, and then Yeshua and Mohammed entered theirs. Mohammed took a quick shower first. Yeshua sat on the bed, still experiencing the mysterious effects of the khat tea. He felt a calm peaceful feeling, and he sensed that whatever the third eye was... his was open. He knew that whatever was going to happen in the future would happen exactly as it was supposed to happen, and when the time came for him to have to make a choice about what to do... he would make the correct choice.

"Okay, your turn," said Mohammed as he walked out of the shower, his white towel wrapped around his torso. I'm going to do my evening prayers while you shower, then get some sleep. It's been one heck of a day."

"You know, they say... 'when you are on an adventure, you are never lost,'" said Yeshua. He stood up from his bed and walked into the bathroom.

"Who the heck is 'they' Yeshua?" joked Mohammed. "I need to know who 'they' are and who says all this stuff. They say 'this' and they say 'that.' I need to talk to them as I have several questions for them."

"Ha-ha... very funny," said Yeshua and he got into the shower. The warm water felt so cleansing as he washed the dirty film of residue off his skin from the muddy waters of the Bath of Queen Sheba. His sensations still seemed quite amplified and enhanced from the khat tea. It felt somewhat intoxicating and blissful. Still in the shower, his mind drifted off and his thoughts ebbed and flowed between many of the happier moments of his life. Then he thought of Taylor... the memory of the first time he saw her in the hospital after he came out of his coma. She was his nurse, and she cared for him the whole time he was there. He remembered her walking into this hospital room after he woke up on the seventh day. She looked like angel.

Yeshua turned the water off, dried himself with a towel and put on some clean boxers. He brushed his teeth, and then got into bed. He felt so relaxed. He closed his eyes, and for the first time in a very long time... after he fell asleep, he didn't dream.

The next morning, Yeshua was awakened to the sound of Mohammed doing his morning prayers on the nearby floor. Rays of light streamed through the slightly open curtains covering the windows across from the beds.

"Good morning, my friend," said Mohammed as he got up off the floor and rolled up his prayer rug. "Did you sleep well?"

"Yes, like a baby," replied Yeshua. He looked at the digital alarm clock on the nightstand next to the bed. It read 7:33AM. "Guess it's time to get moving."

Yeshua and Mohammed packed up their belongings and left the room. They went to the dining area and grabbed a few pastries and fruit for the road. They left the hotel right at 8:00AM and met Avraham at the Jeep exactly on time. They all got into the jeep, and Avraham turned the ignition and started to drive down the hill.

"I had this crazy dream last night," said Avraham. "It

must have been from drinking that khat tea."

"What happened in your dream?" asked Mohammed. "You know, Yeshua is a very good dream interpreter."

"So... I was walking through this barren desert, and then I came upon a beautiful oasis," described Avraham. "It was dark and night-time, but I could see these two figures embracing each other along the edge of the pond in the center of the oasis."

"Ohhh. Who were they?" asked Mohammed.

"Let me guess," said Yeshua. "One of them looked like a demon, and the other was a woman." Yeshua remembered his dream from the previous day as almost exactly identical to Avraham's.

"Yes! How did you know that?" asked Avraham. The man looked like some kind of devil, or demon... and the woman, well... she looked just like Aida, the pretty hotel receptionist. They were kissing and hugging on the ground, you know."

"And that made you very jealous and angry. Correct?" asked Yeshua.

"Yes... again, how do you know what happened in my dream?" questioned Avraham. He made a sharp left turn at the bottom of the hill at the Bath of Queen Sheba in the jeep and drove towards the Obelisk Park.

"He's very good. Isn't he?" interjected Mohammed. "He's like the dream whisperer. So... what happened next?"

"Okay, so I got really pissed off," said Avraham. "Then the Demon attacked me... but this voice came into my head and told me to tie up and bind the devil dude and throw him into a deep black pit. So I smashed him with this giant spear I was holding, then used some rope and bound his hands and feet together."

"Then you parted the water of the oasis and threw him into the pit, then covered him with rocks?" asked Yeshua.

"Oh my God... yes!" yelled Avraham. "That's exactly what happened. The voice in my head told me what to do. The demon, his name was..."

"Azazel," replied Yeshua. "The fallen angel from the Book of Enoch. He was one of the Watchers who betrayed God. You were told to banish him until the day of Judgment."

"Yes. That's him... Azazel." responded Avraham. He parked the Jeep in the parking lot across from the Aksum Obelisks.

"I'm so confused, how do you know what I dreamed?" asked Avraham. "How is that possible?"

They all left the Jeep and started walking towards the large Church of St. Mary's of Zion building with the giant golden dome.

"I had the virtually the same dream, the day before," replied Yeshua. "It's a story from the Book of Enoch. You were the Archangel Raphael in your dream. God commanded Raphael to cast the rebellious fallen Angel Azazel into an abyss for his betrayal."

"But why would I have that dream?" asked Avraham. "Why me?"

They reached the outside of the huge church, and then they entered through the main doors. Just inside, waiting for them in the nave were the two Ethiopian Archbishops they had met the day before standing with another older man wearing dark robes and a black head covering.

Avraham seemed to instantly recognize the old man. He said, "Great uncle! Is that you? I'm Avraham from Israel. You are distantly related to my father... Yonas, from Gondar."

"Yes, I know about you and your father," said the old man in the dark robes. "My name is Negasi... I am the guardian of the Church of the Tablet. It is my honor to meet you, and your companions."

"I wish we had better news to tell you, my young friends," said the older Archbishop. "However, it is forbidden for anyone to see the Holy Ark of the Covenant. We wish you could grant you your wish; however, it is not possible."

"I am so sorry," said Negasi. "We can not take you into the Chapel of the Tablet to see the Ark. I wish we could, believe me."

"Well, then I have a one question for you... before we leave," said Avraham. "I had a vision last night that I was the Archangel Raphael. I bound the fallen Angel Azazel and threw him into the abyss. Why would I have that dream?"

"Raphael, one of the holy Angels, who is over the spirits of men," said Negasi. "That is from the Book of Enoch, and also the story you described from your dream."

"Why would I have that dream?" asked Avraham again.

The younger Archbishop responded immediately as he recited another passage from the Book of Enoch...

"When Enoch asked who the four figures were that he had seen... 'And he said to me: the first is Michael... the merciful and long-suffering, and the second... who is set over all the diseases and all the wounds of the children of men is Raphael, and the third... who is set over all the powers is Gabriel, and the fourth... who is set over the repentance unto hope of those who inherit eternal life is named Phanuel.' And these are the four angels of the Lord of Spirits and the four voices I heard in those days."

"The voice of Raphael has come through you," said Negasi. "And your good friends here with you... Michael and Gabriel have come through them. And there is the fourth Angel Phanuel who is also amongst your midst. This is the will of the Lord, as the day of Tribulation is upon us. The prophecy of Enoch will unfold through your worldly missions."

Avraham, Yeshua and Mohammed stared at Negasi silently for a quite some time. Avraham looked completely stunned.

"How... how do you know this?" asked Yeshua. "Are you sure?"

"It is you who knows for sure," replied Negasi. "I am not telling you something you don't already know. All will be revealed in time, just as it should exactly when it should. All you need to do is have faith, and patience with the process."

"Thank you for your time, your highnesses" said Mohammed and he slightly bowed his head. "We appreciate your hospitality and guidance. And thank you for agreeing to participate in the world peace initiative next year in Jerusalem. We look forward to connecting again."

"We are honored as well," said the older Archbishop. "Farewell, and safe travels with your journeys." The three old Ethiopian clergy turned and walked away.

Yeshua, Mohammed and Avraham quickly left the church and started walking back towards their jeep. Avraham still had a completely stunned look on his face.

"We... we, are some kind Angels?" he asked aloud, almost stuttering.

"Apparently so. It's a long story," replied Yeshua. "We will explain the whole thing to you on the way back."

"Okay," said Avraham, just as they got to the parking lot across from the Obelisk Park. Standing next their Jeep was Aida, the hotel receptionist. She was holding a suitcase. Avraham's jaw literally dropped when he saw her.

"I've changed my mind," she said. "I want to go with

you to Israel. I want to live in the Promised Land."

"Hop on board, ma'am" responded Yeshua. "We can definitely help you with that."

Avraham smiled widely at Aida. He took her suitcase and put it in the back of the jeep, and then they all got inside. He turned on the ignition, and then drove the Jeep out from the parking lot. As they passed the Obelisk Park, Brian and his South African tour group were standing in shadow of the largest monument. He turned and saw his newfound friends driving away, and he waved them goodbye. They all waved back at him from the Jeep, and then they drove down the main street southwards and back towards the Aksum Airport.

Chapter 9

The Vedas

Indira Gandhi International Airport
New Delhi, India
One Week Later

The Israeli EL AL Airlines Airbus A310 flight landed exactly on time at 2:11PM and taxied along a vast series of runways into the international terminal. Yeshua, Mohammed, Avraham, and General Cohen deboarded the plane and entered a very colorful and busy airport in the center of India, a huge and expansive country of well over a billion people. They made their way through a series of extensive security stations and customs checkpoints. The airport was extremely crowded and full of thousands of international travelers from almost every corner of the world. Finally, they reached the baggage claim area and retrieved their large green backpacks from the long conveyor belt carousel.

Two young Indian men wearing simple linen clothes and sandals greeted them at the baggage claim. They both held their hands together in a prayer pose and gently bowed their heads.

The slightly older man then spoke with a heavy Indian-English accent, "Welcome to India, my friends. We have been expecting you. I am Jihan and this is Nihal. We will be your guides and companions during your stay."

"Very nice to meet you," said Yeshua. He slightly bowed his head. "This is Mohammed, Avraham, and Cohen. And I am Yeshua." After being introduced, they all slightly bowed their heads towards their Indian hosts.

"Before our trip, we would first like to honor you with a traditional Tilaka ceremony," said Jihan.

The younger man closed his eyes and started softly chanting and singing verses in a strange and beautiful language. Jihan reached into his front pocket of his shirt and pulled out a small ornately decorated square brass container. He opened the box and touched his finger into the red dye within, then applied a small dot of the ink onto the lower foreheads of Mohammed, Yeshua, Avraham and Cohen. They each bowed their heads again, in appreciation of the ancient Hindu ritual.

Nihal stopped chanting and said in English, the translation of the Vedic prayer...

"Look to this day, for it is LIFE, the very breath of LIFE. In its brief course lie all the realities of your existence... the bliss of growth, the glory of action, the splendor of beauty. For yesterday is only a DREAM, and tomorrow is but a VISION. But today, well lived... makes every yesterday a dream of happiness, and every tomorrow a vision of HOPE. Look well, therefore, to this day."

"Wow! That is a very beautiful and prophetic saying," replied Mohammed. "Where is that quote from?"

"It's a verse of Sanskrit from the Vedas," said Jihan. "That's our ancient spiritual knowledge and wisdom which forms the basis of Hinduism."

"Gentlemen, we have a very long journey ahead," stated Nihal. "We must go to the airport metro station as soon as possible then travel to the New Delhi Railway Station. Does anyone need the use the wash-room, or get some food right now?" Everyone shook their heads 'no' and then Jihan personally handed them all brand new Indrail ticket passes. They left the baggage claim and headed to the nearby Metro entrance via the central airport escalator.

At the very crowed entrance to metro station, they all walked through the main gates after placing their Indrail passes in the automated turnstiles. Once on the crowded Metro train, it was approximately a ten-minute trip to the main New Delhi railway station. They left the metro train and walked across a raised skywalk towards the massively expansive train terminal.

Halfway across the raised platform, Nihal stopped walking. He motioned everyone to join him along an empty observation platform overlooking the huge building full of dozens of trains and tens of thousands travellers below.

"We will be getting on different trains located different terminals in a few minutes," said Jihan. "I will accompany Yeshua and Mohammed onto Hardiwar, and then onto Rishikesh. Nihal will travel with Avraham and Cohen to Mumbai. Your Indrail passes will allow you to have unlimited travel for seven days, which should be more than enough to accomplish all our directives. So for now, it's a goodbye... until all we meet again."

Yeshua and Mohammed shook Avraham's and Cohen's hands and everyone gave each other brief man-hugs as they all said their goodbyes.

"Good luck and Godspeed, my friends," said Mohammed. Then, they all returned back to the skywalk and went their different ways as they entered the enormous main train terminal.

"This is the biggest train station I've ever seen," said Mohammed. Dozens of trains filled the massive room as far as the eyes could see.

"About a half million people travel through this station daily," responded Jihan. They walked along their train's platform, filled with hundreds of people getting into the passenger cabins of a very long train labeled HARDIWAR, written in very large bold white letters near the top of the main railway car.

"Ah... here we are," he said. The three men entered the train in one of higher-class sections and then walked through a few crowded rail cars until they entered a nearly empty air-conditioned cabin. They found some comfortable looking seats in a private area in the back and sat down across from each other, with one empty seat in-between each of them. After just a moment, the conductor came through the cabin and checked their tickets. The train slowly departed the station and then picked up speed as it accelerated towards the north.

"How long is the trip to Hardiwar?" asked Mohammed. He was sitting across the isle from Jihan. "How far is it?"

"Oh, it's only about four hours," said Jihan. "Then we will Uber from there to Rishikesh... it's about a 45-minute drive from the train station."

"Oh nice, just four hours?" replied Yeshua. "I thought it was going to take like four days, thank goodness. And you guys have Uber here, in India?"

"Oh yes, we have very much modernized our country here," said Jihan. As Hindus... and for India as a whole, we do our best honor our ancient traditions and history, while also embracing the technology of the present age... as well as continuing to grow and evolve into the future."

"That sounds like some kind of quote about 'karma'?" asked Yeshua. "Is that another saying from your Vedas you were mentioning?"

"Yes and no," responded Jihan. "In essence, all things, all knowledge, all knowing, all thoughts... come from the Vedas. The actual writings of the Vedas are a manifestation of higher consciousness and understanding. Much like your Hebrew Torah scrolls, yes?"

Yeshua nodded, then turned his head away momentarily and looked out unto the nearly endless city of New Delhi from his window seat. He had never seen so many so many people crowded into one place. The streets were filled with rickety cars, animals, and pedestrians, a truly mesmerizing sight.

"And where exactly are we going in Rishikesh? And whom will we be meeting with?" asked Mohammed.

"The Shankarachraya has spent a year in silence and mediation at the Chaurasi Kutia ashram in the Rajaji Tiger Reserve near Rishikesh," explained Jihan. "We will be so very fortunate and blessed to his presence later today when he breaks his silence and shares his insights and reflections with the world."

"What? Oh no. Are we really going to a Tiger Preserve?" said a very scared looking Mohammed. "I just don't like big cats, that's all."

"And who is this Shankaracharaya?" asked Yeshua. "Is that who we are meeting with?"

"Yes," responded Jihan. "The Shankaracharaya is amongst the holiest men in India, descended from a class of priests called the Brahmin. His knowledge and wisdom have been handed down through all the Shankaracharayas in history, way back to the Adi Shankara... one of the most important sages of Hinduism. He is considered one of the most influential teachers of the Vedas... a true guru."

"So, where do the Vedas actually come from?" asked Mohammed. "I mean... are they written down? Are they in books or scrolls... like the Torah? And how old are they?"

"We have a long train ride ahead," stated Jihan. "So I will be so very happy to share with you some of the longer answers to your questions."

"There are four Vedas," explained Jihan. "The very translation of the word Vedas means knowledge and wisdom. They were passed down as oral stories from generation to generation for thousands of years, and then eventually written down in books in the ancient language of Sanskrit. Their titles are called the Rigveda, the Yajurveda, the Samaveda, and the Atharvavenda. Each of the books, with the oldest one being about 3,500 years old... have a deep wealth and knowledge of philosophy, meditation and spiritual understandings."

Although Yeshua was very interested to learn more about the mystical and mysterious Vedas, he suddenly felt very tired and sleepy. An overwhelming wave of exhaustion came over him. He slowly closed his eyes as he tried his best to continue to listen.

"We also have the Ramayama and Mahabhrata epics... the latter being the longest poem every written," described Jihan. Within its 200,000 verses is contained the Bhagavad Gita, one of the most well know and famous Hindu texts.

"Yes, I've heard of that one," replied Mohammed. "Isn't it about karma, reincarnation, the meaning of life and stuff like that?"

"Indeed it does, yes. Through our Vedas, we are taught that the 'Atman', or what we call our essence or soul... is eternal," explained Jihan. "Simply put, what you do in this life, and the path you take... effects your subsequent lives."

Yeshua could no longer focus on their conversation anymore. He drifted off into a deep sleep with his face pressed up against the train's window, next to his comfortably cushioned seat. After a few moments of experiencing darkness and void... he shifted into a dream state of consciousness.

At first, he felt like he was free falling... like a skydiver after jumping out of an airplane. This was a common and recurrent dream experience for him since his childhood. During this part of all his previous dreams, the falling part... always seemed to be some kind of transition into another dream, like turning the page into a new chapter of a book. Often, when he would free-fall in past dreams... he would end up plunging to his death when he hit the ground below. As grotesque and dramatic as that was in his dreams, Yeshua seemed to know that he was not actually falling to his death... but that the traumatic event was a portal to another experience in the dream. Somehow, within his dreams... he knew he was dreaming.

This time, however, was very different. Rather than free falling like a skydiver in the air, he was sitting in a golden chair and looking out through a large translucent window. Directly in front of him appeared to be some kind of highly advanced dashboard full of controls, knobs and digital displays. To his surprise, everything was made from gold, gems and diamonds.

Was he inside some kind of strange aircraft or flying vehicle? Outside the window, he saw that whatever he was sitting inside... was falling towards the earth at a very high rate of speed. The large, snowcapped mountains below rapidly became closer. He looked to see if there was a steering wheel to control to the plane, without success.

The craft began to spin wildly as it descended downwards towards the Earth. Yeshua held tightly onto a golden orb coming out from the control panel in front of him, like a joystick from a video game. He started to sweat and panic as he saw an inevitable collision into the mountains below within a just a few moments.

Before the impact, Yeshua yelled, "We are going to crash! We are going to crash!" He felt everything shake and rattle.

"Wake up Yeshua. Wake up. We are going to crash?" asked Mohammed as he shook his shoulders. "Wake up! You are dreaming."

"Huh, what?" said Yeshua as he opened his eyes. He was back on the train.

"Are we really going to crash?" asked Mohammed. "Seriously, are we?" Several onlookers in the cabin were looking in horror at them.

"No. No. We aren't going to crash," said Yeshua. "I had this dream were I flying in some kind of golden spaceship. I was about to crash into some snow-capped mountains. I think it was the Himalayas."

"Excuse me Sir," interrupted Jihan. "Did you say you were in a flying craft made of gold?"

"Yes, but I couldn't fly it," replied Mohammed. "It was going to crash."

"You were on a Vimana," explained Jihan. "It's a flying ship from the epic of Ramayana. How fortunate and auspicious for you to have that in your dream, my friend."

"What do you mean?" asked Yeshua. "Are you saying that you have golden spaceships in your legends? And I was in one?"

"I will do my best translate and recite the passages about the Pushpaka Vimana from the Ramayana," said Jihan.

"The great hero Hanuman, who was the son of the Wind God, saw the very great plane, which was made of gold and which was decorated by jewels. That plane whose glitter could not be measured and which could not adequately be described by others was made by Viswakarma with an intention that it should be the greatest plane which could move anywhere in the sky and was parked in the route of wind and was like a sign post of the path of the Sun."

"Wait a sec," said Mohammed. "Did you say plane? As in an airplane?"

"Yes. That is the English interpretation of the Sanskrit," replied Jihan. "It clearly is written as 'plane,' as in a flying vehicle."

"And when was the Ramayana written?" asked Mohammed. "How old is it?"

"I believe it was written approximately 2,600 years ago," answered Jihan.

"So, they were talking about flying spaceships 2,600 year ago here in India?" questioned Yeshua. "I'm not surprised. We also have a description of a flying vehicle in our ancient Hebrew biblical texts."

"You do?" asked Jihan. "Please do share with me. I have always been especially fascinated about this particular legend of flying ships. Perhaps they were the ancients' way of describing what we call UFOs today."

"We have a fantastic story about one of our Hebrew Prophets named Ezekiel," explained Yeshua. "He lived in Babylon, and in the Book of Ezekiel... it describes a vision he had of something called a Merkabah. It was described as a heavenly chariot that came down from the sky."

"How wonderful. And how old is this book? When did Ezekiel live?" asked Jihan.

"The Israelites were taken into captivity in Babylon after the destruction of Jerusalem by King Nebuchadnezzar around the year 597 BCE," stated Yeshua. "So that would make it approximately 2,600 years or so ago that Ezekiel had his vision."

"Oh, how very interesting," said Jihan. "Around the same time the Vimana was written about in the Ramayana. Perhaps they were describing seeing the same thing in the sky. The same celestial chariot. After all, ancient Babylon was not that far from India."

"Perhaps," said Mohammed. "Our eyes are wide open now. We are now seeing things in a different light, and are finding that everything seems to be inter-connected."

"Ahhh... spoken like a true Hindu," said Jihan. "And my young friend with the dreams... next time you are on the Vimana, I have some advice for you."

"Oh really?" said Yeshua. "You think I'll be going back in there? I'm all ears."

"Yes, I do. I am certain you are some kind of Avatar, as your dream proves it," stated Jihan.

"Avatar... like the movie?" asked Yeshua. "The one with the tall blue aliens?"

"No, not like that movie... although it was a very enjoyable movie indeed," replied Jihan. "I use the word in the context of a human having the embodiment or essence of a super-being within them. You certainly have that within you, and so does your friend... and I am so very honored to be in your presence."

Jihan placed his hands into praying position, and closed his eyes and bowed towards Yeshua and Mohammed and recited a passage from the Bhagavad Gita...

"Whenever righteousness wanes and unrighteousness increases, I send myself forth. For the protection of the good and for the destruction of evil, and for the establishment of righteousness, I come into being age after age."

"Thank you Jihan, I'm not sure we are Avatars... however, we are here to help make this world a better place," said Mohammed. "And what was the advice you have for Yeshua?"

"Ah yes, there is another passage from the Ramayana that describes how to control the Vimana, which may help you next time," explained Jihan. He continued...

"The great Pushpaka Vimana was won by the valor gained by full meditation and prayer, which can

go in different styles just by mental wish, which can go at any speed by knowing the wish of it's master, which cannot be stopped by anybody, which can go in the speed of wind."

"So, you are saying I can control the flying spaceship with my mind, by meditating?" asked Yeshua.

"I'm not saying that," responded Jihan. "That's what it says in the Ramayana. So next time you are in that ship… you will know how to control it."

"But I don't really know how to meditate," replied Yeshua.

"It's actually not that hard to learn, it just takes practice," said Jihan. "I know someone who might be able to teach you while you are here in India. And, ah… here we are. We have arrived in Hardiwar."

The train slowed down as they came to their destination. Outside the window, Yeshua could see tall snowcapped mountains in the distance.

"That was four hours?" asked Yeshua. "It seemed like less than a half hour. How long was I sleeping?"

"About the whole trip," said Mohammed. "And thank goodness we didn't crash."

They left the train and walked through the crowded station. Hundreds of Hindu monks, also known as sadhus also left the train and started boarding several old school buses parked across the street.

"They are all going to the Chaurasi Kutia ashram to see the Shankarachraya as well," said Jihan as looked at is cell phone. "We will take an Uber... ah, here it is, right on time."

A small red four door Maruti Wagon pulled up and stopped in front of the travellers. An older man got out of the vehicle and introduced himself.

"Hello and welcome to Hardiwar," he said. "I am Aarav. I will be taking you to the Beatles Ashram. Please, let me help you with your things."

Aarav opened the back of his car, put everyone's packs into the trunk, then closed the door.

"Let us go my friends," he said. "Rishikesh is filled with pilgrims today. It will be very crowded on the main road. We will take the way less travelled through the Rajaji Park."

They all got into the vehicle and headed north, then crossed over the Ganges river at the Bhimgoda Barrage bridge and drove east along the Cheela Dam - Rishikesh Road through the dense jungle. Yeshua and Mohammed sat in the back seat. They passed a large sign that said Rajaji National Park in Hindi and English.

"I'm sorry Sir, Mr. Aarav," said Mohammed. "Did you say we are going to the Beatles Ashram? Did I hear you correctly?"

"Yes, that's were we are going," replied Aarav. "That's where everyone is going today. Very good business day for all the drivers in town."

"I thought we were going to the Chaurasi Kutia ashram, to see the Shankaracharaya," replied Mohammed.

"Ha-ha-ha," deeply laughed Aarav while he drove the car almost too quickly through the nature preserve. "The Beatles Ashram and Chaurasi Kutia are the same place. They are one!" He laughed loudly again. "There are tens of thousands of pilgrims going there today to hear the Shankaracharaya speak after one year of silence and meditation. It is a very special day, my friends."

They drove past a large hydroelectric dam and continued deeper into the jungle along a man-made river canal. Colorful tropical birds flew back and forth across the canopy of tall trees next to the road.

"Are you saying the 'Beatles' Ashram as in the famous musicians?" asked Yeshua. "Those Beatles?"

"Yes. Those Beatles," replied Aarav. "You know... John, Paul, George and Ringo! The fab four. They came here over 50 years ago and were taught meditation by the Maharishi Mahesh Yogi. Their trip to Rishikesh was so influential I believe they composed most of the songs from their White Album while they were here."

"The Beatles Ashram was abandoned in the 90's," interjected Jihan. "Now it's become part of this nature preserve. The Shankaracharaya requested special permission to stay there this past year to be in silence. After he speaks, we will be granted an audience with him at which time you will deliver your message. Then we will be heading to Dharamshala to meet with the Dali Lama."

"The Dali Lama? We will be meeting with THE Dali Lama?" asked a very surprised Mohammed.

"Yes, my friends," answered Jihan. "He is considered the most prominent spiritual leader of Buddhists. As we speak, our other team is on the train to Mumbai to meet with the leaders of the Jain religion, and then they will travel to Amritsar, Punjabi to meet with the Sikhs."

Their car slowed down as they approached a crossing ravine that intersected with their road. There was a short earthworks bridge across what looked like a dry riverbed running up into the mountains. Standing on the bridge were dozens of animals grazing on the surrounding green foliage. They were fairly large, had four long legs and white spots on their brown bodies. Several of the tallest ones had large antlers.

"What are those? Some kind of deer?" asked Mohammed. "They are beautiful."

"Yes, they are called chital," said the Uber driver. He stopped the car in front of the herd. "In English they are also called spotted deer. There are hundreds of them as they are a protected species here in the park. And even more so, the entire Rishikesh district is vegetarian... their only danger is the..."

Suddenly, all the chital perked up their heads and stopped eating. Several of them started running into the dense jungle across the road. Aarav quickly pulled out his cellphone and started to video record the scene unfolding in front of them. He slowly rolled up his window with his free hand. Yeshua heard some high pitch buzzing in his right ear.

"Tigers," said Aarav. "What ever you do, do not leave the car." And almost on cue, a giant orange and black-stripped Bengal tiger jumped out from the underbrush across the bridge and lunged at one of the younger chital deer.

"Oh my God!" yelled Mohammed from within the car. Just as the tiger was about to gorge the stunned juvenile deer, one of the largest males nearby charged the big cat and pummeled him with his sharp antlers. The tiger bounced backwards, and the small deer ran away with the rest of the deer herd. Many of the deer ran right by the car in a full stampede. The entire ground shook as they attempted to flee to safety.

Back on the bridge, the large buck stood guard as his herd ran to safety. The tiger, still stunned and surprised from being laid up on the ground by the male deer, made a loud roar as he got to back on his four feet. He looked directly at the antlered deer in front of him and growled. The deer stood there resolutely, holding his ground. The tiger, now visibly angry... started to run towards the deer.

The tiger leapt into the air, and just at that moment... the very brave chital decided to turn and run. He knew he had saved his herd, and now it was time to save himself. He bolted across the bridge, directly towards the Uber car parked just a few dozens of meters away. The furious and hungry tiger chased him as fast as he could.

"Umm… they are coming right towards us!" yelled Mohammed. "Ahhhhhhh!"

The large deer ran right up to their car, agilely jumped onto the hood and then leapt off the roof as he seemingly catapulted himself into the forest of trees across the dirt road. The frustrated tiger stopped running as he almost crashed his body into the front of the car. He slowly strolled around the car, sniffing the windows and trying to catch the scent of the inhabitants inside.

"Uhhhh. What do we do?" asked a panicked Mohammed. "I really don't like cats. I'm not ready to die."

"Relax," said Jihan. "You're not going die today. You must calm down and quiet yourself. The tiger will leave us. Just be patient."

The tiger circled the entire car, wagging his tail wildly. He continued to sniff the car. As he got to the back-passenger side of the car, where Mohammed was sitting… the tiger got right to the window. He stared right at Mohammed.

"I will be quiet," said Mohammed softly. "I will be calm. I will not die today." He repeated the phrases over and over again very quickly with the tiger's face just inches away.

The tiger let out another loud roar and smashed the window with his huge paw. The glass cracked heavily into dozens of shards.

"Ahhhhhhhhhhhh!" screamed Mohammed as the Tiger hit the window again.

Aarav stopped filming with his phone and floored the gas pedal as he accelerated the car across the bridge. The tiger gave chase, and Mohammed continued to scream as they tried to escape the giant cat. Once across the bridge, they sped quickly along the dirt road next to the canal and the tiger disappeared back into the jungle.

"I can't wait to post that video on YouTube!" said Aarav. "It will go viral with millions of views on the 'Watch People Die Inside' channel. You should have seen your face, Mohammed. It was priceless."

"Are we safe now?" asked Mohammed. "Can I breathe again?"

"Yes, we are safe now," said Jihan. "I'm really surprised that Tiger attacked us. It's very rare for tigers to become man-eaters. There are many, many more fatalities from poisonous snake bites here in India."

"Snakes? There are killer snakes here too?" asked a still shaken Mohammed. "What have we gotten ourselves into?"

"My poor car, it's trashed," said Aarav. "I guess we should have taken the other route. Although, I've never seen a tiger attack like that. If I only could have a crystal ball and seen into the future."

"You know, everything happens for a reason," said Jihan.

"Yes, sometimes the reason is you are stupid and make bad decisions," said an agitated Aarav. "And I don't mean you... I mean me. I thought we could take a short-cut through the jungle and get to the ashram faster, but to be completely honest... I did hear there was a man-eating tiger out here, I just didn't think we would come face to face with it."

"You knew there was a man-eating tiger in the jungle, and you took out here?" questioned Mohammed.

"Yes, I am truly sorry," apologized Aarav. "And look at my punishment... instant karma. My car is all dented up and window smashed. It will cost many rupees to fix, and I will not be able to take you to Dharamshala from Rishikesh. You will need to take the bus from Hardiwar now."

"We will pay you to fix your car," said Jihan. "Everything will be okay."

After a period of uncomfortable silence in the car, the Cheela Dam road ended at another bridge crossing the over Ganges river. On the other side of the wide river was the remarkable and scenic city of Rishikesh. The tall spires of giant multi-tiered temples dotted the landscape. Aarav turned the car to the right just before the bridge and drove along a windy dirt road up into the Indian jungle. They passed a large sign that said Chaurasi Kutia Ashram in Hindi and English. A few small grey monkeys with cute pink faces were playing around the sign.

"What kind of monkeys are those?" asked Yeshua.

"They are called rhesus macaques," answered Aarav. "They are very smart, friendly and social. As a matter of fact, they launched these monkeys into orbit during the space race of the 50s and 60s. Two of them were the first living beings to travel into space and return alive."

"Nice. Monkeys flying spaceships. I love it," replied Mohammed.

As they travelled along the windy dirt road, they passed by many Hindu monks walking towards the ashram, all wearing bright orange linens. They would smile and wave towards the passengers inside the car each time they drove by a group. After 15 minutes or so, they came to a large parking lot surrounded by huge trees. Dozens of parked school buses filled the lot, and hundreds of the Hindu monks strolled around the area.

"And here we are. We made it alive!" exclaimed an exhausted looking Aarav. He left the vehicle running and got out of the car. Everyone got out of the car and collected their things from the trunk. There were huge dents in the hood and roof of the car from the jumping spotted deer.

"Good luck my friends, I will leave you here," said Aarav. "I'm going to head back to Rishikesh and find somewhere repair my poor car."

"Thank you, Sir," replied Jihan. He handed him a stack of rupees. "This will take care of your repairs, and some extra. Just remember, in the future… you should listen to your intuition more carefully. It will usually tell you the right thing to do. Sometimes, it's not worth taking the short cuts in life… as we learned today."

"Thank you for the tip," responded Aarav. "I hope you find great value in what Shankaracharaya says today. Good luck on your trip to Dharamshala. And watch out for those tigers!"

"Please, no more tigers," half-joked Mohammed. "We've had enough excitement already."

Aarav made a prayer gesture with his hands, and then slightly bowed. Everyone reciprocated, and then he got back in his damaged car and drove away.

"Nice chap, that Aarav," said Jihan. "But he did almost get us killed. I'm sure that not the first-time you gentlemen have been in harms way."

"You have no idea," said Mohammed. "We could write an epic Sanskrit poem with at least 100,000 verses."

Jihan smiled and put his backpack onto his back. Yeshua and Mohammed followed, and then they walked to an ancient looking stone entrance of the ashram on the far side of the parking lot. Hundreds of monks, pilgrims and western tourists also filed through the main gateway, which was topped with three large pyramidal cones made from tiny round stones.

As they walked under the main gate, one of the young Hindu monks (sadhu) standing nearby seemed to recognize Jihan.

"Jihan, Jihan!" the sadhu said as he waved his hands in the air. He wore an ochre colored robe and had medium length dark hair with a beard and mustache. He pushed his way through the crowd to get closer.

"Pavhari!" responded Jihan. They shook hands and smiled. Rather than following the hundreds of people moving towards the center of the ashram, Pavhair brought them to a narrow path along the outer wall of the complex and stopped walking for a moment.

"This is Mohammed and Yeshua," said Jihan. "They are Israeli emissaries with a very important message for the Shankaracharaya."

"I am Pavhari, the Shankaracharaya's assistant," he said. "It is truly a blessing to meet you. Thank you for making the long trip to be here today. As you already must know, the Shankaracharaya has spent the last year here in meditation. In just an hour or so, he will break his silence and share a message with the entire world. After he is done speaking, you will have the honor of meeting with him privately."

"Thank you so very much," replied Yeshua. "We greatly appreciate your assistance in this most important matter."

"Follow me please along this path as we will avoid the huge crowds of pilgrims," said Pavhari. "We estimate at least 20,000 people here today; it's unbelievable."

They walked along the narrow stone path in the dense jungle forest. After a few minutes, they came to a grotto of round stone buildings that looked like ancient ruins. It looked like something out of science fiction movie, as the pod shaped structures appeared to be otherworldly.

"These are the meditation pods," said Pavhari. "The Shankaracharaya spent almost the entire year in one of them. I brought him his food and water. It was a great honor."

They continued along the stone path and went through another heavily forested area. Ahead, there appeared another ruined building that was several stories high. There were hundreds of people walking along the courtyard of the old stone structure.

"What is that place, up there?" asked Mohammed.

"Oh, that was the residence building," answered Pavhari. "That's were the meditation students would live. It's been abandoned for many years. We are almost at the meeting hall."

Pavhari led them behind the residence complex to a large rectangular building nearby. It had a triangular roof and there many open windows and doorways. Inside were hundreds of the Hindu sadhus monks with their orange and ochre colored robes as well thousands more standing outside as far as the eye could see.

"This way," said Pavhari as he pointed to the back of the structure. They made their way through the large crowd of onlookers and entered the rear of the building through an open window.

Inside, there was a raised wooden platform along the back wall. In the center of the platform, sitting crossed legged... was an old dark-skinned Indian man wearing white robes. He had long white hair and a long white beard. His eyes were closed. He held a beautiful pink lotus flower in-between his hands. Behind him, on the wall... was a large and colorful mural of the Maharshi Mahesh Yogi, flanked by Ringo, John, Paul and George of the Beatles. They wore their circus-like outfits from their St. Peppers Lonely Hearts Band album cover. The image of Maharshi's face glowed and smiled, as his gaze seemed to be looking directly towards momentous event unfolding in front of him.

All the sadhu monks sat in the lotus position in front of the silent Shankaracharaya, patiently waiting. Pavhari motioned with his hands for Mohammed, Yeshua and Jihan to sit in the corner of the room near the raised platform. As they sat down, Pavhari grabbed a cordless black microphone and a glass of water from a nearby table and walked onto the platform. He sat right next to the Shankaracharaya and then placed the glass of water in front of him. Pavhari then closed his eyes and began to meditate. All of the sadhus in the room also closed their eyes and began to meditate.

Yeshua suddenly felt something shift in the room. He had never experienced this kind of powerful feeling before. Some kind of energy was amplifying intensely in the room as the monks went into a deep meditative state. He looked at Mohammed sitting next to him, who had closed eyes and in a meditative state. Somehow, Yeshua could see into his mind. He saw the electrical currents streaming through the neurons within his friend's cortex inside his head. They appeared like lightning bolts, travelling in an organized coherent pattern between the two sides of his brain. Yeshua decided close his eyes and tried to meditate as well.

After approximately 20 minutes, the Shankaracharaya opened his eyes. His pupils seemed to glow with a beautiful luminescence. He reached for the glass of water in front of him and took a sip, still holding the lotus flower in his other hand. Everyone in the room opened their eyes and focused on the Shankaracharaya. He smiled, then put his hands together in praying position and gently bowed his head. All the sadhus, pilgrims and tourists in the entire surrounding ashram reciprocated.

Pavarhi handed the microphone to Shankaracharayah who spoke a few words in Hindi. His strong voice broadcast in the room and throughout the entire Beatles Ashram via strategically placed audio speakers. The massive sea of sadhu monks in the main building and all the other Hindus within the entire grounds of the ashram smiled and nodded their heads as they responded to his statement.

The Shankaracharayah handed Pavarhi the microphone to translate his declaration in English. "After one year of silence, meditation and deep reflection, his Holiness's wants to share a most important message with everyone. He says... be excellent to each other!"

The Shankaracharayah smiled and laughed like a child. After his joyous outburst, he took the microphone back and spoke for some time in Hindi, then handed it back to Pavarhi. He glanced at the old bearded sage with a very confused look, and then the Shankaracharayah motioned him to speak by waving his pink lotus at him.

Many of the sadhus were looking at each other with confused looks. Some of them even started to make questioning comments under their breath.

Pavarhi paused for a moment until there was once again total silence in the ashram. He continued translating the guru's words... "As the dark age of the Kali Yuga comes to an end, his holiness says it is the utmost importance that we treat each other with more love, compassion, empathy, respect and civility. We are all brothers and sisters of the same human family and we must do better to help each other as we are all connected. He also says most of us have been meditating the completely the wrong way."

Pavarhi gave him the microphone again, and the Shankaracharayah spoke for quite some time, then handed the microphone back. There was some laughter from the crowd during his speech.

"We should no longer do mind-full meditation," said Pavarhi. "We should be doing mind-less meditation. The true goal of meditation should be to empty the mind of thoughts, and release the mind's focus of all objective thought. At that point, there is total silence. The mind will find bliss and fulfillment in the silence. Your conscious mind, or 'subject' ... is always focused on the thought of an 'object.' We are always thinking... thoughts, thoughts, and more thoughts all day long. We think about the food we eat, the plans for the day, and our many daily stresses like paying the bills and those constantly annoying relatives. And many of us waste our time and energy on these silly things called cellphones. They are a distraction and have become a curse to humanity as we have become slaves to them. You all should spend less time on them and more time in nature and focus on real connections. These horrible phones... they don't make us less stressed; they make us more stressed and unhappy. You know this to be true."

Many of the westerners and tourists nodded their heads in agreement. The Shankaracharayah took the microphone and spoke again for a long time, in a calm and almost musical way.

Pavarhi continued to translate, "The stressed mind desires total and absolute silence, as that will allow the mind to truly calm down and rest. It is the silence that you seek, to empty the mind of all thoughts, and not to fill it. No thoughts also mean no stress, and that is very charming to the mind indeed. Without any specific focus on conscious thoughts, the mind will naturally detach from the subject-object relationship. When the mind, or 'subject' loses the focus of the 'object', it also loses the experience of being the subject. The mind no longer focuses on anything, including sense of self. At that point, with no focus on any objects... there becomes a state of self-less. There becomes no self. There becomes no 'subject', and no 'object'... only pure silence. When that happens, the bound mind becomes boundless. There are no thoughts to bind the mind anymore. And what is another word for boundless? That which is boundless is also infinite. In the silence of the boundless mind... is experience of infinity, of pure being. There is nothing. Only silence. No thoughts and no things, and no stress! That is what your soul is seeking... to dive into the absolute silence. But you can not do that by filling the mind, you must empty it."

The Shankaracharayah took the microphone back. He smiled and made his childish laugh again. He then spoke for some time and then Pavarhi continued to translate...

"Just over 50 years ago, these wonderful musicians called the Beatles painted on wall behind me came here to this place to learn meditation from the Maharishi Mahesh Yogi. He was a disciple of my predecessor, the Shankaracharayah Swami Brahmananda Saraswati. Everyone called him Guru Dev. The Maharishi would always place a photo of Guru Dev behind him out of respect as he taught tens of thousands of students meditation and share with them the experience of infinity. He would never claim the teachings as his own. He would always humbly say the knowledge was passed down to him from Guru Dev."

Again, Pavarhi handed the microphone to the wise sage and he spoke at length in Hindi some more. Pavarhi continued to interpret...

"Just as the Maharishi taught the Beatles 50 years ago, the same technique is just as effective today. The meditation teacher bestows a special 'mantra' to the initiate, or student... to utilize as a tool to calm the mind during their meditation. This 'mantra' is specially designed to have no meaning, or definition to the student. It's just a word that transmits a vibratory signal. There should be no specific meaning of the word for the mind to attach to... so a 'mantra' word such as 'peace', or 'love', or 'ommmm' won't really work, as the mind will cling unto the meaning of those words. There should be no attachment to the mantra. The 'mantra' is then gently repeated as a faint idea by the meditator as they calm their mind. As normal thoughts will just bubble up naturally during the beginning of the meditative process, the student is also instructed to gently begin the manta again if the mind becomes consciously aware of a new thought. Eventually, the calm and relaxed mind loses even the thought of the mantra as it dives deep into the ocean of no thoughts. There it will find total silence, as that is what the mind actually desires. The mind then becomes self-less and bound-less. As the mind becomes empty of thoughts, it will find bliss and true fulfillment. This is called the method of Transcendental Meditation, and how the mind achieves a state of Transcendental consciousness. The mediator does this twice a day for approximately twenty minutes each time. That is my message to all of you... to learn this meditation. It will change the world."

The Shankaracharayah held both his hands together, with the lotus flower still in-between and he bowed his head slightly with his eyes closed. Everyone sitting inside the room and standing outside did the same gestures back. He abruptly stood up and started walking out of the back of the building towards one of the open doors. Pavarhi followed him and motioned with his hands for Yeshua, Mohammed and Jihan to join them. They all left the building together, then walked along the narrow trail behind the abandoned residence hall and went into the densely wooded area with the dozens of stone meditation pods.

The Shankaracharayah entered one of the pods, and sat in the center of the floor. A group of rhesus macaque monkeys played just outside. Pavarhi, Yeshua, Mohammed and Jihan followed the old guru inside the pod and sat in front of him. Almost humorously, one of the adult monkeys ran inside and sat lotus style with the group. Surprisingly, the macaque made a 'namaste' pose with his hands towards the Shankaracharayah who smiled and reciprocated.

"Pavarhi," said the Shankaracharayah. "I want to personally thank you and let you know how I am grateful for all of your assistance this past year. I wouldn't have made it without your help. Now, who are your friends here?"

"This is Yeshua and Mohammed, from Israel. And this is their guide, Jihan," replied Pavarhi. "They have a very important message for you."

"From Israel, huh? All the way from the Holy Land? A very far trip indeed," said the Shankaracharayah. "This must be a very extraordinary communication. What do you have to tell me?"

"One of our friends in Israel, let's say... she is what we call a prophet. She had an incredible prophetic vision, and we are here to share that vision with you," said Mohammed.

"You say she is a prophet," replied the Shankaracharayah. "How do you know that for sure? Because she sees into the future means that she is a prophet?"

"Actually, I'm not sure she is a prophet," responded Mohammed. "That's the best word I can find to describe who she is... to be more precise, I think she is the re-incaration of the Archangel Phanuel. That is the one of the Angels from The Book of Enoch who is said to be set over repentance and those who hope to inherit eternal life. Phanuel is one of four Archangels that help banish evil from the Earth"

"I am not familiar with these Archangels you describe, or this Book of Enoch," said the Shankaracharayah. "However, it sounds like she is actually an avatar... an incarnation of a divine being. In Hinduism, we have many Gods... however, they are all just manifestations of a singular and undeniable universal principle that permeates all of existence. This ultimate truth will sometimes manifest, or incarnate itself into special humans in order to achieve certain goals. It sounds like she is an avatar of Ganesha, a divine being who incarnates to destroy demons and help pious people. In the ancient Sanskrit text of the Ganesha Purana, Ganesha is described as having four avatars. Their names are Mohotkara, Mayuresvara, Gajanana and Dhumraketu. Their common purpose is to slay demons and bring fulfillment to humanity."

"So, are you saying the four Archangels from the Book of Enoch could be the same beings as the four Avatars of Ganesha as described in your ancient texts?" questioned Mohammed. "Because in the Book of Enoch, I believe in Chapter 40, it names the four Archangels... Michael, Raphael, Gabriel and Phanuel... they are sent to defeat 200 fallen Angels who had betrayed God."

"Yes. How wonderful! She has incarnated to stop the dark ones and their demon minions from returning," said the Shankaracharayah. "They are trying their escape from their bondage and banishment. We are so blessed and fortunate that Ganesha has returned. Is that her message to me?"

"Wait. No," responded a confused Mohammed. "Wait a sec. The Watchers are returning? How do you know that?"

"The Watchers?" said the Shankaracharayah. "I'm not sure who they are. But I've had horrible dreams about the evil demons called the Rakshasas returning. They're a horrible race of giant warrior man-eating demons with dark magical powers who terrorized the world many thousands of years ago. They could use their powers to shape shift and assume the form of any creature. The avatars of Ganesha supposedly destroyed them all; however I keep on having a dream where several survived, and they have been secretly plotting the return of the evil ones. They and the Danavas must be stopped."

Suddenly, the monkey sitting next to them made a strange grunting sound, stood up and ran out of the pod and disappeared into the surrounding jungle.

"The Rakshasas? They sound like they might actually be the Nephilim," interjected Yeshua. "They are described in the Genesis Chapter of our Hebrew Torah. They were the giant monstrous offspring of the Watchers, or fallen angels... who betrayed God and mated with human women. You are saying they, the Rakshasas you described, are coming back? They are going to return?"

"That has what has been in my dreams, young man," replied the Shankaracharayah. "But dreams are just dreams, and perhaps I watched far too many Bollywood horror movies. Anyhow, after having many of those horrible nightmares... I decided to come here and isolate myself from all TV, technology and meditate for the entire year. Thankfully, the dreams have now stopped."

He closed his eyes for a moment and smiled. "So, what was the prophetic vision from your Israeli friend? I am so happy beyond words to hear this! Please do tell."

"Her vision was at the Temple Mount, in Jerusalem," said Yeshua. "She was a silent observer, watching from above. She saw a dozen or so figures walking towards the Dome of the Rock shrine from different directions. She said there was the Pope, the Dali Lama, a Hassidic Rabbi, a Muslim Imam and several other important religious men. She said there was a man there that looked just like you, representing the Hindus."

"How spectacular!" said the Shankaracharayah. "What happened next?"

"They walked into the Dome of the Rock together," said Yeshua. "She said she flew through the top of the golden dome to see inside. All the religious leaders stood in a circle around the ancient Foundation Stone, in-between the tall columns holding up the golden dome. They all closed their eyes and seemed to be in deep thought or meditation. Then, after a few moments, they all raised their arms to the sky and started chanting a prayer in unison."

"How miraculous," replied the Shankaracharayah. "What did they say?"

"All is one. All is one. All is one... over and over again. Then she woke up from her dream," stated Yeshua.

"Yes. All is one," replied the Shankaracharayah. "There are many religions, but just one truth. As I said in my message... we are all brothers and sisters of the same family."

"So, we came all the way to see you," continued Yeshua. "To ask if you will come to Jerusalem next year and collaborate will all the other world spiritual leaders and join together in the Dome of the Rock and declare world peace."

"Yes, of course I will," said the Shankaracharayah. "What an auspicious day. I will be honored to travel there and join with the others. All is one."

"Thank you," responded Mohammed. Yeshua smiled. He, Mohammed and Jihan all made the Namaste pose with their hands and again said "Thank you." The Shankaracharayah reciprocated, and then closed his eyes.

"His Holiness now will require some silence during afternoon meditation," said Pavarhi as he stood up. "It has been a momentous day. I will coordinate with you soon and arrange for his journey to Jerusalem. Thank you for coming to Rishikesh. You can find transportation back to town outside ashram entrance. Safe travels, my friends and we will be in touch."

Yeshua, Mohammed and Jihan stood up and quietly shook hands with Pavarhi. They left the pod and were greeted by what looked like a small army of rhesus macaque monkeys. The dozen or so primates all made hooting noises as they pumped their arms up into the sky.

"This way, quickly," said Jihan as he led them along the narrow stone path from the meditation pods and towards the main entrance through the dense, overgrown jungle. Hundreds upon hundreds of people crowded the entrance area as they made their way back to the main parking lot.

"How do we get out of here?" asked Yeshua. "How will we find someone to take us back? Can we use that Uber app on your phone?"

Jihan looked at his phone. "Dammit," he said. "I don't have a signal."

"So, we need to find a ride back to Hardiwar?" asked Mohammed. "Then take a bus to Dharamshala? Ahhh... what a mess, and it's going to be night-time soon."

Jihan left Yeshua and Mohammed and walked over to a group of bald men wearing robes. Their skin was much lighter than the sadhu Hindu monks, and they didn't even look Indian... they looked more like Chinese. Jihan spoke with one of the older bald men for a few minutes and then returned back to Yeshua and Mohammed.

"Our prayers have been answered," said Jihan. Those Buddhist monks over there have agreed to let us go in their bus back to Dharamshala. We will be arriving at the Dali Lama's Temple around sunrise tomorrow morning. How fortunate is that? Perhaps your so-called guardian Angels are looking over you?"

"Perhaps they are," replied Yeshua. "Maybe they've been guiding us every step of the way."

"Come, let us go now," said Jihan. "They are leaving immediately." Jihan motioned with his hands to follow the group of the Buddhist monks as they left the ashram entrance area and then made their way through the very crowded parking lot.

"We are going in that thing?" asked Mohammed as he pointed to a large old bus decorated with a rainbow of technicolor designs and decorative stickers. It looked like something hippies would drive to Woodstock from the

1960s. Dozens of the bald Buddhist monks piled into the magical looking bus, and many of them sat on the second tier of seats on the roof.

"Yes, that's our bus," responded Jihan. "Very nice, eh?" Mohammed smiled and slightly bent his neck and head to the left and acknowledged him. They continued to make their way through the vast crowd of people leaving the ashram and finally reached the bus, which they got on. The three of them sat down in the only unoccupied bench in the front of the vehicle near the driver's seat.

After a few moments, an older Buddhist monk entered the bus and sat down in the driver's seat. He looked in the rear-view mirror and saw that the bus was completely full. He said a few words loudly in Tibetan; then all the monks replied by clapping and cheering, and many of them gave a thumbs up sign. The driver smiled; turned on the ignition, and started the engine.

They slowly left the parking lot as the driver navigated the large bus through a mass of humanity. The sun was setting in the western sky, over the foothills of the Himalayan Mountains. Yeshua, sitting next to the window, looked out at the beautiful valley below where the Ganges River flowed to the south. He reflected on the day's incredible events... and thought deeply about everything the Shankaracharayah had said. In his mind, he re-played the Hindu guru's message to the world about learning meditation and then contemplated his story about the demons and evil ones coming back.

"Do you really think the Rakshasas demons are actually the Nephilim?" Yeshua asked Mohammed, sitting next to him.

There was silence... no response. Yeshua turned his head away from gazing through window and looked at Mohammed. He was totally out, sleeping with his head slumped against the back of the seat. So was Jihan, fast asleep. It was almost night outside as thousands of stars appeared in the dark sky as the twilight transformed into blackness.

"Where are you from, traveller?" asked the driver in very bad English. He was directly across the aisle from Yeshua.

"I am from Israel," answered Yeshua. "We came all the way here to meet the Shankaracharayah."

"You got to meet the Shankaracharayah?" replied the driver. "Oh how very nice! What did he say? And ... by the way, my name is Sakya."

"I am Yeshua. Nice to meet you. He told me just what I needed to hear. That everything just may be even more connected than I thought. And, just curious... how long is the drive to Dharamshala?"

"We have about nine more hours," replied Sakya. "A very long drive, but worth the trip. It was a wonderful to hear the insights of the Shankaracharayah after his one year of silence. We all decided to learn this form Transcendental Meditation he spoke of, as meditation is part of the path of our Four Noble Truths."

"The Four Truths? What are those?" asked Yeshua.

"The Truths are from the teachings of the Buddha," replied Sakya. "I am happy to describe them, as we have a very long ride ahead."

"Yes please," responded Yeshua. "I would very much like to learn about them. Thank you."

"The first Truth is called **Dukkha**," explained Sakya. "The concept has to do with the persistent suffering of the human experience. It's the truth about all the pain, sadness, sickness and disappointing unsatisfactoriness that comes from the endless cycles of birth and death. The teaching of the Buddha is to how to liberate one's self from all pain and suffering through a development of deep self knowledge and understanding."

"So, the Buddha taught how to end all suffering?" asked Yeshua. "How do you do that?"

"Well, that is called the Noble Path," replied Sakya. "I will get to that in a few minutes. The second Truth is called **Samudaya**. It teaches us that much of our affliction stems from the disappointment of basing our happiness on fleeting pleasures and material things. That craving, clinging and attachment to impermanent things keep us trapped in a cycle of dissatisfaction."

"Yes! That makes total sense," responded Yeshua. "And that reminds me of one of my favorite quotes... it goes something like this... 'Without expectations, there can be no disappointment.'"

"Perfectly said," replied Sakya. "You could be an honorary Buddhist. So, the third Truth is called **Nirodha**. This is the teaching of letting go. The Buddha shows us that suffering can end by renouncing the cravings and desire of attachments. Once we release ourselves from clinging to these attachments, we are no longer bound to the cycle of suffering. The Buddha reached enlightenment by doing this, and achieved a state of what we called Nirvana."

"Nirvana, yes... I heard of that," said Yeshua. "Isn't that like reaching heaven?"

"Well, no. We don't have a concept of heaven in Buddhism," explained Sakya. "Achieving Nirvana is the ultimate goal of the Buddhist spiritual path. By liberating one's self from suffering, we each can become our own Buddha. Once awakened, we no longer are bound to the cycle of birth and death. That is the state of Nirvana."

"So, isn't the desire to reach Nirvana and become enlightened, or awake as you say... a desire and craving unto itself?" asked Yeshua. "Aren't you clinging to the idea of reaching Nirvana and personally suffering because you aren't there yet?"

"That is a good point," replied Sakya. "I've never thought of it that way; however... what you are saying is somewhat correct. I want to reach enlightenment. And something you 'want' is a craving, also called **Tanha**. The Buddha teaches that Tanha is the root cause of suffering. But if I shouldn't 'want' or desire Nirvana, then how could I find the will to seek and achieve it?"

"I'm sorry, I didn't mean to disrespect your teachings," said Yeshua. "And sooo... what is the Fourth Truth?"

"No disrespect taken," replied Sakya. "Your observation is very insightful, and I will discuss your question with my teacher when we get back to Dharamshala."

"Oh, very good," replied Yeshua. "Just curious...who is your teacher?"

"My teacher is named Tenzin Gyatso," answered Sakya. "He is also known as the Dalai Lama. Have you heard of him?"

"Yes, I have," replied Yeshua. "I think everyone has heard of him. Actually, we are going there to meet with him. We have a very important and timely message for him... that is why we have come here from Israel."

"You know, they say... everything happens for a reason," said Sakya. "I will be honored to take you and your friends for a private audience with His Holiness."

"I have always wondered, my new friend Sakya... who 'they' is," joked Yeshua. "I mean, who are 'they'?"

"Ha-ha-ha, very funny!" laughed Sakya. Yeshua laughed too. They both laughed hard for quite a while.

"And what is the Forth Truth?" asked Yeshua? "There's one more, correct?"

"Yes, the Forth Truth is called **Magga**," described Sakya. "This is the teaching of the path to liberation. Buddha shows us how to liberate ourselves from the painful cycle of rebirth. This path includes the principles of having the right view, right resolve, right speech, right conduct, right livelihood, right mindfulness and right conscious concentration."

"Oh, I see," replied Yeshua. "How very interesting, so many good and righteous behaviors. But I have another question...you said mindfulness. But didn't the Shankaracharayah mention something about mindlessness? He said the purpose of meditation is to lose focus of all objects and sense of self... and experience pure silence, or otherwise lose the conscious sense of perception altogether and merge with infinity."

"Yes, that is similar to what we call the four **Arupas** in Buddhism," replied Sakya. "Those four meditative states also known as The Formless Dimensions, and consist of infinite space, infinite consciousness, infinite nothingness and infinite perception. A Buddhist meditation master will achieve a complete dwelling in emptiness when all of those dimensions are transcended. It takes years of meditation practice to get there."

"But the Shankaracharayah said this Formless Dimension can be experienced with just the simple tool of a basic 'mantra' and learning a few basic principles of gently repeating the 'mantra' as a faint idea," replied Yeshua. "It sounds like anyone can do it; you don't have to be a Buddhist master."

"Yes, that is what he said," responded. "And I will be discussing that subject with my teacher as well when we return to Dharamshala. We, I mean... all of us who went to Rishikesh want to learn this form of Transcendental Meditation. It seems so easy and simple."

"Yes. I want to learn it as well," said Yeshua. "Can I ask you one more question? Then I might close my eyes for a bit. I'm getting very tired. We've travelled thousands of miles today."

"Yes, of course," replied Sakya. "You can ask anything. I am very much enjoying our conversation."

"You said something about the cycle of rebirth... are you talking about re-incarnation?" asked Yeshua. "Often, I think I have memories of my past lives. Is that possible?"

"Yes, reincarnation," answered Sakya. "We call this **Samsara**, or the endless cycle of birth, death and rebirth. Everyone comes back life and after life, and we are each reborn in accordance with one's own karma. It is through the Buddhist teachings of the Four Truths and following the Noble Path that one can reach Nirvana and break free of this endless chain. The goal of Buddhism is to end the painful cycle of rebirth."

"But what if we want to come back?" asked Yeshua.

"What? Come back?" said Sakya.

"Like, what if we want to come back... and help others here on Earth?"

"Yes. I believe that can happen," answered Sakya. "You can choose to come back once you reach Nirvana, the perfect state of enlightenment. I believe that is why the Dali Lama is here. He is the 14th human incarnation of an enlightened being named Avalokitesvara... a Bodhisattva of compassion who keeps coming back to help humanity."

"So, is that the difference between incarnation and re-incarnation?" asked Yeshua. "Human beings are bound to reincarnate until they shed all their negative karma and reach a state of enlightenment. Once they reach Nirvana, they become a divine being who can then choose to incarnate back on earth in a human body as an Avatar?"

"Yes, I supposed more or less that is all correct, my friend," replied Sakya. "Although karma is much more complex than what you might think. We could talk the whole rest of the bus ride about what exactly karma is and how works, but why don't you get some sleep, my friend. It has been a long day for you."

"Yes, it has..." replied Yeshua as he closed his eyes. He was fading fast. As he began to drift off to sleep, he remembered watching the movie *Groundhog Day* when he and Mohammed lived at the orphanage in Beersheba. The main character in the movie... who was not a very good person, kept repeatedly waking up at the exact same time on the same day. He had to figure out a way to do everything 'just right,' to become a good person and then be allowed to finally move onto the next day. He wondered if that's how karma worked... you had to do good deeds and evolve spirituality in your current lifetime in order to move onto a better next lifetime. And perhaps after many lifetimes full of honorable deeds and actions, one could reach a state of enlightenment... like the Buddha, and become a divine being.

After a few minutes of replaying the 'Groundhog Day' movie in his mind, Yeshua drifted off into a deep sleep. At some point, within the darkness and void of his dream state... he sensed something. He became fully awake and aware within his dream, like so many times before. He heard the sound of people walking in the dark... their footsteps seemed to echo into the distance.

Suddenly, a small flame of light appeared in front of him. The flickering light came from Mohammed, but he was not holding a candle. The fire came directly from his left hand and illuminated two other human figures nearby... they were Avraham and Taylor! Everyone, including Yeshua, were wearing long and flowing colorful robes. Surprisingly, Mohammed held a fancy steel sword in his right hand and Avraham held long spear. Yeshua recognized their outfits; he had seen them before, painted on the wooden doors of the St. Mary of Zion Church in Ethiopia. They were dressed as the Archangels Michael and Raphael. Taylor, as the Archangel Phanuel, held a tall wooden staff with a beautifully carved lion's head on it's top.

They seemed to be in a long, dark tunnel... cut from stone bedrock. There were no lights at all, as it was pitch dark except for Mohammed's small flame emanating from his hand. Yeshua looked down at his himself, as he also was wearing an ornately colored robe. He was shocked when he saw that he was holding a large golden pinecone in his right hand and held a leather satchel connected to a short handle in the other hand. On both his wrists were colorful wristbands with what looked like large watch faces in their centers. Displayed on watch faces were some kind of holograms with rotating spiral galaxy images. Yeshua realized he looked similar to the Apkallu genie figure they had recently unearthed in ancient Babylon while in Iraq.

Mohammed turned his head and silently motioned for everyone to continue moving along the hallway. After some time, they came to a large empty alcove on the left side of the dark hallway. Mohammed held his right arm upwards towards the ceiling of the tunnel and the flame coming out of his hand became much larger and brighter. They could now see further down the hallway, and there were six more recessed large alcoves on each side. Within each alcove was a massive black granite stone box, totaling 12. Each box appeared to be hermetically sealed with a huge stone lid.

Some strange distant sounds came from the opposite direction of the long tunnel, from which they had just come. Yeshua's right ear began to emit a high pitch buzzing sound as a sign of imminent danger. All four Archangels turned and looked down the hallway towards the direction of the scampering sounds. From the most distant part of the corridor, three sets of ominous glowing eyes appeared. They were coming closer and closer, and their shadowy forms seemed to dance in darkness.

Mohammed, as the Archangel Michael... turned his body and held the flame in his left hand towards the direction of the oncoming creatures. They made loud grunting and growling sounds as their forms became illuminated from the light of the fire. They were clearly visible now: they were giant grotesque monsters. Their jackal-like heads looked demonic, and their bodies were rippled with exaggerated musculature. Their clawed hands each held a large spiked club made from bones.

"Holy shhhhh…" said Yeshua as all three giants started to gallop and run towards them. They were each approximately ten to twelve feet tall and they had to awkwardly contort their massive bodies in order to rapidly navigate along the tunnel. Mohammed closed his eyes and concentrated. A large burst of flame from his left hand shot down the hallway and as it reached the proximity of the demons, the closest giant swung his bone club and extinguished the entire fireball almost effortlessly.

"Incoming!" yelled Avraham as he knelt down on the ground in front of Mohammed. As the first giant was upon them, Avraham lifted his spear from the ground and impaled the monstrous being through his chest. Black blood immediately poured out from his ribcage as the demon made a deafening scream as it fell to the ground.

The second giant lunged at Taylor and she immediately hit him hard with her lion's staff in his groin as she nimbly sidestepped the attack. He fell to the ground in agony, and then she smashed his skull with the head of her staff. His body went limp and motionless.

The last demonic giant jumped over his two fallen comrades and swung his spiked club at Mohammed, who blocked the fierce blow with his sword. Sparks flew everywhere as the two weapons collided. The giant pulled his body closer to Mohammed… then said in a deep voice, "You can't kill us all. We will outsmart you."

Mohammed pushed the giant away, and then with one swift motion... decapitated the demon's head with his sharp sword. The giant's dead body immediately fell to the floor in a heap with the other corpses.

"Are those... the Nephilim?" asked Yeshua, still in shock from the horrific encounter.

"Yes," said Mohammed, as the flickering flame from his left hand continued to provide warm light within the stone corridor. "They came here to defend their masters. Somehow, they thought they could hide them from us... but, they were dead wrong."

Taylor stood next to the three dead demons lying motionless on the smooth floor. Their black blood formed a slowly enlarging pool around them. The dark blood started to bubble and morph into strange and rippled forms. Yeshua's right ear began to buzz again as he looked down at the evil, animated fluid in horror.

Avraham closed his eyes, and then pointed his left hand towards the demon's blood while holding his spear in his right hand. Amazingly, electricity sparked from the tip of his sharp spear-point, like shooting stars and lightning bolts. The energy leaped and pulsed into the demon's dead bodies on the ground and the surrounding pool of blood. After a few moments... everything was completely burned and disintegrated into a fine ash and dust. Then, a strong wind formed and all dust slowly swirled up from the floor and disappeared.

"Gabriel, come here," said Mohammed to Yeshua. He stood below in the nearest recessed alcove next to one of the huge black granite boxes. "It is time. Open this box with your mullilu."

Yeshua looked down at the golden pinecone in his hand. He remembered that Professor Taylor had called the pinecone 'a mullilu' at the Babylon archeological dig. He clearly was supposed to use the object to somehow open the black 100-ton hermetically sealed rectangular granite box in front of him.

He closed his eyes and deeply concentrated as he pointed the pinecone towards the box. Yeshua envisioned the massive lid being lifted off the box in his mind. He could feel the tremendous weight of the stone lid, and then he pushed it upwards with his thoughts.

"It's working!" said Avraham. Yeshua opened his eyes and saw that the lid was slowly levitating as a beam of golden energy flowed out from the pinecone. Heavy smoke poured out from the opening of the box below. The flame from Mohammed's hand became larger and brighter as the black stone lid lifted up higher into the air. Avraham descended down into the alcove from the corridor and pushed the floating lid towards the back of the room with the sharp point of his long spear.

As the top of the rose granite box opened more, like a coffin... two huge hands appeared as a giant humanoid figure started to climb out of the ancient stone casket. Yeshua recognized this evil being when he saw his blood red eyes... he was one of the Dark Angels from his vision at the Well of Abraham at Beersheba. He remembered all the corrupt and evil angels climbing out from the bottomless well. At the sight of the terrifying colossus, Yeshua's concentration broke and the beam of glowing golden light stopped flowing from his pinecone. The lid slammed down hard, although it had opened enough from the unholy creature to fully pull himself out from the box. He stood on the top of the edge of the box, and then his black wings unfurled and stretched out to fill the room. He let out a bone-chilling scream as he flexed his ripped muscles of his arms and chest.

Taylor, still standing in the stone passageway above the alcove… pointed her lion's staff towards the Dark Angel. A vortex of spiraling wind formed from the lion's mouth and blew directly at the red-eyed beast. The giant calmly held out his hand and easily pushed the wind away. Avraham pointed his spear upwards and blasted him with wide bolts of intense lightning. The electrical energy pulsed around the giant man, like an anaconda snake would wrap itself around its prey. Mohammed followed suit by holding his sword in both hands and he unleashed a steady flow of fire from his blade towards the Dark Angel. The fire engulfed his wings and upper torso as the wind tornado from Taylor's staff redirected itself and lifted the giant into the air. He let out another deafening scream that echoed loudly into the darkness of the underground labyrinth.

"Gabriel, now!" yelled Taylor. Yeshua looked down at his giant golden pinecone again. He knew exactly what he had to do, as he pointed it towards the levitating Dark Angel entrapped by his friend's fire, lightning and wind. After a moment of concentration, a golden beam of light flowed out of the pinecone and into the chest of the giant man. Ripples and waves of bright energy pulsated throughout the entire body of the creature, as the fire and electricity amplified even more strongly.

The Dark Angel exploded, like a supernova. Then, all the energy collapsed into itself and formed what looked like a black hole above the granite stone box. The vortex swirled like a spiral galaxy for a few moments and then transformed into floating black orb. The sphere contracted and became smaller, then fell to the ground in front of Mohammed. It looked like a black marble. Mohammed leaned forward and picked the marble off the floor and held it up looked at it using the light from the fire in his other hand. He smiled, then walked over to Yeshua and opened his leather satchel he was holding and placed the marble inside.

"That was... one of the Watchers?" asked Yeshua. Mohammed looked at him with a strange expression.

"Yes, of course it was," responded Mohammed. "And we have a lot more work to do."

"Mr. Yeshua. Mr. Yeshua... we are here," said a voice in a bad English accent. "Welcome to Dharamshala."

Yeshua opened his eyes. He was back on the bus, and the morning sunlight streamed from the east through the tinted windows. The snow-capped peaks of the Himalayan Mountains were visible in the distance to the north. Mohammed and Jihan were still sleeping next to him on the bus seat.

The bus stopped in front of a beautiful temple complex and the Sakya, the driver... pulled the large black lever next to him and the opened the front door. The dozens of Buddhist monks started to leave the bus.

"We made it... we are at Tsuglagkhang. The Dalai Lama's Temple," said Jihan. "I slept the whole ride."

"I will take you to meet the Dalai Lama," said Sakya. "He will be very pleased to meet you. Let's just wait until everyone has left the bus."

"How wonderful," replied Mohammed, now awake as well. "And thank you for driving us here."

"We will only have a few minutes, as his Holiness has a very busy day scheduled," explained Sakya.

Once the bus was empty, Sakya stood up from his driver's seat and walked down the stairs and onto the street below. Yeshua, Mohammed and Jihan followed. Overhead were hundreds of colorful multicolored flags hanging from ropes crisscrossing throughout sprawling complex. As the four men passed through the main entrance, Sakya took off his sandals and placed them into a long wooden shelving unit full of hundreds of shoes and sandals. Everyone else removed their shoes and put them into the cubbyholes.

Sakya led them through several colorful hallways decorated with prayer wheels and adorned with many statues of sitting Buddhas in various meditation poses. Finally, they came to a wonderfully carved wooden door the end of a long corridor. Sakya made a "shush" gesture with his index finger as he brought his hand close to his pursed lips. He quietly opened the door and stepped inside, and everyone followed him into the room.

Sitting alone in the room was the Dalai Lama. He sat in deep meditation, just like all the Buddha statues... in a very large, plush beige sofa-chair. His red crimson robes were wrapped around his relaxed body as the morning sunlight shined through the tall windows in the back of the room. A single beam of light illuminated his head and created a rainbow of reflective prisms all over the room.

Yeshua had never seem a man look so calm, and at peace. On either side of the 14th Dalai Lama's chair were two end tables containing several bouquets of beautiful flowers.

"Sakya, welcome back," said the Dalai Lama, still with his eyes closed. "And who are your friends?"

"These are the gentlemen from the Israeli delegation we were notified about a few weeks ago," said Sakya. The Dalai Lama opened his eyes and gently smiled at his visitors. He bowed his head slightly and made a 'namaste' gesture with his hands. Everyone reciprocated.

"This is Yeshua, and Mohammad," said Sakya. "And their Indian guide Jihan. We all met in at the Chaurasi Kutia ashram in Rishikesh after the Shankaracharayah came out of silence."

"Sakya, I have the most wonderful joke to tell you," said the Dalai Lama. "One of our visitors just told me. I just can't stop laughing."

"Yes, your Holiness," replied Sakya. "Please do tell."

"Okay. So... the Dalai Lama walks into a pizza shop," he said. "And the man in the pizza shop asks 'What do you want?' and then the Dalai Lama says 'I'll have one with everything.'"

The Dalai started laughing hysterically. "Get it… One with everything!" He continued to laugh some more. Sakya started laughing too and then everyone else began laughing as well. "One with everything!"

After a few moments, the laughing calmed down and there was once again silence. The Dalai Lama motioned for his guests to sit down on the surrounding couches and chairs and everyone followed his cue.

"They have a special message to tell you," said Sakya.

"Ah, I am not a such special person to receive a special message," responded the Dalai Lama. "I am just an human being, a simple Buddhist monk."

"Your Holiness, I believe you are an incarnated avatar of the divine being Avalokitesvara," replied Yeshua. "You are a very special person. And we have a very important request for you of the utmost importance."

"Before you share with me your message," requested the Dalai. "I want each of you to ask me a question. That is usually what I do after my morning meditation. I answer questions. What would you like to know?"

"My question is… was Jesus an avatar too?" asked Mohammed almost immediately.

"Jesus. Yes of course. Jesus Christ lived many previous lives, and eventually became a fully enlightening being," answered the Dali Lama. "And then, at certain period, certain era... he appeared as a new master and teacher. Jesus taught many of the same exact religious and spiritual values of Buddhism as being patient, tolerant and compassionate. This is, you see, the real message in order to become a better human being. And that is what our world needs so much more of... compassion."

The Dalai Lama smiled. "And your question, young man?" he said while looking at Yeshua.

"If there are so many different religions... how can they all claim to be the only correct one?" asked Yeshua.

"Ah, yes. Wonderful question," replied the Dalai Lama. "And that is one of the biggest root causes of suffering of our entire human history. So, have you ever heard the story of the elephant and the blind men?"

"No your Holiness, I have not," answered Yeshua.

"I will tell you, then. Many years ago, a powerful king asked for all the blind men in his kingdom to be shown a elephant. They were all assembled together in the same room with a large elephant. None had ever been in the presence of an elephant before. One of the blind men felt his head, and one his ear, and one his tusk, and one his trunk, and one his body, and one his back, and one his tail, and one the end of his tail. After this, the king asked all the blind men... 'Do you now know the elephant?' and they all replied 'yes we have'. And then the king asked, 'What is the elephant like?' and then the blind man who touched the elephant's head said, 'the elephant is like a pot,' and the blind man who touched the tusk said, 'the elephant is like a plough pole,' and the blind man who touched the trunk said, 'the elephant is like a plough,' and the blind man who touched the body said, 'the elephant is like a granary,' and the blind man who touched the leg said, 'the elephant is like a pillar,' and the blind man who touched the back said, 'it is like a mortar,' and the blind man who touched the tail said, 'it is like a pestle,' and the blind man who touched the end of the tail said, 'it is like a broom'. Then, all the blind men began to argue and bicker about how the elephant 'was like this, or was that like' until they started to fight with each other. You see, all the religions claiming their perspective is the only correct one is the same story as the blind men describing only part of the elephant. They just like the blind men. They are both correct and incorrect. They don't see the whole picture… they only see their part of the whole. The moral of the story is clear; we shouldn't have closed minds to only what we perceive or experience. We should be open, respectful and compassionate of each other's views. We are one race of human beings, one family of brothers and sisters. We should not be arguing and fighting about limited views and narrow realities. We are all part of the same oneness. The same pizza!"

The Dalai Lama started to laugh hysterically again, and the room once again erupted with laughter for some time.

"And what is your question, Jihan?" asked the Dalai Lama.

"Yes, your Holiness," said Jihan. "Who will be the next Dalai Lama?"

"Very good question, young man," he replied. "So many people ask this question. It seems everyone wants to know. As for now, I am in no rush to incarnate any time soon. When I turn 90, I will consult with my Tibetan Buddhist friends and a decision will be made as to how and when I come back. And written instructions will be left describing how to locate the 15th Dalai Lama. Now, my new friends… what is your message for me?"

"One of our friends had a prophetic vision," explained Yeshua. "She saw dozens of world spiritual leaders coming together in Jerusalem. She said the Pope, a Hebrew Rabbi, a Muslim Imam and several other important religious men walking on the Temple Mount. You were there too."

"How wonderful!" interjected the Dalai Lama. "What happened next?"

"You, and the others… walked into the Dome of the Rock together," said Yeshua. "Then all the religious leaders stood in a circle around the ancient foundation stone, in the center of the shrine. You all closed your eyes went into deep prayer and meditation. Then, everyone raised their arms and started chanting a prayer in unison."

"Ahhhh. What did we all say?" asked Dalai Lama.

"All is one. All is one. All is one… over and over again. Then vision ended," stated Yeshua.

"Yes. All is one indeed," replied the Dalai Lama. "This was a very good vision."

"That's why we are here," said Mohammed. "We've come to personally ask you to come to Jerusalem next year and fulfill the vision. We want you and the all the other spiritual world leaders to go into the Dome of the Rock and declare world peace."

The Dalai Lama stared at Mohammed for a few moments, deep in thought. He smiled. "It appears some of my prayers have been answered. Yes, of course I will do this. That is why I am here."

CHAPTER 10

AVARIS

2 Weeks Later

The white and blue Gulfstream C-20G flew from the east towards Cairo, Egypt. The massive pyramids on the Giza plateau were visible in the distance. After landing at the Cairo International Airport at 420PM, Yeshua and Mohammed de-boarded with Elijah Spencer, the American diplomat. They got into a black Land Rover waiting for them on the tarmac and headed north on the Cairo-Belbeis Desert Road towards the Nile delta. The driver was a handsome, young Egyptian man.

"So, where exactly are we going?" asked Mohammed, from in the back seat.

"We are going to meet with the leaders of the Coptic Church in Alexandria," said Elijah. "But first we are taking a short detour to meet some friends in place called Tell el-Daba."

"I've never been to Egypt before. At least not in this lifetime," half-joked Yeshua. "Will we have an opportunity to visits the Pyramids and the Sphinx? It's my dream to go there." Yeshua looked down at his backpack on his lap containing his Shofar.

"I don't think so. Unfortunately, we won't have enough time," answered Elijah. "Maybe on the next trip."

"How was your trip to India?" asked Elijah.

"It was very successful," replied Mohammed. "We got to meet with the Dalai Lama and one of the top spiritual leaders of the Hindus. They both agreed to participate in the peace initiative. Avraham and General Cohen met with the Jain and Sikh leaders, and they also agreed as well."

"Fantastic," said Elijah. "I love when a plan comes together. And how was it meeting the Dalai Lama?"

"It was really good; he actually has a very funny sense of humor," responded Mohammed. "I wasn't expecting that."

"How far is it to this Tell el-Daba place?" asked Yeshua.

"Depending on traffic, it will be about a two-hour drive," said the driver in a slight Egyptian-English accent. "And by the way, my name is Ahmed. I am one of the official guides of the US Embassy."

"Nice to meet you," said Mohammed. "I am Mohammed, and this is Yeshua. And sitting next to you is Elijah."

"Yes, I know Mr. Elijah well very, my friend," replied Ahmed. "I hope you enjoy your stay here in Egypt. I will take you anywhere you need to go and will always keep you safe and out of harms way."

"Keep us safe? Is it dangerous here?" asked Yeshua.

"Let's just say there are many here who do not appreciate Americans and Israelis being on Egyptian soil," replied Ahmed. "And that's tragic... our tourism industry has suffered greatly due to some deplorable violent elements."

"Yes, perhaps someday there will be more tolerance of visitors here in your country," said Elijah. "It's a shame we can't just all get along."

"Well, this is nothing new," said Ahmed. "For thousands of years... there has been conflict between Egypt, its neighbors, and beyond. As a matter of fact, the place where we are going was once the capitol city of occupying invaders who came from the east and controlled ancient Egypt for over one hundred years time in-between the Middle and New Kingdoms."

"Really? I never heard of that. Foreign invaders controlling ancient Egypt?" questioned Yeshua. "What's the story there?"

"Their capital city was called Avaris, and the invaders were called the Hyksos people," explained Ahmed. "They took control of the region around 1650 BC, and eventually were defeated and expelled by the Pharaoh Ahmose around 1550 BC... who founded the Eighteen Dynasty of Egypt and began the period of time we now call the New Kingdom."

"Hmm. Isn't that around the timeframe of the biblical story of the Hebrews here in Egypt? Were the Israelites from the Exodus story somehow related to these Hyksos people?" asked Yeshua.

"I can not comment on that," sternly replied Ahmed. "We are not supposed to discuss such things. But I will say, supposedly some archeologists who excavated an area in Avaris claim they found the palace and tomb of the Hebrew Prophet you call... Joseph."

"What? Joseph?" replied Yeshua. "The biblical Joseph who came to Egypt and became the vizier of the Pharaoh? The man who interpreted the Pharaoh's dream?"

"Again, I am not supposed to discuss such things," said Ahmed. "But yes, they found a rare pyramid tomb which housed a giant statue of a man with red hair and pale skin that dated well before the Hyksos period. Perhaps it was really the Joseph you speak of. And nearby that site is a huge section of an ancient city containing thousands of houses that were built in the Canaanite style dating to the 12th dynasty. Our contemporary Egyptian archeologists are denying the possibility that these findings could be evidence of the biblical Hebrews as described in the Torah. As a matter of fact, they make sure everything is re-buried and covered back up after any archeological excavations... it's like they want to cover up all the evidence."

"I'm sorry, did you say red hair?" asked Yeshua. "The statue had red hair?"

"Yes Sir," replied Ahmed. "Just like yours! Although, he had more of a 'bowl' haircut. Like the musicians, who do you call them? From the 60s... the Beatles."

"So, let me get this straight," said Elijah. "We are going to the place where the biblical Hebrews actually lived, in the Land of Goshen?"

"Shhhhhhh," said Ahmed as he held his index finger up to his lips. "You did not hear that from me."

They drove through miles and miles of irrigated, lush green farmland. After passing through the large town of

Faqus El Balad, then continued north on the Al Husseineya-Fakous highway. Next to the road, directly to the east was a wide canal with a flowing river streaming northward.

"Is that the Nile River?" asked Yeshua, pointing to the water.

"Well, technically yes. But it's just a small tributary of the Nile," answered Ahmed. There're dozens of these canals all over the delta that supply the water for irrigation for the hundreds of miles of farms you see around us. In ancient times, the Nile used to flood unpredictably every year... but now the Aswan dam controls the flow of the water."

"Are we almost there?" asked Mohammed. "I have to, you know. The call of nature."

"Yes, we are approaching the village of Tall az Zahirah," replied Ahmed. "We are just a few minutes away."

Ahmed made a right turn and drove the Land Rover over a small bridge and crossed the canal. They continued along a narrow dirt road and traversed dozens of farms full of crops.

After a few minutes, they drove up to small town of mostly small white stucco houses, nestled along a large mound of dirt. Ahmed parked the Range Rover in front of one of the larger white buildings at the base of the hill.

"The rest room is inside this building, my friend," said Ahmed as he pointed to one of the doors of the house in from of them. Mohammed quickly opened his door and ran into the house.

Ahmed, Yeshua and Elijah left vehicle somewhat more calmly and walked towards the hill behind the house.

"What is this big sand mound behind here?" asked Yeshua. "Are these the ruins of Avaris?"

"Yes, it's not much to look at anymore," replied Ahmed. "However, this used to be one of the largest cities in the ancient world at its height. It was estimated to have a population of 25,000 souls."

"It just looks like a pile of dirt, surrounded by all this farmland," stated Elijah. "It's hard to image anything of that magnitude ever being here."

"The Nile used to come right through here, and there were massive temples and palaces all along the water," explained Ahmed. "It was also a port city as one could boat from here all the way north to Mediterranean. The archeologists have determined there was continuous occupation at this site from at least the 12th Dynasty all the way through the 18th Dynasty and beyond."

"It all gone now. What happened to the city?" asked Yeshua. "Why did it become ruins?"

"The current theory is that the Nile River gradually shifted and moved away from here, and then city was eventually abandoned," explained Ahmed. "Many of the statures, monuments and building materials were eventually repurposed and moved to city of Tanis, just north of here by Pharaoh Ramses the second of the 19th dynasty. Then the city was slowly reclaimed by nature."

"Wait a sec, wasn't Ramses the Pharaoh of the Exodus?" asked Yeshua. "Isn't he the Pharaoh in the famous *10 Commandments* movie with Charlton Heston and Yul Brynner?"

"Yes, he's the one from that movie. Ramses the Second," replied Ahmed. "But I think that movie, and most of the historians are wrong. I think the Pharaoh whom Moses dealt with was from the late 14th dynasty; right before the Hyksos peoples took over this city. Around three hundred years before Ramses the Great."

"How do you know so much of the history?" asked Mohammed, now standing with the group men after finishing up at the nearby house.

"You will find out my source soon. I have a surprise for you, as I will introduce you to some of my friends," explained a smiling Ahmed. He started walking up the Tell el-Daba mound along a narrow dirt path and everyone followed him up the hill. In the distance just to the north, some large white tents were set up along a medium sized pond.

Under the shade of the tents several people worked on an archeological dig site. Yeshua could clearly see Professor Noah Taylor and his beautiful daughter Miriam amongst the ruins. He immediately felt his chest tighten and a warm rush of happiness overcame his entire body.

"Taylor, and the Professor!" yelled Mohammed as he waved to them from the top of the dirt mound. Under the tent, they both looked up at their new visitors and waved back. Taylor immediately raced up the hill and greeted

Yeshua, Mohammed, Elijah and Ahmed with hugs and smiles.

"It's so good to see you all," said Taylor. "It's seems like it's been such long time. Welcome to the ancient city of Avaris, well... at least what's left of it."

"Thank you, and it's so good to see you too," said Yeshua. He still felt quite elated and frankly overwhelmed with happy emotions to be in Taylor's presence again. He did his best to keep calm and cool on the outside.

"Please, come down to the tents and let's get out of this insane heat," suggested Taylor. "We've just found something amazing in the rubble of an old palace."

"Oh gosh... I love all this archeology stuff," said Mohammed as they all walked down the hill and then went under the tents. About a dozen or so dark skinned Egyptian men were digging into the earth around some stonewalls partially buried in the sand and dirt. The entire site of the dig was at least four feet below the adjacent ground level of the surrounding farmland fields.

"Elijah, Mohammed, Yeshua, Ahmed... welcome to our little slice of paradise," said the Professor, standing next to a table full of interesting looking pottery shards. "I hope your trip was uneventful." The Professor shook hands with everyone.

"Yes, it was all smooth sailing," replied Elijah. "We decided to pay you all a visit on the way to Alexandria and see what you're up to. By the looks of it, you're having a very productive endeavor."

"Well, just like in Babylon… with the exception of a bunch of jihadist terrorist trying to kill us, you came at a very good time," said the Professor. "We just found something remarkable here in this particular layer dating to the 14th dynasty. It's a scarab seal of one of the Pharaohs."

"Oh, which one? And when was the 14th Dynasty? I don't remember anything about that one," questioned Mohammed.

"The 14th Dynasty dates between 1725 and 1650 BCE, right before the Hyksos invasion. As for which Pharaoh… let's take a look and figure it out; we literally just found the relic," said the Professor as he grabbed a small oval stone object from the table. He wiped off some sand from the seal with a small brush, and held it up to show all his visitors. They all gathered in together to see it more closely. There were some distinct engraved markings on the round piece of carved stone about the size of a silver dollar. There appeared to be the shapes of coiled snakes on its edges and some kind of bird at the top of the artifact. Three rectangles surrounded by an oval filled the center of the seal and at the bottom was triangle shape and an image of an Ankh.

"I can read this… I think," proclaimed Ahmed. "I've been studying hieroglyphics for years."

"Please, go ahead," said the Professor. "Let's see if you read it the same as I do."

"It says… **The son of Ra, Sheshi, given life**," said Ahmed. "It's the inscription of a Pharaoh named Sheshi. I've never heard of him though."

"Yes! Yes! That's exactly who it's from. Pharaoh Sheshi Maaibre, from the 14th Dynasty. Very good Ahmed," replied the Professor. "Hundreds of these scaraboid seals bearing his name have been found all over Egypt, Nubia and Canaan. The exact details of his reign are somewhat controversial; however, I have enough archeological evidence that points to Sheshi ruling over lower Egypt for approximately 40 years... likely from 1745 BCE to 1705 BCE."

"Daddy, tell them why those dates are so important," said a very excited Taylor.

"Well, I'm not ready to publish this yet; however... I believe that Sheshi's daughter was the princess who recused baby Moses from the Nile. Therefore, I believe the Exodus happened around the year 1650 BCE."

"What?" questioned a very shocked Elijah. "Are you sure? That contradicts almost every known historian. Your timeline is at least 200 hundred year before what is considered by mainstream biblical experts. What other evidence to you have?"

"Yes, I understand that most biblical historians would call my theory heresy," explained the Professor. "However, we've found hundreds of structures here that were built in a Canaanite or early Israelite style in a much deeper layer, dating well before the 14thDynasty. They originate back to the 12th Dynasty, from around the year 1850 BCE. Two hundred or so years before Pharaoh Sheshi. And furthermore, the ruins of a palatial estate were found nearby with what several of my archeological colleagues are now calling the Tomb of Joseph. We can look it up on-line later. It will blow your mind."

"Here? The Tomb of Joseph... in Avaris?" questioned Yeshua. "The Joseph who was sold into slavery by his brothers and eventually became the Pharaoh's second in command?"

"Yes, exactly that Joseph," replied Taylor. "Although, no bones were found in the tomb. Just the remnants of a giant statue with red hair... just like yours Yeshua. And we think based on several other archeological considerations that the Pharaoh of Joseph's time was named Amenemhat the Third. His reign, from approximately 1860 BCE to 1814 BCE, was considered the golden age of the Middle Kingdom."

"So, again... you've shifted all the biblical timelines back hundreds of years," said Elijah. "You certainly have some chutzpah!"

"It's really not chutzpah," said the Professor. "It's archeology."

The sun was slowly approaching the western horizon as the long, hot Egyptian day was coming to a close. The entire archeological crew continued to excavate the surrounding dig site.

"Wait a second, if I recall correctly it says in the Book of Exodus that the Jews were in Egypt for a total of 430 years," said Elijah. "So you timeline doesn't make sense. I'm not the best person at math... however, if you are saying that Joseph came to Egypt around 1860 BCE and then the

Israelites left with Moses around 1650 BCE... that's only 210 years. How could your theory be correct if the math doesn't add up?"

"Ah... good point," replied the Professor. "However, I've done some extensive research about the biblical dating and found that the one of the foremost experts on the Torah, named Rabbi Rashi calculated that indeed the sojourn was 210 years and not 430. That would fit perfectly with the timeline between Pharaoh Amenemhat 1860 BCE and the end of the 14th Dynasty around 1650 BCE."

"How can you be so sure about 1650 BCE being the date that Moses led the Israelites out of Egypt?" asked Elijah.

"Because a group of my contemporary archeologists confirm the dates by looking the evidence from Jericho," explained the Professor.

"Jericho... where Joshua brought the walls down and destroyed the city at the end of the Exodus?" asked Yeshua.

"Yes," replied the Professor. "After walking around the city for seven days with the Ark of the Covenant, the high priests blew their shofars and the walls crumbled down and the city was burned to the ground."

"So, what did your fellow archeologists find?" asked Elijah.

"They did extensive excavations over many years," explained the Professor. "Not only did they find there had been habitation at the site for at least 12,000 years... they also used carbon dating and found that the city had been severely burned and destroyed around the year 1600 BCE."

"Ah, I see," replied Elijah "That would have been 40 to 50 years after the Israelites left Egypt with Moses in 1650, which was exactly the amount of time the Hebrews were supposedly wandering around in the desert. And I assume based on your new timeline... you are claiming that after Egypt suffered the 10 plagues, death of their first born and destruction of their army from being drown in the Red Sea after chasing the Israelites, it left a huge political power vacuum which allowed the Hyksos people just to move right in and take over?"

"Exactly, correct," said the Professor. "I think you are getting the big picture now. The Exodus story is the exactly the same, it's just the timeline and dates have been off by a few hundred years as to what most traditional historians have proposed. And, oh... and I have another mind-blowing revelation that we will be discussing at the next major biblical archeology exposition in Paris."

"Ohh... nice. And what's that?" asked Elijah.

"That Mount Sinai is definitely not in the Egyptian Sinai," declared the Professor. "It wasn't in Egypt at all. Not even close. Mount Sinai is in Saudi Arabia. As per described in the Book of Exodus, it's located the biblical land of Midian, which is in Saudi Arabia."

"Mount Sinai is Jabal al-Lawz, the mountain of God, in Saudi Arabia," said Yeshua. "Across the Gulf of Aqaba."

"Yes, that's it!" exclaimed the Professor. "How did you know that?"

"I've seen it... in a dream," replied Yeshua. "Its peak is burned black at the top. It's the place where Elijah's cave is across the valley... and there's a giant split stone nearby where Moses brought forth the water."

"Yes, yes. We are going there soon to do some primary field work," said the Professor. "The Saudi government is now giving permits to study the area. But, I am getting ahead of myself. It's almost sun set. Let's head back to the headquarters building and get some dinner, then it's time for bed. It's been a very long day."

The Professor, Yeshua, Mohammed, Elijah, Ahmed and Taylor hiked back up the dirt mound and then towards the white building where their Range Rover was parked. As the sun went under the horizon in the west, they all went inside the large white house and into a simple rustic dining hall. The other Egyptian workers joined them after a few minutes and they were all served a delicious traditional meal of ful medames, kushari, lentils, mashed fava beans, molokhiya and okra by a very friendly and hospitable wait staff.

During their dinner, Yeshua and Mohammed told everyone about their fantastic recent adventures in India. They described their frightful run in with the lion, the ancient Vedic words of wisdom conveyed by the Shankaracharaya at the Beatles' ashram and the thoughtful insights about world peace from the Dali Lama.

After dinner, the Professor excused himself and told the group he was retiring for the evening. Then, everyone left the dining hall and went outside behind the house and surrounded themselves around a large blazing campfire. The dark night sky was filled with thousands of stars as the impressive constellation of Orion shone the brightest overhead.

Several of the Egyptian men brought out their musical instruments including an Oud, a lute, a lyre, double pipes, percussion cymbals and small drums. In unison, they all started playing a wonderful rhythmic jam. A few of the men also started clapping their hands and then Taylor began to dance slowly around the fire. She closed her eyes and turned in circles as she raised her hands up into the air. The musician's beat became faster, and Taylor responded ecstatically by dancing more swiftly.

"This is called Zar music," said Ahmed to Yeshua and Mohammed, now sitting across from the campfire and listening to the pleasing sounds of the impromptu concert.

"This is one of Egypt's oldest folk music traditions," continued Ahmed. "Some say this kind of music is for healing and cleansing, and others say these songs originated as rituals to exorcise evil spirits."

"I love it," said Mohammed. "It reminds me of the Sufi whirling dervishes dancing. I want to dance too!"

Mohammed stood up and joined Taylor dancing around the campfire. Her long blonde hair twisted and turned as she danced in circles. Mohammed began clapping and howling as he turned in circles as well. The elated Egyptian musicians reacted by playing even faster.

Taylor looked at Yeshua, sitting next to Ahmed on the ground and smiled at him. She motioned with her hands for him to join her, and he jokingly pointed to himself as to confirm if she was asking him to dance with her. She smiled and shook her head up and down to signify that she wanted him to join her.

Yeshua hesitated as he knew wasn't a very good dancer; however, Ahmed immediately pushed him up to a standing position and towards the direction of Taylor. She beckoned him with her outreached hands, and then he joined her as she moved to the music like a belly dancer. He could feel the intense heat from the flames of the campfire as they crackled and sparked upwards.

Taylor drew her body closer to Yeshua and she seemed to merge her vibrant energy field with his. They danced together as one, as the music continued in an almost trance-like fashion. Yeshua could feel a shift in his state of consciousness as he felt waves of bliss come over his entire being. He touched the fingertips of his hands to Taylor's hands as they moved to the music, and he experienced an incredible jolt of electrical energy. Suddenly, dozens of tiny balls of light emanated from their fingertips and spun around Yeshua's and Taylor's bodies as they continued to dance around the campfire. Several of the musicians began to howl and cheer as a few of Egyptian workers joined Taylor, Mohammed and Yeshua and pranced about.

The festivities continued for another hour or so, and then everyone said goodnight and found their appropriate sleeping quarters in the large white house. Before going to her private chambers, Taylor kissed Yeshua on his cheek and hugged him tightly.

Yeshua found his small room adequate. It had a single bed with clean sheets. Along the wall was a sink and a dresser. He put his backpack on top of the dresser and opened the outer compartment. He pulled out his Shofar and held it in his hands for a few moments, reveling in the mysterious power of the magical horn. He placed the Shofar on an empty shelf on the far wall of the room then and changed into his sleeping attire. He looked out of the small window along the far side of the room and could see the dirt mound that was once great city Avaris. He thought to himself if this was the place where his ancestors toiled under slavery and the oppression of the Pharaoh thousands of years ago.

Yeshua lay down in his bed, completely exhausted and closed his eyes. It had been yet another epic day of adventure and discovery. He thought back to his dance with Taylor around the campfire, and the fireflies that appeared when they touched. He felt again the emotion of the wonderful feeling when Taylor kissed him earlier.

Soon, Yeshua was asleep and entered his dream state some time later. He felt that familiar falling sensation, then landed hard on the ground of a place he did not recognize. It was some kind of shadowy place, with mostly darkness all around. He saw ahead in the haziness a large creature with four legs standing near him. It was a stunning chestnut colored horse, with a beautiful long red mane. Instinctively, Yeshua walked up to the horse and held out his hand for the stallion to smell him. He had one of those déjà vu feelings, as he had seen this horse before. And the horse somehow knew him. Although he had no saddle, Yeshua easily mounted the horse and began to ride through the foggy mist.

Ahead, Yeshua saw the faint outline of another horse with a familiar man riding on it. As he got closer, he clearly recognized the long-bearded Enoch on top of an exquisite white mare. Yeshua pulled his horse closer and greeted the old man.

"I am your humble servant," said Yeshua. "What will you have of me?"

"You have always been a loyal and selfless soul, my dear old friend," said Enoch. "There is always so much to do… in the past, the present and the future. In this world and all the others."

"I will always do anything you ask of me," responded Yeshua. "But I may I ask you a question?"

"Yes, what do you need to know that you don't know already?" replied Enoch.

"Am I the Angel Gabriel?" asked Yeshua. "And why did you give me the Shofar? Why me?"

"That's actually three questions, not one," half joked Enoch. "Come, follow me. We have somewhere important to go. I will explain to you everything along the way."

The two riders approached a misty rift in between two tall cliffs. The wind began to howl. Shadowy figures seemed to follow them high up along the heights of the rocky spires.

"I am known to this world as Enoch," said the old man on the white horse. "However, I'm actually the custodian of many worlds, many earthlike planets in this galaxy you call the Milky Way of 300 billion stars. You earthlings aren't the only ones. There are thousands of habitable planets with life at all different stages of developing consciousness. Let's just say… for lack of a better term, I'm in charge of all of them."

"So are you God?" asked Yeshua. "You are in charge of all the planets, and all the stars. You control all things here on Earth?"

"Hardly, my son," responded Enoch. "I am certainly not God. And I don't control all things. I'm just here to help things along in the right direction. Sometimes in a gentle way, and sometimes in a more dramatic way. That's why I need you. I need you at times to intervene on my behalf. You see… I can't be here all the time. I have many worlds to guide."

The two men came through the slot canyon, and beyond was vast flat plane that seemed to go towards infinity. The sky above was full of fast moving, dark billowing clouds that seemed to be morphing into one another in a strange, almost psychedelic way. An occasional pulse of massive lightning shot across entire sky, followed by loud, rumbling thunder.

Awaiting the two riders at the end of the trail were two more impressive figures on horses. The first rider was a very muscular dark-skinned man seated on top of a black horse who looked just like Avraham. He wore an ornately crafted suit of chain mail armor and held a lengthy silver spear. Mohammed, riding on his dark brown horse and dressed in platinum scale armor... held his demon slaying sword. Flames of fire shot out of the blade as he raised it up high, illuminating the four riders of the storm.

"We are here to do the Lord's work," said Enoch. "Our destiny is to make things right as the Fallen Ones have betrayed their covenant and defiled this world. In every generation, they attempt to rise back up... and I need you to help me stop them. That's why I gave you the Shofar. We are here to do battle, and you are my soldiers."

Enoch softly spoke into his horse's ear, and then the brilliant white horse started a full gallop into the dark plain. Yeshua, Mohammed, and Avraham's horses followed in full stride. The four riders swiftly approached what appeared to be a huge army in front them. The wind howled louder. Thousands of giants and ogre like creatures wore armor and held weapons as they held a steady formation. In front of the army, hundreds of tall winged humans with red eyes stood patiently. The tallest one, Yeshua recognized... was the Dark Angel from Abraham's Well in Beersheba.

As the riders got closer to the massive evil army, the dark clouds above separated, and beams of light shone towards the ground. When the light rays hit the army of giants below, it burned them with intense fire. This caused chaos amongst their group and they started to break their ranks and disorganize.

Suddenly, 18 winged angels holding swords flew down from the heavens, led by a woman in beautiful gold armor who held a carved wooden staff with a lion's head on its top. She looked just like Taylor. She pointed her staff downwards, and huge blast of wind in the shape of a tornado vortex streaked downwards and wreaked havoc with the giant army below.

Dozens of the Watchers flew upwards to engage battle with the Angels coming from above, while the others raced towards Enoch's group. Mohammed held his sword forward and a fireball erupted from the blade and into the charging giant winged men. Several of them immediately disintegrated. While still riding full speed ahead on his horse, Yeshua turned his head and looked upwards... trying to locate Taylor.

Just as he was able to track her flying hundreds of feet above, one of the Watchers flew right at him and smashed into his body. It was Azazel. Yeshua was immediately knocked off his horse and fell down to the ground below. As he hit the ground violently... he woke up.

Yeshua opened his eyes and found himself back in his small bedroom at the archeology outpost. His heart was racing, as his dream seemed so real. He was sweating profusely, and then got up out of bed and drank an entire bottle of purified water. He looked outside the small window overlooking the Tell el Daba mound as the first rays of light from the new dawn were coming in from the east.

Yeshua looked at his Shofar on the dresser table. It seemed to glow and pulsate with energy. Almost immediately, Yeshua decided to take the Shofar and go out into the ruins. He slung it over his back with the leather sling attached its front and back, then quietly opened the door and left his room. He exited the white house through the back porch, and then he walked up the dirt mound, using the flashlight from his cellphone to guide his way through the darkness.

Yeshua walked down the to the tent excavation area next to the small pond. He sat down on one of the folding chairs next to the table full of 3700-hundred-year-old pottery shards. Shofar in hand, Yeshua brought the mouthpiece up to his lips and blew hard into it with all his might. The horn beamed out a really big, long blast.

Ba-ba-baaaaaaaaaaaaaaa...

He blew the Shofar two more times.

Ba-ba-baaaaaaaaaaaaaaaa...

Ba-ba-baaaaaaaaaaaaaaaa...

Then, everything changed. Yeshua began to lose consciousness, and everything faded to black. There was nothing. He was completely out of his body, as in a dream. It felt as if he was moving through the darkness, like floating. He could sense some movement forward. Then, he saw something up ahead. Out of the darkness came a steady stream of flowing lights. First it was quite dim, and then as he got closer, he saw that he was flying through some kind of mystical tunnel formed of repeating concentric circles. The lights became much brighter, and then he saw a magnificent display of multicolored circular patterns rotate around him. He seemed to glide through the magical infinite space.

The kaleidoscopic patterns morphed and shifted around him, as he seemed to fly even faster and deeper into the tunnel. From the end of the tunnel he saw a bright light approaching rapidly. He was flying incredibly fast and literally he came out through the light at the end of the tunnel.

Suddenly, his spirit seemed to hover above a small pond of water. Reeds of papyrus grew from the edges of the pond while the light from the dawn continued to illuminate the landscape. Although, everything had changed, Yeshua was no longer at the ruins of Avaris… he was in the ancient city of Avaris. The Shofar had transported him back in time 3700 years.

Surrounding his angelic ethereal form were dozens of large brick buildings. Hieroglyphics decorated several of their walls, and Yeshua moved his spirit to look closer at one of the nearest buildings. Two Egyptian guards stood motionless as they protected the entrance to structure, and then Yeshua moved between them to see what was inside the building. The guards were unaware of his apparition as he floated between them.

Inside the building were huge piles of grain and barley. It was a food storehouse. A small black cat walked along the edge one of the heaps of grain, hunting for invading rodents. The cat turned and looked at Yeshua, as it somehow felt a presence in the room. Its eyes glowed in the morning light and she hissed loudly. The felines tail stuck up in the air and grew much larger, and then the cat ran away into the darkness. Triggered by the cat's loud growling, the two guards ran into the building so see what was causing the commotion.

Yeshua decided to leave the storehouse and head north through the city. He passed a large temple with massive columns flanked by several granite statues of majestic sphinxes. A few short bald men in white robes walked into the temple from the main road.

After passing through a residential area, the road forked and Yeshua continued to the north. He saw some large buildings ahead, and then he came to a full stop at a large closed gate connected to a large barrier wall. Four Egyptian guards with spears stood in front of the gate.

Above the wooden gate, carved into the stone above... Yeshua recognized the large symbols written in hieroglyphics. There was the bird with the sun, the three rectangles surrounded by an oval and an ankh next to a pyramid. Four snake-like figures surrounded the images. It was the cartouche of the Pharaoh Maaibre Sheshi, from the 14th Dynasty. Yeshua realized he was standing in front of the palace of the Pharaoh.

Several minutes passed by while Yeshua hoped someone would open the gate so he could sneak though unnoticed. As no one came though, he decided to come up with a different plan. He focused all his energy and set his intentions above the gate in front of him. After a moment, his formless apparition lifted upwards and floated above the gate and wall of the palace. He continued to fly up into the morning sky as the sun was coming over the distant horizon to the east.

Yeshua marveled at the immense scale of the palace and temple complex of Pharaoh Sheshi. Dozens of sandstone structures with huge columns decorated with colorful hieroglyphics filled the multi-level tiered royal complex. Beyond the palace to the north flowed the wide Nile River. Yeshua stopped moving upwards and focused on moving himself towards the river and over the palace buildings.

As he reached the banks of the river, he saw below a beautiful young Egyptian woman walk out of a palatial building. She wore an exquisite long turquoise robe; her black hair was braided with gold bands. Three young women wearing white robes followed her while holding folded linens. Two of them had darker skin and black hair, while the third woman had lighter skin and auburn hair.

Yeshua decided to cross the Nile and explore the more of the surrounding area as he moved his spirit form upstream and flew west along the river. He descended down closer to the water's surface along the opposite of the Nile from the Pharaoh's palace, and then something caught his eye. A small papyrus basket covered in tar and pitch slowly floated along the reeds of riverbank.

From the basket, Yeshua could hear the sounds of a crying child. Then, a dark figure appeared in the shadows of some dense vegetation near the basket. It was an enormous Egyptian crocodile, at least 20 feet long. The huge reptile started swimming rapidly towards the basket, just a couple dozen feet away. The sun was now rising over the horizon, due east... and millions of shimmering rays of light reflected over the ripples and waves of the water of the Nile River. The crocodile's eyes gleamed red as it swam directly at the crying baby's floating basket.

With the power of his thoughts, Yeshua immediately pushed the water behind the basket and towards the other side of the Nile River. As the crocodile saw his potential morning meal dash away, he lunged forwards in attempts to catch the elusive child's cradle. Upon seeing the monstrous creature hurdle itself forward, Yeshua willed the water around the basket to move even faster. The crocodile just missed crunching the tiny bassinet with its huge open jaws, and then it came crashing down into the water with a huge splash and then disappeared into the darkness. Startled by the huge commotion in the water, dozens of white ibis birds flew up into the sky from the edge of the water.

Yeshua saw across the Nile along the Pharaoh's estate, where the beautiful Egyptian woman had just submerged her naked body into the river water to bathe. He saw that she had just turned her head and looked upstream in response to the giant splash from the crocodile and the panicked birds as they took flight nearby. She then locked her gaze on the pitch and tar covered basket that seemed to being moving in the water towards her side of the Nile along the dense reeds.

This all seemed so familiar... thought Yeshua in his mind, as he had a very powerful déjà vu. The Nile River, the Egyptian woman... the Pharaoh's palace. The crying child in basket... it was baby Moses! It had to be. This moment was exactly as described in the Book of Exodus.

The beautiful woman in the water was the Pharaoh's daughter. She was the daughter of Pharaoh Maaibre Sheshi, one of the Pharaohs of the 14th Dynasty of Egypt who ruled his kingdom from Avaris. She called out to her two attendants as they walked along the edge of the riverbank. Somehow, Yeshua could understand their Egyptian language. She asked her servants to fetch the basket... and almost instinctively, Yeshua moved water behind the cradle and pushed it into the waiting arms of the closet maidservant.

She opened the cradle, and was shocked when she discovered a small baby inside.

As the Pharaoh's daughter swam back to the shoreline, another maidservant came and saw the baby in the boat-crib. Yeshua moved his spirit close to the two servants and baby Moses.

"This is a Hebrew child," said one of the servants as she looked at the babt. "The Pharaoh has decreed that all the male Hebrew children in the land be put to death, so we must not defy his order, or we will be severely punished."

"What should we do?" asked the other servant. "Should we float him back down the river?"

"No. It's too late. The Princess has already seen the basket," replied the first servant. "I think... um, we should drown him before she gets here."

"What?" responded the other handmaiden. "That's horrible. It's just an innocent baby. Let's let the Princess decide."

"No. We will be held responsible by the Grand Vizier," said the first servant. "I will do my duty. I will drown it."

Yeshua looked in horror as the Egyptian woman bent down to pick up Moses from his crib. The baby was quietly and peacefully sleeping. Almost instinctively, Yeshua used all of his energy and directed it at the murderous woman to stop her. He felt a rage and anger that he had never felt before, and channeled all of it towards the Egyptian woman. Before she could grab the child, she clutched her chest… then fell to the ground and became unconscious. The other maidservant looked in shock at what had just happened to her fellow attendant.

The maidservant picked up the basket, closed the lid and walked back to the palace courtyard along the riverbank. Yeshua followed her closely. The Princess, now dried off and wearing her turquoise robe, stood next to the paler skinned woman with auburn hair. The maidservant placed the basket in front of the Princess and bowed down.

The Princess knelt down and opened the lid to the small crib. The baby opened his eyes and started to cry loudly.

"This is one of the Hebrew children," said Pharaoh's daughter. "Poor thing. He must be hungry."

"Shall I go and call one of the Hebrew women to nurse the child for you?" said her auburn-haired slave.

"Go ahead, Miriam," said the Princess. "I think we will keep him, and raise him as my own child."

"As you wish," said Miriam. She walked back into the palace complex from the riverbank.

Miriam… Miriam, gently repeated Yeshua in his head, like a meditation mantra. "Miriam," he continued thinking in his mind several more times. He then remembered that Miriam was Moses's sister. "Miriam!" he then said out loud.

"You can call me Taylor," said Miriam. "I would prefer that."

Yeshua suddenly opened eyes. He was sitting on a folding chair under the archeological tent and holding his Shofar in his lap. Taylor and Mohammed were standing in front of him as the early morning sun shined directly behind them. They both looked like Angels with majestically golden auras surrounding their bodies.

"Why are you out here with your Shofar this early in the morning?" asked Taylor.

"Go ahead, tell her," said Mohammed. He was smiling. "It's time to let her in on our secret."

"Secret?" asked Taylor. "What secret? What are you guys up to?"

"Do you remember ever seeing this Shofar before?" questioned Yeshua. He held it up with both hands. "Does it look familiar to you?"

"Well, ehhh... I think so," responded Taylor. "Yes! That's the Shofar the old rabbi brought to you when I was your nurse in Beersheba. You were in a coma, and you finally woke up the day after he brought it to you."

"Yes, very good memory," said Yeshua. "I was 13 years old when that happened. And I am forever grateful you took care of me. The Rabbi left explicit instructions with Mohammed that I should wait until my 18th birthday to use the Shofar, which I then did later at the ancient ruins of Tel Be'er Sheva."

"You are very welcome. And what happened then, after you sounded the Shofar?" asked Taylor.

"Well, I was transported back to biblical times as the Archangel Gabriel," explained Yeshua.

"What? Excuse me," replied Taylor. "That doesn't make any sense. Are you on drugs?"

"No. I'm not on drugs, I swear," responded Yeshua. "As it turns out... the old Rabbi is actually the Prophet Enoch, and we are his team of Archangels to help him defeat the Watchers."

"What? What do you mean we?" asked a very confused Taylor.

"You're doing really good Yeshua so far, tell her all of it," interjected Mohammed. He was smiling and nodding his head.

"You, me, Mohammed and Avraham," continued Yeshua. "We are manifestations of four Archangels from the Book of Enoch. I am Gabriel, Avraham is Raphael, Mohammed is Michael and you are Phanuel. We are modern incarnations of the four Angels of Presence."

"What? I'm an Angel?" responded Taylor. "We are Angels? And you are saying I'm called Phanuel... I've never heard of that particular Angel."

"Yes, that's you," said Yeshua. "From the Book of Enoch. You are called the demon-slayer. And it's written in the Book that you are set over the repentance unto hope of those who inherit eternal life. Enoch told me that we are here to do the Lord's work. And this Shofar is some kind of mystical time machine that will transform us into our biblical angelic forms."

"Yes. It's true," said Mohammed. "We've both gone back to biblical times and changed the world."

"Is that where you two went in Babylon?" asked Taylor. "I heard you sound the Shofar then you both basically disappeared."

"Yes, we went back to the time of the Prophet Daniel and King Nebuchadnezzar," described Yeshua. "Let me ask you a question, Taylor... have you ever seen a carved wooden staff with a lion's head on top of it?"

"Umm... yes!" exclaimed Taylor. "I've seen that in my dreams. But how could you possibly know that? I've never told anyone."

"And in your dreams... what do you do with that staff?" asked Yeshua.

"Well, recently... I've been having these recurrent dreams," replied Taylor. "Often, I am using that staff, and I'm in some kind of war or battle. I can't remember all the details; however, it's like a good versus evil conflict in the dream. But seriously... how do you know about the lions staff?"

"Because I'm in your dreams too, and Mohammed," said Yeshua. "We are fighting the same bad guys. They are fallen angels called the Watchers, and their evil offspring are called the Nephilim."

"The Nephilim... from the Book of Genesis?" asked Taylor. "The mighty men, who were of old, the men of renown?"

"Yes, exactly them," replied Yeshua. "In the Book of Enoch... we were tasked with destroying them, and the Watchers... as they had betrayed God."

"So... if that's true, that's all in the past. Correct? Then why we are needed now, in modern times?" asked Taylor.

"Because, they are trying to come back," said Mohammed. "And we need to stop them."

"Yes, exactly," said Yeshua. "Enoch choose us to help him, and that's why we've each been given special superpowers."

"What do you mean, superpowers?" questioned Taylor.

"Don't act like you don't know," said Mohammed. "I saw what you did during our Krav Maga training at the Nitzanim Army Base. You put your hands in a triangle shape and did some kind of telekinesis to stop all the falling airplane debris from killing us."

"So you do have a super power," said Yeshua. "You can move things with your mind. I'm sure you have some other abilities as well."

"Okay, yes," agreed Taylor. "I've had this gift, or superpower as you call it… since I was a young child. It's been both a blessing and a curse. I only use it when I have too. And what are your powers?"

"I can go into deep meditation and remote-view out of my body and mind control people," replied Mohammed. "That's how I saved your archeological team in Babylon. I mind controlled one of the armed jihadi terrorists to neutralize the other ones. And that's how I saved Yeshua after he was kidnapped by the Iranians."

"That's a quite a superpower," responded Taylor. "And what about you, Yeshua?"

"Well, I have this built in warning system," explained Yeshua. "When something bad is about to happen, I get a high-pitched buzzing in my right ear. Somehow, I am alerted about danger before it happens."

"Is that how you know how to diffuse bombs from blowing up?" asked Taylor. "Your ear buzzes and helps you as to what to do?"

"Yes, exactly," said Yeshua. "And there's more… so much more. We each have a superpower in our angelic forms when we go back in biblical times after sounding the Shofar."

"What? Really? What kind of superpowers?" asked Taylor.

"It has to do with the elements of nature," explained Yeshua. "Each of us can control one element. Mohammed, as the Archangel Michael controls fire, Avraham as the Archangel Raphael controls electricity and I... as the Archangel Gabriel controls water."

"What about me?" asked Taylor. "What can I control?"

"As the Archangel Phanuel, you control the wind," replied Yeshua. "I've seen you make tornados and stuff like that, when we were battling the Watchers and the Nephilim."

"Wait a sec... you've seen me in battle as the Archangel Phanuel?" questioned Taylor.

"Yes, several times," described Yeshua. "Just last night in my dream for example. As I said, you are a demon slayer."

"Yes, I know what you did last summer!" joked Mohammed.

"Very funny," replied Taylor. "Wow. Mind blown. I need a few minutes to process all of this."

"Okay, while you are doing that... I have something to tell you about my dream from last night," said Mohammed.

"What happened?" asked Yeshua.

"In my dream, I was riding on a brown horse... and that Enoch dude rode up to me on his white horse," described Mohammed. "He kinda looked like Gandalf from the Lord of the Rings, anyhow... he told me we need to go to a place called Nuweiba and sound the Shofar. Does that sound familiar too you at all?"

"Did you say Nuweiba?" asked Taylor. "I told you both about that place when we were at Eilat. It's a small port city in Egypt along the Gulf of Aqaba."

"Then we must go there!" said Yeshua.

"Go where?" said Elijah Spencer. He had just walked down the Tel el-Daba hill completely unnoticed with Ahmed and joined the three Israelis under the archeology tent.

"We have a slight change of plans," said Yeshua. "Mohammed and I need to go to a place called Nuweiba. Going to Alexandria will have to wait."

"Nuweiba? I am familiar with that place," said Ahmed. "It is on the Gulf of Aqaba across the Sinai Peninsula. It's at least 6-hour drive from here through difficult terrain; however, I can take you there if you wish."

"And I can go with Elijah to Alexandria," said Taylor. "I have a Jeep we can take. I'm ready to leave this desolate place anyway."

"Perfect," said Yeshua. "I love when a plan comes together."

"Wait, I changed my mind... I want to go with you guys," declared Taylor. "Ahmed, do you mind to go with Elijah without us."

"You wish is my command," replied Ahmed. "But here, take my diplomatic pass… I don't think the Egyptian border patrol would take kindly to three Israelis randomly driving around the Sinai Peninsula."

CHAPTER 11

NUWEIBA

Mohammed drove the old four door black Jeep south on the El Qantra Shark – Ras Sedr Road along the eastern bank of the Great Bitter Lake. Taylor sat in the front passenger seat, and Yeshua sat in the back. Near the city of Suez, they came to a security checkpoint at a crossroads. Mohammed showed the Egyptian guard his diplomatic pass and they exchanged some words in Arabic. The guard motioned them to pass, and they turned due east along Route 50. The hot noon sun was directly overhead as they drove through the wide-open desert.

"What did he say?" questioned Yeshua.

"He asked me where we are going," responded Mohammed.

"And what did you say?" asked Taylor

"I told him the truth. That we are going to the town of Nuweiba to meet with some friends," replied Mohammed.

"Well played Sir, very well played," said Taylor. She nodded at Mohammed and then looked back at Yeshua, and they exchanged warm smiles.

"So, what's the plan when we get to Nuweiba?" asked Taylor. "I hear there's great snorkeling and scuba diving there on the gulf."

"We are going to sound the Shofar… all three of us together, just before sunrise tomorrow," answered Yeshua. "Then you will see what happens."

"You mean, I'm going to go into some kind of magical time vortex and become the Archangel Phanuel and enact great miracles during biblical times?" half-joked Taylor.

"It's no a laughing matter," stated Yeshua. "There's something much bigger going on here that we're just now starting the understand."

"Oh come on, Yeshua," replied Taylor. "Lighten up a bit. Why do you have to take everything so seriously? You act like this is a matter of life and death."

"Perhaps it is," responded Yeshua. "Perhaps it is…"

"I agree with her," said Mohammed. "You need to need to chill out a bit. Let's please all try to have a little fun out here and blow off some steam. Maybe let's go snorkeling when we get to Nuweiba… I've never done that before."

"Okay, you're absolutely right," responded Yeshua. "I do think I need to calm down and relax. Although, it seems as though we shouldn't get too distracted from our primary mission."

"Listen, bro!" exclaimed Mohammed. "We've got this. Nothing wrong with a little R&R in-between all this saving the world stuff."

The terrain changed from alternating sand dunes and vast flat desert to more of arid hills and valleys. Along the road, there were many dry riverbeds and large patches of what looked like burned, scorched earth.

"How could anything live out here? It's brutally hot and dry," said Taylor. "Do you really think this could be the path the Moses and the Israelites took from Avaris to Mt. Sinai?"

"It certainly could be," replied Yeshua. "In the Torah, it describes Moses as taking the Israelites through the wilderness to the land of Midian, which is location of Horeb... the mountain of God. That's the same place where he spoke to God at the burning bush while in exile after killing one of the Egyptian slave masters. A more northernly route would have taken them into the land of the Philistines. This southern route we are on leads towards Saudi Arabia, which is also considered the biblical land of Midian."

"I've always been so impressed with your biblical and historical knowledge," said Taylor. "It's like you memorized the entire Hebrew Bible."

"Well, I've read and studied it since my childhood," replied Yeshua. "I find it all so fascinating as well as deeply spiritual. And I'd say after reading the stories over and over again... I've seemed to have recognized a repeating and recurrent pattern in almost every story."

"What's that?" asked Mohammed.

"It's really pretty simple," explained Yeshua. "When you, and I mean when a rhetorical 'you'... does the right thing, or the moral or ethical thing... then there is usually a good consequence. And when you do the wrong thing, then there are usually bad consequences."

"You mean, like karma?" said Taylor. "That 'you' get positive points for good deeds and negative points for bad deeds. And hopefully 'you' end up with more positive than negative points."

"I guess that's one way at looking at it," replied Yeshua. "However, when you look at each particular story in the Torah, if 'you' scored too many negative points... at some point, there would literally be hell to pay. And it wasn't just limited to individual actions, but would also include the entire society's actions. Like eventually an entire people would collectively get punished for their negative actions."

"Hmm. I've never thought about it that way before," said Taylor. "Give me an example."

"Okay, let's look at the entire Israelites population who left Egypt with Moses. How many adult men who left with Moses eventually stepped foot into the Promised Land?" asked Yeshua.

"I have no idea," replied Taylor. "They wandered in the desert for 40 years, correct? And by the looks of this horrible place... maybe half of them made it."

"And how many do you think made it, Mohammed?" asked Yeshua. "Of the reportedly 600,000 men who left on foot with Moses after the 10th plague."

"Wow, 600,000?" questioned Mohammed. "That's a lot of slaves. I supposed at least 100,000 would have made it? I don't know. What's the answer... how many made it?"

"Two," answered Yeshua.

"Two? Are you serious? Just two made it?" Mohammed. "That's shocking. They all died in the desert?"

"Yes. Only two made it," said Yeshua. "Joshua and Caleb. The rest of the adult men, including Moses... weren't allowed to make it there collectively, because when things got tough in the wilderness, they betrayed God. Over and over again they would fall short in honoring their savior. From worshipping the golden calf to the persistent complaints that they would prefer to be back in Egypt as slaves rather than suffer in the desert as free men."

"So, you are saying they lost their faith in God?" questioned Taylor. "Even after being shown miracle and after miracle?"

"Yes. They lost their faith," replied Yeshua.

"What I don't understand is, after witnessing all the of 10 plagues against the Egyptians, and being delivered out of slavery, and witnessing the parting of the Red Sea, and all the other miracles... how could all the Israelites lose their faith?" asked Mohammed.

"Well, I believe they were called a 'stiff-necked' people," replied Yeshua. "They should have been more grateful and appreciative of being freed from slavery and observing so many miracles... yet they behaved and acted so poorly."

"So they were all punished then?" asked Taylor. "You are saying God on purpose killed them in the desert, rather than let them make it to the Israel? That sounds horrible. I thought God is supposed to be forgiving, benevolent and loving. Why would He do that?"

"Well, first of all," replied Yeshua. "I don't think God is actually a he, like a male, or man. I think God is a divine being that doesn't have a sex, either male or female."

"Good point," said Taylor. "Then why would the omnipotent divine being, creator of the Universe... purposefully make all the Hebrew adult men, save for two... die in this horrible desert?"

"I don't think we can truly understand the mind of God, and the all the reasons behind each decision," explained Yeshua. "However, we can look at overall patterns of actions and make some observations, especially when you apply the teachings of what is called the Kabbalah."

"Isn't Kabbalah something about ancient Jewish mysticism?" asked Taylor.

"Yes, it's a deep and spiritual esoteric knowledge that was passed down for generations and eventually written down into several books, probably the most important one called The Book of Zohar. Kabbalah explains the process of creation, and also unlocks the metaphysical meaning of the Torah stories. Traditionally, these teachings were only taught to scholarly religious Jews who were deemed worthy."

"Whoa. Where did you learn Kabbalah? How do you know so much about all of this?" asked Taylor.

"Let's just say he spends many late nights looking up this stuff on the Internet," joked Mohammed.

"Well, that's partially true," said Yeshua. "It's only in past few generations that these teachings have become more widespread and accepted."

"So, what are the teachings? And how does that apply to the bible stories?" asked Taylor.

"Well, there are many philosophies and understandings," answered Yeshua. "Probably more that one can absorb in one lifetime... however, I've have figured out at least three main themes."

"Oh, please do tell!" said Taylor. "This is all so fascinating." She smiled and her blue eyes sparkled in the Egyptian sunlight.

"The first thing, which is absolutely tremendous in my opinion," began Yeshua. "Is that your soul is eternal and infinite, and that you reincarnate from one lifetime to another."

"Reincarnation? That's a Jewish belief?" asked Mohammed. "I thought only the Hindus and Buddhists believed in that."

"Well, the Kabbalistic reincarnation philosophy is not taught in traditional Judaism," explained Yeshua. "And probably for good reason. One of the main focuses of Judaism is doing Mitzvah, or good deeds in this lifetime. The focus of being Jewish is in the 'here and now,' and not in the afterlife."

"So how does that related to all the Hebrews who died in this desert?" asked Taylor.

"Well, precisely that… God did not want their collective unworthy behaviors to be brought into the Holy Land," explained Yeshua. "In their betrayal, they no longer deserved salvation. So, in essence their souls were taught an important lesson. That certain repeated behaviors that cross moral, ethical or spiritual lines can and will lead to ultimate consequences."

"Wow, that's harsh," said Taylor. "Is that what the Kabbalah taught you?"

"Well, yes and no," replied Yeshua. "But if you look at life and death from the perspective that the soul is eternal and is continually reborn… the perspective of dying in one lifetime completely changes."

"So, you are saying that all the Hebrew men in the Exodus who perished in the desert didn't really die… they just reincarnated into new bodies afterwards?" asked Mohammed.

"Yes! Exactly," replied Yeshua. "And most likely their reborn souls were reincarnated into Hebrew children who did eventually reside in the Promised Land."

"So, technically speaking… they did make it to Israel. Just in different bodies in a subsequent generation?" questioned Mohammed. "Honestly though, that's a bizarre concept and it's hard to grasp my head around all of this. I suppose it's like that *Groundhog Day* movie you were talking about… you can't move onto the next day until you make appropriate corrections to your soul. And if you can't seem to make them for yourself, God will eventually have to push the reset button."

"That's an overly simplified way to look at it... but that is actually quite a good analogy, my friend," said Yeshua. "The reset button!"

"What about the Holocaust?" asked Taylor. "Was that God pushing the reset button? What about all those Jews dying in the extermination camps at the evil hands of the Nazis?"

"I don't know... I've never considered it in that way before," replied Yeshua. "Although if you think about it... it was basically the next generation of Jews after the Holocaust that made it to Israel. That's very similar to the slavery and purge story from the Exodus. There's a definitely a similar pattern there, just like all the other stories."

"Hey... we are running low on gasoline," said Taylor as she looked at the Jeep's dashboard. "We definitely don't want to run out of fuel out here in the desert."

"I saw a sign for a town called Nekhel a few kilometers back," said Mohammed. "It should be coming up here soon. We can refuel there."

"Okay great," replied Taylor. "So, Yeshua... what's your second epiphany about the Kabbalah?"

"Well, have you ever seen the image or diagram of the Sefirot?" asked Yeshua.

"The Sefirot?" questioned Taylor. "I'm not sure. What's that exactly?"

"There's this geometric design with 10 connected spheres where each sphere represents a specific divine attribute," explained Yeshua.

"Yes, yes! I've seen that image," replied Taylor. "It's also called the Tree of Life?"

"Precisely," responded Yeshua. "Each sphere has a specific name and like a spiritual ladder, there's an ascending and descending pathway that connects God with humanity. There's literally endless information and concepts within the system. Recently, I've made a breakthrough in my understanding of how it all works."

"This is awesome," exclaimed Taylor. "I could just talk hours and hours about all this. What was your epiphany?"

"I could too!" replied Yeshua. He smiled. "I'll do my best to simplify the basic concepts. At the top of the diagram is a sphere that represents God, and at the bottom of the diagram is a sphere that represents man, or the human soul. There are lines connecting all the spheres. Again, most of this system is described in the Book of Zohar written during the Middle Ages. Anyhow, divine or spiritual 'Light' emanates from Crown or Godhead sphere at the top and descends through the other spheres to the bottom one called Malkuth, which in essence represents our physical world and the location of humanity."

"Wait, did you say Crown? Like the Crown Chakra?" asked Taylor.

"Umm. Chakra?" asked Yeshua. "What's that?"

"You know, the Chakras," replied Taylor. "It's from Hinduism and eastern philosophy. There's seven connected physiological and spiritual points in the human body that channel and flow energy up and down that help create balance and harmony. The top point is called the Crown Chakra."

"I don't know, but maybe the spheres of the Tree of Life and the Chakras are possibly related," said Yeshua. "It sounds like a similar pattern. After all, everything is connected."

"Okay, sorry. I didn't mean to interrupt you," stated Taylor. "You were saying…"

"Yes. So, spiritual 'Light' energy flows downwards from God through each sphere and eventually arrives at our physical world… and specifically directed towards our human souls. This also explains the path of creation. And furthermore, by understanding the spiritual pattern… it also teaches us how to evolve our souls and travel upwards towards God as the entire construct is like a two-way ladder."

"And how do you do that? How do you climb the spiritual ladder?" asked Taylor.

"Yes, it's quite simple," answered Yeshua. "You do as God would do."

"Whoa," said Taylor. "My mind is totally blown. And how would one do that?"

"So, here's how it works," said Yeshua. "When God sends 'Light' from the other side towards us, it is without expectations. God, as the divine Creator... has given us everything. Through this metaphysical concept of 'Light" or energy, everything is created for us. After all, Einstein's famous equation wraps all this into a mathematical formula. Energy equals mass, times the speed of light squared. Energy, light and physical mass are all connected and interchangeable. That is the divine gift of creation, as it all comes from God and everything is a gift... like a Christmas or Hanukah present from a parent to their child. Simply put, we are given this Universe, this planet, this body you live in, all your possessions, everything you eat is given to you by God, correct?"

"Yes, I suppose so," said Taylor. "That is actually quite a beautiful way to look at it. Everything is a gift, from God."

"And what does God ask for in return?" asked Yeshua. "Does God condition all of these gifts on getting something in return?"

"Well, I suppose if you look at it using your Christmas present metaphor... then no," replied Taylor. "When a parent gives a Christmas present to their young child, it's a selfless act. There are no expectations of anything in return, at least physically. Perhaps the only things the parent wants to see is the joy and happiness in their child's face upon opening the gift and then maybe even some gratitude or appreciation."

"Exactly, when something is given as a gift by God... it's essentially a selfless act," explained Yeshua. "God does not want anything physical in return, save for some appreciation and gratitude as you perfectly stated."

"Okay, and how does that related to the Kabbalah and evolving your soul?" asked Taylor.

"So, it has to do with you the intentions behind your actions," described Yeshua. "When you do something for someone else, what is the root cause of why you are doing it? What is your motivation behind doing something for someone?"

"Is that a rhetorical question?" asked Taylor.

"Yes and no," replied Yeshua. "For example, Mohammed... would you go out of your way to help someone you didn't know that would potentially cause you a great inconvenience."

"In general, of course not," answered Mohammed. "Why would I help someone I didn't know to my own detriment?"

"Exactly, you wouldn't," said Yeshua. "And you, Taylor... would you help them?"

"Well, I usually try to help everyone when I can," explained Taylor. "But I supposed there would be a limitation of what I would do, especially if it was very inconvenient."

"Now, let me change the scenario a bit," said Yeshua. "Same question… would you help someone you didn't know, resulting in a great personal inconvenience, but you would be getting a million dollars for it."

"What? For a million dollars? Heck yes," said Mohammed.

"And you Taylor, would you do it?" questioned Yeshua.

"Of course. It's an obvious answer," said Taylor. "As long as it wasn't something illegal or brought me significant danger or potential harm."

"Well said," replied Yeshua. "So, my dearest friends… your honest answers precisely illustrate my point about the intentions behind most of our actions as they relate to doing things for others. When we do something for someone else, we are often expecting some kind of reward… like the millions dollars you said would motivate you in my hypothetical situation. It may be subtly subconscious… however, every time you do something for someone else, a little voice in your head asks 'What's in it for me?' and then you decide if the reward is good enough to perform the deed."

"Interesting. You are describing what is called a quid pro quo," explained Taylor.

"Quid pro quo? What's that?" asked Yeshua.

"It's a Latin phrase," described Taylor. "It means a favor or advantage granted or expected in return for something."

"Yes! That's exactly what I'm trying to describe," said Yeshua. "Most of what we do, as humans is a quid pro quo. I do something for you, with the intention of getting something in return. That's the motivation for our many of our actions."

"Okay, that's a very good point. But, again, what does that have to do with the Kabbalah stuff you are talking about? How does basic human nature relate to all of this?"

"It has everything to do with it," replied Yeshua. "The un-evolved human soul is very selfish. It only thinks of itself. When it does do something for someone else, it is usually conditioned with getting someone back in exchange. You scratch my back, and I'll scratch yours. So, with that in mind... how does the soul evolve? How do you elevate yourself from selfishness? How do you become more like God?"

"I totally get it now," said Mohammed. "You change the intentions behind your actions. You stop doing things for the sole purpose of getting something back. You give, without the expectation of receiving back."

"Yes, bingo!" exclaimed Yeshua. "That's how you evolve yourself and climb the Kabbalistic ladder."

"Wow. That's called unconditional love," said Taylor. "That means you love someone so much that you selflessly give yourself without expectations or conditions."

"Yes, that's exactly what you do... to evolve your soul," replied Yeshua. "Like the love between a mother and her newborn child. It's selfless, and pure."

In the vast Sinai desert, their Jeep passed a large green sign next to the highway written in Arabic. Ahead, there was a fork in the road.

"What does the sign say?" asked Yeshua.

"It says Nekhel to the left, and the Nekhel bypass and Route 55 to the right and towards the Taba Airport," answered Mohammed."

"We should probably stop here to refuel... we are on a quarter tank," said Taylor as she looked at the dashboard. "Make the left towards Nekhel."

Suddenly, Yeshua's right ear began to have a loud, high pitch buzzing sound. He held his right hand up to his head and winced in pain.

Mohammed looked in the rear-view mirror and saw his best friend holding his ear in the back seat and knew exactly what that meant... danger!

"I think we will continue on towards the airport," said Mohammed. He veered the Jeep towards the right at the fork in the road and drove due east on Route 55. Yeshua's right ear stopped ringing and he removed his right hand away from his head and he immediately looked much more relaxed and calmer. Yeshua saw that Mohammed was looking at him in the rear-view mirror, and he nodded at him.

"Okay, do you think we have enough gas to get to the next station?" asked Taylor.

Mohammed looked nervously at the fuel meter on the dashboard. There was less than a quarter tank left.

"We should have at least 50ish miles of fuel left," said Mohammed. "We should be fine."

For the next hour or so, there was uneasy silence in the Jeep. The three Israeli friends seemed be in silent prayer as they were all hoping they wouldn't run out of gas and get stranded in the middle of the extremely arid and hostile Sinai Peninsula. Occasionally, an Egyptian military vehicle would pass them travelling west.

The barren desert road began to turn slightly to the southeast. On the dashboard panel of the Jeep, the external thermometer showed that it was 113 degrees Fahrenheit and 45 degrees Celsius outside. Along the hot, black asphalt of the straight highway... the illusion of a smooth surface of water on the road seemed to magically appear and disappear as a heat mirage.

After a few minutes, the gasoline gauge dial moved squarely into the red area of the 'E' zone and an emergency light started to blink on the control panel indicating low fuel. The dashboard clock read 1:13PM.

"Oh snap, I think we are almost out gas," said Mohammed.

"I thought you said we had enough?" said a very disturbed Taylor. She looked quite upset.

"I know, I thought we did," replied Mohammed. "However, it looks like we might not make it to the next gas station. Unless one just magically appears in the next little bit."

"Ffffff...." muttered Taylor under her breath. "We should have stopped back there at Nekhel. Why didn't we go there?"

"Just relax," said Yeshua. "We are going to be okay; everything will be fine."

"Don't tell me to relax," said Taylor in an angry tone. "Everything is not fine. We might die out here."

"Yeshua my friend, don't you know by now? You should never, ever, ever tell an upset woman to relax. That's a cardinal rule."

"Shut up, Mohammed," barked Taylor. "You're not being funny. This is no laughing matter."

"As God guided Moses and the Israelites through this wilderness over 3600 years ago, so to will we be led to safety," said Mohammed. "I am sure of it."

Suddenly, the Jeep rattled and shuttered as the last few remaining droplets of gasoline combusted within the six-cylinder engine. Black smoke poured out of the rear exhaust pipe. The vehicle started to de-accelerated slowly.

"Or maybe I'm dead wrong," half-joked Mohammed.

"Do you know what they do with three Israelis here in Egyptian territory with a borrowed diplomatic pass?" asked Taylor. "They'll put us in jail. And that's if we are lucky. There are plenty of hostile jihadists elements roaming around out here that would shoot us on sight."

"Well that doesn't sound very pleasant at all," responded Yeshua. "What's our plan B?"

"Yeah, let's come up with a plan B quickly," said Mohammed. The Jeep slowed down and almost completely stopped as it crested a small hill. Luckily, it gained some momentum and speed as it rolled downwards within a mountainous valley. Ahead was another vast, flat arid desert plain as far as the eye could see.

"I think I see a gas station, far off in the distance... there!" yelled Mohammed as he pointed from the driver's seat and towards the eastern horizon. A tiny reflection of light was visible along the distant road far off in the distance.

"That must be at least five or six miles from here," said Yeshua. "I don't think we have any chance of making it."

Miraculously, the Jeep seemed to gain speed and accelerate quickly down the road. A strong wind blew from the west, pushing the vehicle forward. Yeshua turned his head around and saw a massive sandstorm bearing down on upon them, with several tall sand twisters dancing along the periphery of the billowing wall of sand and wind.

"Eh, we got a problem here," said Yeshua.

"Actually, I don't think we do," whispered Mohammed, still with both his hands on the steering wheel. "It appears Taylor has everything under control."

Yeshua unlocked his seatbelt and pulled himself up from the backseat and looked at Taylor in the front passenger seat. Her eyes were closed, and she held out both her hands together and formed a triangle shape with her thumbs and index fingers.

"That's what she did during training when she stopped the crashing plane from hitting us," said Mohammed softly. "It looks like she's in a meditative trance and pushing us with wind from the sandstorm behind us. She's controlling the wind."

The Jeep reached a maximum speed of 100 miles (160 kilometers) per hour as the immense sandstorm engulfed the entire surrounding road, and then just as quickly as it formed... it dissipated and disappeared. Taylor slumped over and seemed to pass out.

"Is she okay?" screamed Yeshua. Mohammed took his right hand and placed it on Taylor's neck.

"Yes, she okay," said Mohammed. She has a strong pulse and is breathing. She's fine, thank God."

"She did all that?" asked Yeshua. "She made the wind and the sandstorm to propel us towards the gas station?"

"Yes, and we are almost there!" said an elated Mohammed. "I can see it just ahead. I think we have just enough momentum to get there."

The Jeep gradually slowed down as it rolled along the black asphalt road. The Watanya Petrol Station was just ahead, and almost with perfect precision… their vehicle had just enough momentum to make to the nearest gasoline pump. Mohammed guided the Jeep next to the pump and he gently put his foot down on the brake.

"That was a long strange trip, my friend," said Mohammed. "Stay here inside. I'll go pay for the gas and get some water and supplies. I guess let's let Taylor sleep it off. That whole X-men thing she pulled back there must really have taken the wind out of her."

"Ha-ha, very funny… always joking," replied Yeshua.

Mohammed left the Jeep and walked into the entrance of the convenience store. An Egyptian man who was working behind the counter greeted him and they started talking in Arabic. Outside, a few Egyptian truckers were filling up their vehicles with gasoline.

Suddenly, Yeshua's left ear started a gentle high pitch buzz. Every time in the past if his right ear had buzzing… it meant danger or warning. If his left ear buzzed, it often meant to pay attention for a good omen or a positive event. He quickly looked around outside the Jeep through the windows and noticed an old, gravel road to the south across the street. When he looked down the unmarked old road, the buzzing in his left ear got louder.

Yeshua got out of the Jeep and closed the door. Almost in a trace, he walked away from the petrol station and he started to cross the street.

His attention was immediately interrupted by the horn of an 18-wheeler truck that was barreling towards him. He hadn't looked both ways before crossing the street, and he walked right into the path of a huge cargo truck. Fortunately, someone's hand grabbed his right shoulder and pulled backwards just before the truck would have surely crushed and pulverized his body. The truck whizzed by, as the driver continued to push down on his loud horn.

"Mohammed, you saved my life yet again," said a grateful Yeshua.

"What the heck were you doing?" yelled Mohammed. "I told you to stay in the damn Jeep. You almost got yourself killed. For like the 1000th time!"

"I'm sorry," apologized Yeshua. "My left ear started buzzing and led me to that road across the street. There's something about that road. Maybe we are supposed to go that way, south?"

"That way? I don't think so," replied Mohammed. "The GPS shows that we are supposed to continue east along this Route 55 and then to the Gulf of Aqaba. From there we take the coastal road to Nuweiba."

Yeshua stared at the southern road, still somewhat in a trance and said…

"The Lord spoke to Moses, saying speak to the children of Israel, and let them turn back and encamp in front of Pi-hahiroth…"

"What? What does that mean?" asked Mohammed. "Another Torah passage?"

"Yes, that's correct," replied Yeshua. "It's from the Book of Exodus. Moses and the Israelites were leaving Egypt on foot and heading toward the land of Midian and safety, which is due east... towards Eilat and Saudi Arabia. That's the route we are taking. Ancient Midian is only about 20 miles from here due east. I looked it up on the GPS. It would have been a half day's walk for the Israelites to get there and to have finally escaped Egypt. But in the passage I quoted, God tells Moses to 'turn back.' God commands them to go back, deep into the Egyptian wilderness rather than go onto nearby Midian.

"Umm... why would he do that? I mean why would God want them to do that?" asked Mohammed.

"Let me recite the next verse from the Book of Exodus as it will explain God's decision," explained Yeshua.

"And Pharaoh will say about the children of Israel, they are trapped in the land. The desert has closed in upon them. And I will harden Pharaoh's heart, and he will pursue them..."

"Wait a sec, God sent the Israelites back into the wilderness of Egypt instead of Midian to bait the Egyptians and then mind-control the Pharaoh to send his armies after them?" asked Mohammed. "It was a biblical set up? And you think that's the way God told Moses to go?" questioned a bewildered Mohammed as he pointed his finger south towards the old, crumbled unmarked road.

"Yes, I know it," said Yeshua. "That's exactly the way they went. That's where they turned back into Egypt instead of towards Midian. At this very spot."

"Listen, let's talk about this more in the Jeep," said Mohammed. "And we need to check on Taylor ASAP."

"Okay, yes," replied Yeshua as he looked up into the sky. "Let's get moving. I'm starting to get a sunburn."

They walked back to the Jeep and Yeshua looked at Taylor through the glass of the front passenger window. She was still peacefully sleeping. He quietly opened the back-passenger door and got inside. Meanwhile, Mohammed pumped the gas until it was full. After he returned the nozzle to the pump and closed the gas cap, he walked over to one of the truckers who was filling up his vehicle. Yeshua watched as Mohammed had a brief conversation with the trucker in Arabic. He pointed towards the southern road a few times. After they shook hands, Mohammed returned to Jeep and got inside. He started the ignition and the engine revved up loudly.

"I will never take the sound for granted, ever again," joked Mohammed.

"What were you talking to that trucker about?" asked Yeshua.

"Oh yeah," replied Mohammed. "I asked him about that road. I think you might be right."
"How so?" asked Yeshua.

"He said it goes through a bunch of windy canyons, but eventually leads to Nuweiba Beach... our final destination," answered Mohammed. "It's about 60 miles — 100 kilometers from here to Nuweiba. We can make it before sun set. So, let's hit the beach."

"I love when a plan comes together, my friend," said Yeshua.

"What about her?" asked Mohammed about Taylor. "Should we try to wake her up?"

"No, I don't think so," replied Yeshua. "Let's let her sleep it off I suppose."

"Maybe you will need to kiss her to wake her up, just like Snow White," joked Mohammed.

"Ha-ha, very funny again," replied Mohammed. "Always the joker."

Mohammed put the Jeep into gear and drove out of the petrol station parking lot. He crossed the interstate and drove south onto the unmarked gravel road. After a few minutes, it transformed from gravel into finely paved asphalt. The surrounded terrain was mostly flat, arid desert with large patches of rolling sand dunes.

"Nice, a very smooth road indeed," said Mohammed. "I hope it's like this all the way to Nuweiba. Hey... Yeshua, I have a question for you. You said something in that Exodus story... that God hardened the Pharaoh's heart. Was that really some form of mind control? I thought we are all supposed to have free will."

"Yes, that comes up a few more times in the Exodus story," replied Yeshua. "God would harden the Pharaoh's heart and force him to make choices and decisions he wouldn't normally make."

"Wow, I didn't realize that," responded Mohammed. "What other times did the Pharaoh get mind-controlled by God?"

"Well, during the 10 Plagues… God hardened the Pharaoh's heart twice and made him say no when Moses asked him to free the Israelite slaves," explained Yeshua.

"What? Are you serious?" asked Mohammed. "I don't remember that part of the story at all. I thought that God just wanted the Israelites to become free. If the Pharaoh was really ready to just let them go, why would God mind control him and make him say NO? That doesn't make any sense at all."

"I know, right?" replied Yeshua. "I thought about that for a long time. But there's a pattern and an ultimate purpose that I saw, just like everything else."

"And what's that?" asked Mohammed.

"That God purposefully wanted all the 10 Plagues to happen, including the death of the first born AND for the Pharaoh's entire army to be destroyed in the Red Sea," explained Yeshua. "It was retribution and punishment for the horrible and absolute evil perpetrated onto the Israelites by their Egyptian overlords. But there's something else there too… maybe even more important. If you read the scriptures carefully, you will see that God wanted to show the

Egyptians the power and glory of Yahweh, the one true God."

"So, it was all basically a big lesson of karma for the Egyptians?" questioned Mohammed. "God put them in their place with severe punishment. He... I mean God, could have just had Moses walk away with the slaves after a few plagues, but there was much more retribution ultimately planned."

"Yes, and what I learned at Avaris supports that even more," said Yeshua.

"How so?" asked Mohammed.

"That Avaris was the Royal Egyptian city where Moses was raised as a prince, and it's where the Hebrew slaves lived and toiled under horrible conditions for generations. The Egyptians were judged for their crimes against humanity collectively as they suffered through the 10 Plagues, and then their entire chariot army was destroyed in the Red Sea. This led to their land becoming essentially defenseless, and that's exactly when the Hyksos people moved in and took over the majority of Egypt for over 100 years. It was one of the darkest periods of time in Egyptian history. They were humiliated, conquered and subjugated by a foreign occupier. That part of the story isn't mentioned in the Bible, but while Moses and the Hebrews were wandering the wilderness for 40 years, it appears the entire Egyptian society was pushed to the brink of extinction. It was the end of the Middle Kingdom for the Egyptians."

"Wow, that's pretty harsh," replied Mohammed. "I guess the moral to the story is don't piss off God. So, I have another question for you. The 10th Plague… it was the killing of all the Egyptian's first born, correct?"

"Yes, that's correct," answered Yeshua. "It was an eye for an eye situation, as previously the Pharaoh had ordered all the newborn Hebrew male children to be murdered."

"Yeah, again. Pretty dam harsh," said Mohammed. "So, how were all the Egyptian first born killed? I can't remember all the details."

"God sends the destroying Angel," answered Yeshua. "Some call him the Angel of Death. He would 'Passover' the Hebrew homes and go into the Egyptian dwellings and snuff the life out of all the first-born males."

"Do you think, if we are truly connected with the Archangels Michael, Gabriel, Raphael and Phanuel… that one of us is the Angel of Death, the Destroyer?"

"Oh Gosh, I hope not," replied Yeshua. "I don't think I could bear the weight of knowing that we killed all those people. All those innocent children."

"Yes, that wouldn't be a fun job at all," joked Mohammed. "Professional hit man killer Angel of Death. Divine clean up duty. "

"Why are you making jokes here?" questioned Yeshua. "This is serious."

"You are right, I apologize," said Mohammed. "I shouldn't be joking about any people suffering. My bad. But I have another question for you… we were talking about

God hardening the Pharaoh's heart. Do you think God routinely mind controls other people? Like in modern times?"

"I don't know," replied Yeshua. "But that is very, very possible."

Yeshua leaned forward and looked at Taylor. She was still in a deep sleep. Outside, the terrain changed from rolling sand dunes to dry riverbeds and slot canyons. The paved road turned into gravel and dirt, and they drove deeper into narrow valleys formed by thousands of years of weathered erosion.

"I don't think we're in Kansas, anymore," joked Mohammed as he activated the 4-wheel drive mechanism. "Hold, on back there... we're in for a bumpy and windy ride."

"Do you really think this is the way the Israelites made their way to the Red Sea?" asked Mohammed.

"I do, I can feel it in my soul," replied Yeshua. "I'm having one of the intense déjà vu feelings. It's like I've been here before."

"I am too," said Mohammed. "I feel like I've been here before too. It's all so very familiar, this deep canyon. It's like I know every twist and turn of this road."

"Just, making sure... do we have enough gasoline to get there?" asked Yeshua.

"Very funny, ha-ha!" laughed Mohammed. "It looks like you finally decided to have a sense of humor. We have over ¾ of a tank."

The two best friends stayed in silence for quite some time while Mohammed drove through the rugged mountainous landscape. Although it was a harsh and desolate land, it had a certain mesmerizing beauty. It looked almost like it was a different planet rather than Earth.

After about 20 miles of difficult driving, the serpentine dirt road turned eastward, and the surrounding mountains became much taller and more ominous. Several stretches of road were quite narrow, as the passage seemed to almost be swallowed up by the steep cliffs.

Finally, the valley opened up and the sunlight from the late afternoon sun illuminated a vast sandy peninsula surrounded by the brilliant deep blue waters of the Gulf of Aqaba.

"We made it! Nuweiba," said Mohammed. "Thank God. Where to now?"

"Let's take the road straight to the beach," suggested Yeshua. "We need to find somewhere to rest for the evening."

"Where… are we?" asked Taylor. She had just woken up from her long nap.

"Sleeping beauty, your chariot has arrived at Nuweiba," joked Mohammed.

"Gosh, I had the strangest dream," said Taylor as she stretched her arms outwards. "Someone stole your Shofar, Yeshua. This dark man, however... I couldn't see his face. He had deep blood red eyes. I tried to pull it away from him, but he was too strong. We struggled over it. He said he was going to go back and change everything. He pushed me away, and I started to free-fall into some kind of void. Then as I was hopelessly falling, he sounded the Shofar and disappeared."

"Whoa, that's some dream," replied Yeshua. He felt his backpack and made sure his Shofar was still there... and to his relief it was. "Just curious... did you happen to catch that bad man's name at all?"

"I think so," answered Taylor. "I mean, he didn't say his name. Although somehow... I knew his name. It was Sam, I think. Yes, pretty sure it was Sam. Or something like that."

"Was it Samyaza?" asked Yeshua. "More than just Sam... Sam with a 'yaza' at the end?"

"Yes! It was," answered Taylor. "I believe so. But how would you know that? And who the heck is Samyaza?"

"In the Book of Enoch, Samyaza was the leader of the fallen angels," replied Yeshua. "He commanded the Watchers, the rebellious sons of God who betrayed their orders and came down to earth to mate with human women and corrupt the Earth."

"It's the four Archangels... Michael, Gabriel, Raphael and Phanuel who were tasked with defeating the Watchers and the offspring, the Nephilim," explained Mohammed.

"And you guys are saying I'm somehow connected to the Archangel Phanuel," stated Taylor. "And that we are here to stop the Watchers from coming back?"

"Yes, and that's exactly what makes your dream so disturbing," said Yeshua "All the Watchers were either destroyed or imprisoned in an fiery apocalyptic prison by the Archangels in the Book of Enoch. So, if somehow Samyaza could get a hold of the Shofar and go back in time, he could change all of history."

"Holy Back to the Future, Batman," joked Mohammed as he parked the Jeep in front of a small beachfront hotel. "So… ladies and gentlemen. Enough of all this gloom and doom stuff. Let's hit the beach. It's time for some much-needed R&R. We have just a few hours before sunset."

"Yeah, I totally could go for a swim," said Taylor.

They all got out of the Jeep with their gear and walked into the tropical entrance of The Aten Nuweiba Beach Resort. A young Egyptian woman greeted them in Arabic at the reception desk. The quaint hotel was decorated with interesting sandstone columns and beautiful tile mosaics. Mohammed had a long discussion with her, and then he pulled out a small stack of Egyptian currency and placed it in front of her. The receptionist shook his hand and they both smiled, then she handed him three keys numbered 10, 13 and 18.

Mohammed thanked her and said "Shukran," then motioned for Yeshua and Taylor to follow him into the central courtyard of the hotel complex. There was a beautiful pool with sparkling turquoise water surrounded by lush tropical plants and ornately carved ottoman styled columns.

"And of course, you get room 18, my friend" said Mohammed as he handed Yeshua his key. "Your lucky number." He handed Taylor the key to room 13.

"Okay, this is quite fortunate for us," continued Mohammed. "Apparently, the last group here had to leave early and cancel their guided sunset snorkel trip. So, we are going to take their place. Get your swimsuits on STAT let's meet at the dock of the beach in fifteen-ish minutes."

"Sir, yes sir!" replied Yeshua.

"Oh, and Taylor," said Mohammed. "Be mindful of how revealing your bathing suit is... they are quite conservative here."

"Whatever," said Taylor as she rolled her eyes and shrugged her shoulders as she turned around and walked to her nearby hotel room. She placed the key in the door lock, opened the door and went inside.

Fifteen or so minutes later they all met at an old wooden dock along the water's edge of the Gulf of Aqaba. A young Egyptian man waited for them in a large skiff boat made from papyrus reeds. There was a large travel bag full of snorkel gear in the middle of the boat, along with a couple of oars.

Everyone got into the boat carefully as Mohammed introduced himself and the others to the Egyptian. He said his name was Youssef. After a short conversation in Arabic,

Youssef grabbed the oars and starting rowing out from the beach towards the east.

"He says he's going to take us out to the coral reef a few hundred meters away," explained Mohammed. "He says he has something special to show us, but he won't tell me what it is. He wants it to be a surprise."

The bright sun started to set in the west. Directly to the east across the dark blue waters... just a few miles away, the towering mountains ranges along the coast of Saudi Arabia were clearly visible. The vibrant colors of the ocean and all the distant landscapes began to glow as the sun descended towards the horizon. Several large bands of glorious sunrays radiated from the sun and through the scattered clouds in the western sky and down towards the Egyptian Sinai.

Youssef started talking in Arabic to Mohammed for a few minutes while he rowed the boat. He seemed to be very animated with his facial expressions.

"What did he say?" asked Taylor after Youssef stopped talking.

"He said he's never seen a more beautiful woman as you," replied Mohammed. He grinned widely.

"Shut up," exclaimed Taylor. "You've joking, right? That's not what he said."

"Actually, he did," responded Mohammed. "But then he told me more about the local lure about this place. He said this was the exact location where Moses and the

Israelites crossed the Red Sea on their way to Mount Sinai. And he will prove it to us."

"Prove it? Really?" questioned Yeshua. "How is he going to do that?"

"He says all will be revealed," explained Mohammed.

Youssef rowed for a few more minutes, then lowered and small anchor on a chain from the back of the boat into the water. He opened the travel bag and pointed to the snorkel gear and motioned everyone to go in the water.

"It's time to swim, my friends," declared Mohammed. He took off his tee shirt and placed the snorkel mask on his face, then jumped in the water. Taylor removed her beige shawl that covered most her body, exposing her white two-piece bikini. She grabbed and put on her snorkel gear, then jumped into the water with a big splash.

Yeshua had tried his best not to stare directly at Taylor while she prepared to get in the water; however, he was just mesmerized by her allure.

"Come on, last one in is a rotten egg!" yelled Taylor as she treaded water a few feet from the boat. "What are you waiting for? Get on in here Yeshua."

Yeshua grabbed his mask and snorkel and placed them snuggly on his head. Then he leaped into the gulf from the reed boat and made a huge cannonball splash as his body impacted onto the water's surface. He came up for air, and then treaded for a moment. Yeshua saw that Yosseuf was trying to get his attention as he pointing to an area of coral reef just to the east of the boat. Mohammed and Taylor were already swimming in that location.

Yeshua placed the snorkel in his mouth and looked down into the water through his mask. The surface of the ocean floor was about 10 to 15 feet below. There were dozens of strange looking coral formations scattered along the white, sandy bottom. Hundreds of small, colorful exotic looking fish swam among the almost geometrically shaped coral structures.

Suddenly, Taylor grabbed Yeshua's hand and motioned for him to swim with her. She excitedly pointed towards one of the geometric shapes below.

They both dove down, and inspected the colorful, living coral more closely. There seemed to be something serving as a foundation for the coral to grow around. It had a definite circular shape, and there were impressions of spokes going towards a central point. Multiple areas were bare of coral, and it was clear that the underlying circular object had the blue-green color of weathered copper metal. It was undoubtedly in the shape of a chariot wheel. Nearby, Mohammed was inspecting another chariot wheel covered in coral. Evidently, there were dozens of these ancient wheels scattered over the entire seabed.

Yeshua saw something glistening and white in sand near the coral encrusted chariot wheel. He nudged Taylor to get her attention and pointed towards it, then swam down deeper and put his fingers around the object. He slowly loosened it from the sand and gravel and carefully removed what seemed like a smooth white orb from the ocean floor.

He turned the orb to examine it more closely while Taylor watched nearby. They were both shocked to discover it wasn't an orb at all... it was a human skull.

Yeshua completely panicked, and the skull slipped out of his hands and floated down towards the sandy floor. He started to hyperventilate and inhaled some water through his snorkel as he attempted to swim back up to the surface. He started choking and lost his bearings as he began to drown. He breathed in even more water.

Seeing Yeshua struggle, Taylor rapidly swam over to him and pressed her body against his. She wrapped her arms under his shoulders and began swimming upwards with all her might. Nearby, Mohammed saw them entwined together as Yeshua seemed to lose consciousness and stop breathing entirely. Mohammed swiftly swam towards his two friends and helped Taylor push him up towards the edge of the boat.

Seeing the events play out below him, Youssef quickly grabbed Yeshua's limp body as Taylor and Mohammed brought him up back up to the water's surface along the skiff boat. They all pulled Yeshua into the boat and Mohammed felt his pulse and checked if he was breathing.

"He's not breathing and barely has a pulse!" screamed Mohammed.

Immediately, Taylor tilted Yeshua's head back and lifted his chin. She pinched Yeshua's nose closed and gave him two deep rescue breaths into his mouth. After the second breath, Yeshua vomited a bunch of water and starting coughing. They rolled him onto his side as he coughed some more and then he drifted into unconsciousness. Mohammed felt his pulse again and saw that he was breathing normally.

"He's alive, thank God," exclaimed Mohammed. He smiled and looked at Taylor with tears in his eyes.

To the west, the sun set beautifully over the crest of the Sinai Mountains. Rays of pink, purple and orange light reflected and refracted in a wonderful technicolor display. In the distance, dozens of African sacred ibis flew upwards into the sky as Youssef rowed the boat towards the shoreline.

CHAPTER 12

THE CROSSING

The next morning, 4AM
Aten Nuweiba Beach Resort
Gulf of Aqaba

"Yeshua, Yeshua... wake up!" yelled Mohammed as he shook his best friend awake in the bed.

"Ughhhh," muttered Yeshua. "Go away... just let me sleep."

"Get up right now and grab your Shofar," commanded Taylor. "It's time to show me how it works."

"Now?" asked Yeshua as he pulled himself up from bed and looked at the bedside clock. "Really? It's freaking 4AM?"

"Come on, let's go down to the beach and sound the Shofar," said Mohammed. "Don't you know? You never want to keep a woman waiting."

"He's absolutely correct," stated Taylor as she plunked Yeshua's backpack unto his lap. "Grab the Shofar and let's roll."

"Okay... okay," replied Yeshua. He opened his backpack and removed the ancient spiraled shaped ram's horn. He stood up and slung the Shofar over his back using its attached leather sling.

They all left Yeshua's room and heading down towards the beach through the central courtyard. Just a subtle hint of morning light appeared in the eastern sky across the Gulf of Aqaba over Saudi Arabia. A strong wind began blowing towards the east

"Did I die yesterday?" asked Yeshua as they reached the wide sandy beach. The crashing waves along the shoreline became quite loud as they walked closer to the water's edge. The full moon, now setting in the west, illuminated their path.

"No, you came close though," replied Mohammed. "You drowned while we were snorkeling. Taylor had to perform mouth to mouth resuscitation on you."

"Really? Mouth to mouth?" questioned Yeshua. He looked at Taylor and smiled. "You saved my life again; I am forever grateful."

"You are very welcome Yeshua. I would do anything for you, as you know," responded Taylor. "So, tell me more about the Shofar. I know the old Rabbi gave it to you the day before you came out of your coma when you were 13. And that it's some kind of time travel device. But where did it originally come from?"

"We think it's from the ram that Abraham sacrificed on Mount Moriah instead of Isaac," answered Mohammed.

"And the old Rabbi is actually the Prophet Enoch," said Yeshua.

"Enoch?" asked Taylor. "As in the Enoch from the Book of Enoch. The one who walked with God?"

"Yes, exactly," answered Yeshua. "He's also called the Angel Metatron and is basically God's chief emissary here on Earth."

"So, he's like in second in command to God?" questioned Taylor. "And he gave you that Shofar to do what exactly?"

"I think he actually gave it to us," replied Yeshua. "It's opened our eyes to our true nature. That we are here for a specific purpose."

"And what is our purpose? Why are we here?" asked Taylor.

"Sound the Shofar, and you will see," said Yeshua. He removed the Shofar from his back and handed it to Taylor. She held it upwards as both Yeshua and Mohammed placed one of their hands on it as well.

Taylor put the Shofar up to her lips and blew with all her might.

Ba-ba-baaaaaaaaaaaaaaa...

Ba-ba-baaaaaaaaaaaaaaaa...

Ba-ba-baaaaaaaaaaaaaaaa...

Everything went black.

Out of the darkness came a wonderful array of magical lights. At first everything was quite dim, and then a tunnel of infinite concentric circles formed in front of them.

The glowing lights became much brighter, and Yeshua, Mohammed and Taylor seemed to be flying through a streaming tunnel full of multicolored patterns and rotating circles.

"Taylor, are you there?" asked Yeshua, telepathically.

"Yes, I think so, I'm here," replied Taylor. "Although, I'm not exactly sure where 'here' is."

"We are in a time-space-continuum vortex," explained Mohammed as they zoomed though the mystical tunnel. "The Shofar portals us through a transcendental worm-hole that goes back in time as we are transformed into spiritual angelic forms. When we arrive on the other side, we won't be in our bodies, just apparitions. And we will have special powers: Yeshua can control water. I can control fire. And you… I assume you will be able to control the wind."

"And you said Avraham is one of us too? And that we are incarnations of the four Angels of the Presence?" asked Taylor. "What can he control?"

"Yes. That is who we are… the four Archangels. We stand in duty before the Lord of Spirits. And Avraham can control electricity," answered Yeshua. "The lightning."

From the end of the tunnel they saw a rapidly approaching bright light. Then they came out through the light at the end of the tunnel.

Their formless spirits were on the same exact spot on the beach. It was still dark and nearly dawn, and the enormous full moon hovered just above the western Sinai

Mountains. A strong wind still blew towards the east, making millions of ripples and waves in the Gulf as the tide appeared to be going backwards.

There was no hotel resort, or any buildings at all along the coastline. Tens of thousands of people in simple cloth garments were sleeping on beach as far as the eye could see. Surprisingly, from the water's edge... Mohammed's spirit seemed to be channeling smoke and dark vapor upward that formed a huge pillar of cloud above the Gulf of Aqaba. At the top of the cloud appeared some flames and fire.

"Mohammed, what the heck are you doing?" asked Taylor. "And who are all these people on the beach?"

"I'm not sure," replied Mohammed. "As soon as we came through the tunnel... I was channeling this huge pillar of smoke up into the air."

Suddenly, like alarms going off... the sounds of several shofars could be heard far to the west, closer to the opening in the mountains that led into the beach peninsula. A loud rumbling sound and a rising dust cloud could be seen from the slot canyon that Yeshua, Mohammed and Taylor had driven through the day before. Something was rapidly approaching the beach from the mountain trail. It sounded like hooves of hundreds of horses running in unison.

Almost all the people on the beach woke up at the sound of the shofars and the oncoming earthquake-like rumbling. Most of them looked scared, and the women and children huddled together in fear. Some of them started to cry, others started to scream in anger.

"I recognize exactly what is happening here," said Yeshua telepathically to his two friends. "This is the Exodus. We are here with Moses and the Israelites on the edge of Red Sea. The Egyptian army is approaching from the west."

"Oh my God," responded Taylor. "Are you sure?"

And Yeshua spoke some verses from the Book of Exodus...

"The Egyptians chased after them and overtook them encamped by the sea... every horse of Pharaoh's chariots, his horsemen, and his forces beside Pi-hahiroth, in front of Ba'al Zephon. Pharaoh drew near, and the children of Israel lifted up their eyes, and behold! The Egyptians were advancing after them. They were frightened, and the children of Israel cried out to the Lord."

"And what are we supposed to do now?" asked Taylor. "What is our purpose?"

"I know exactly what we need to do," replied Yeshua. "Mohammed, take your pillar of cloud and go behind the Israelites. Use the cloud pillar and block the Egyptians from coming through that mountain pass. NOW, Go!"

"Yes Sir!" said Mohammed. He quickly moved his spirit aura through the Israelite camp and pulled the huge pillar of cloud and smoke with him to the opening of the mountains, about two miles west of the edge of the water.

And Yeshua spoke some more verses of the Book of Exodus…

"Then the angel of God, who had been going in front of the Israelite camp, moved and went behind them, and the pillar of cloud moved away from in front of them and stood behind them. And he came between the camp of Egypt and the camp of Israel, and there was the cloud of darkness, and it illuminated the night, and one did not draw near the other all night long."

Just as the hundreds of chariots led by the Pharaoh arrived to attack the Hebrews, Mohammed channeled the clouds and smoke and made a fiery wall as a blockade at the opening of the pass. The angry and frustrated Pharaoh signaled for his army to immediately halt.

"And what should I do?" asked Taylor telepathically from her spirit aura, next to Yeshua's.

"When an old man holding a staff comes here and stretches his hand out of the sea, use your power to control the wind and blow it as hard as you can towards the east," explained Yeshua. "You will part the Red Sea."

"As you wish," replied Taylor.

Then, like clockwork… an old bearded man wearing a long white robe and holding a giant wooden staff walked up to the edge of the water and stood next to Yeshua and Taylor's spirit. He was certainly Moses, the great Jewish Prophet. Thousands of the frightened Israelites had followed him to the shoreline from their camps.

And Yeshua said…

"And Moses stretched out his hand over the sea, and the Lord led the sea with the strong wind all night, and He made the sea into dry land and the waters split."

The old man raised his right hand towards the ocean and held his wooden staff up high towards the sky. Taylor immediately channeled all her might and the already strong breeze blowing towards the east kicked up and changed into gale force winds. The surface of the water rippled and contorted as a narrow channel began to form in the ocean towards the other side of the Gulf.

Yeshua telepathically reached out to his best friend across the and sandy Nuwieba peninsula and said, "Mohammed, how's is going over there?"

"It's going well, my friend," communicated Mohammed. "These Egyptians are stuck in the valley and look pretty pissed off. I have them pinned down with this very awesome dark fiery cloud that seems to be flowing out of my ghost-like hands."

"Perfect, just keep them there until I give you the signal," replied Yeshua. "Then let them go."

"Yes Sir," responded Mohammed, telepathically.

Meanwhile, back on the beach… the entire population of hundreds of thousands of Hebrews had gathered on the shoreline as Moses held his outstretched hand towards the Red Sea. The strong wind continued to flow eastwards and separate the waters to the north and south. The light of dawn approached quickly from the east.

After some time… Taylor said to Yeshua, "I can't do this much longer anymore. That's as strong as I can make the wind blow. I can't seem to completely split the water all the way across the entire Sea down to dry land."

"Oh, I thought it was just the wind that splits the sea," replied Yeshua. "As the crow flies."

"Well I guess not!" yelled Taylor, seemingly struggling to channel the wind harder. "Can't you control water, as your special power? Get down there and help me out, Yeshua. Complete the miracle and make the entire tunnel of sea down to dry land."

"Yes ma'am," responded Yeshua. "On it!" He moved his formless spirit apparition down the beach and into the tunnel of wind coming from Taylor that was splitting the water apart within the long channel.

Yeshua focused all of his concentration on either side of the wind tunnel. With all his might, he pushed the water as strongly as he could with his powerful thoughts. Slowly, the water came apart as the all the land below became exposed. Along the shoreline, the Israelites stared in disbelief. Moses stepped down from his place on the beach and towards the opening in the water; however the whirlwinds were still super-strong coming from Taylor's hands. Moses almost fell over from the tornado-like blast of air.

"Yeshua, we have a problem," said Taylor telepathically. "My wind is too strong; the people won't be able to walk through the water tunnel."

"Oh gosh," replied Yeshua. "I hadn't thought about that."

"What's going on over there?" asked Mohammed, still controlling the cloud of smoke and fire.

"The wind from Taylor is way too powerful and will prevent anyone from walking out into the Red Sea," explained Yeshua. "And I've had to move out into the waters and push everything apart as the wind wasn't strong enough."

"Well, if Taylor stops the wind... can you just continue to push the walls of water apart?" asked Mohammed. "It's simple physics. Can you hold it until all the Hebrews have walked to the other side?"

"I hope so," replied Yeshua. "Actually, yes. I know so... I can do it. Taylor, you stop channeling the wind."

Taylor, now completely exhausted from her divine channeling... stopped blasting the wind forward. As the gusts subsided, Yeshua felt the full force of millions of gallons of water rush backwards towards the dry channel in the middle of the Gulf.

He prayed to God for strength and again, with all his might, he pushed the waters back and said...

"Then the children of Israel came into the midst of the sea on dry land, and the waters were to them as a wall from their right and from their left."

Along the shoreline… the thousands of Hebrews, led by Moses, began their trek across the floor of the Red Sea. They calmly moved forward, in-between the tall walls of water. In the east, the sun crested over the Saudi Arabia Mountains. Glorious sunlight poured over the Gulf of Aqaba and the vast beaches of Nuweiba.

"Guys, I have a problem," said Mohammed telepathically to his friends.

"What's that? Are you okay?" asked Taylor. She had just watched the last few Israelites enter the water tunnel and follow the rest of the Hebrews towards the other side of the Sea.

"I thought I could do this indefinitely," said Mohammed. "However, I'm getting very tired. I don't think I can keep this cloud going much longer. It's been hours now, and I'm literally running out of steam."

"Okay, hold on a bit longer," said Yeshua. "Moses and the Israelites are almost halfway through the tunnel. They've just passed me and are almost out of harms way."

"I'm really sorry," said Mohammed," I can't seem to hold on anymore. My power seems to have been drained… and I'm fading."

"What? No… don't let the cloud barrier go just yet," exclaimed Yeshua, still holding the walls of water apart.

"They need more time... or the Pharaoh's army will catch up with them."

"I... I... can't anymore," cried Mohammed. "I'm fading."

Suddenly, Mohammed spirit collapsed. The massive pillar of fire and cloud slowly lifted up from the mountain pass and upwards in the new mornings sky. Instantly, hundreds of Egyptian chariots surged forward and toward the beach's shoreline and the water tunnel filled with the fleeing Israelites.

"I'm fading too," said Taylor telepathically. "I can't seem to stay awake... I'm... I..."

"Taylor, Mohammed! Are you there?" yelled out Yeshua as the last Israelite passed his spirit form along the dry tunnel at the bottom of the Gulf of Aqaba. In the distance, to the west... he could see the oncoming legion of Egyptian charioteers racing towards him.

Above, in the sky... Mohammed's cloud of smoke and fire had moved directly over the Egyptians. Ominous lightning bolts shot out in all directions from tall cloud and loud thunder rumbled in the valleys. An intense glowing light emanated from the top of the cloud.

Yeshua looked up at the cloud in awe, as the Egyptians scrambled in fear. He felt his strength disappearing, and he knew he couldn't hold up the water much longer.

Yeshua recited one more time from the Book of Exodus...

"It came about in the morning watch that the Lord looked down over the Egyptian camp through a pillar of cloud, and He threw the Egyptian camp into confusion. And He removed the wheels of their chariots, and He led them with heaviness, and the Egyptians said... Let me run away from the Israelites because the Lord is fighting for them against the Egyptians."

In the distance, on the Saudi Arabian coast to the east, in the land of Midian... the last Hebrew reached dry land. The entire Egyptian Chariot army, save for the Pharaoh and his Generals who watched from the shoreline... were stuck in the channel of water in the Red Sea. Moses stretched out his hand over the waters... and Yeshua lost consciousness as all his energy was finally depleted. Everything went black.

CHAPTER 13

SAMYAZA

The relaxing sounds of gentle waves washed up on the shore, and seagulls filled the air. The warm mid morning sun slowly ascended in the eastern sky. Yeshua, face down in the sand… felt a splash of salty water on his face as the high tide approached. He opened his eyes and saw the empty small wooden dock of the Aten Nuweiba Beach Hotel just a few feet away. Next to him were the motionless bodies of Mohammed and Taylor lying on the beach.

"Guys, guys… wake up!" yelled Yeshua as he tried to pull himself up from the sand. He was very weak. He crawled over Taylor and shook her firmly.

"Taylor, are you okay? Wake up!" said Yeshua. "Please, get up…"

Taylor opened her eyes. She looked up at Yeshua and smiled.

"We did it. We went back and parted the Red Sea," said Taylor very softly. "Or was is just a dream?"

"A dream you dream alone is only a dream," replied Yeshua. "A dream you dream together is a reality. That's one of my favorite quotes from John Lennon."

"Ugggh… did you get the license plate of that chariot?" joked a very groggy Mohammed. He pulled himself up to a sitting position on the beach. "I feel absolutely wiped out."

"I guess being an Archangel and changing the world is pretty hard work," said Taylor. "You weren't kidding when you said the Shofar is a biblical time travel device."

"Speaking of the Shofar, Yeshua... where is it?" asked Mohammed.

"It should be right here," responded Yeshua. He looked around calmly, then stood up and seemed to panic when he couldn't locate it. "Where is it? It's always lying nearby when we come back."

Mohammed and Taylor also stood up and looked around the nearby beach for the Shofar, without luck.

"Hey guys, it that Youssef rowing away in the skiff boat out there in the water?" asked Taylor.

"I think so," replied Yeshua. "And wait a sec... he's got the Shofar slung around his back. What the heck!"

"Youssef! Youssef!" yelled Mohammed and Yeshua, standing on the edge of the water and waving their arms. Mohammed yelled some more words in Arabic very loudly.

The man on the boat turned and looked back at the three Israelis on the beach. His eyes were bright red, almost glowing and there was a deep scar on the left side of his face.

"I don't think that's Youssef stealing your Shofar," said Taylor. "That's the dark Angel from my dream. That's Samyaza, leader of the Watchers."

TO BE CONTINUED...

ABOUT THE AUTHOR

Joshua Kreithen was born on a Sunday morning, October 18th, 1970 in Albert Einstein Hospital in Philadelphia, Pennsylvania to Leslie and Marvin Kreithen.

His parents are descendants of Eastern European Jews who escaped religious persecution and arrived in America as immigrants in the early 20th century. His Grandfather, 'Zayda' Jacob Kreithen came to Ellis Island as a teenager and spent most of his lifetime supporting his family as a 'cutter' in a men's clothing manufacturing warehouse in Philadelphia. His favorite hobbies were listening to opera and painting, and his artistic creative passion has been passed down to all of his descendants.

At the age of 13, Joshua became a Bar Mitzvah at the Ohev Shalom of in Bucks County in Richboro, PA. As a customary practice during this ancient rite of passage into adulthood, all Bar Mitzvas would choose a special project to share during their Bar Mitzvah service. Joshua's project was focused on Kabbalah, based on ancient Jewish Mysticism.

Joshua went on to go to medical school and become a surgeon; he completed a plastic surgery fellowship at the University of Florida. He chose to combine all of his artistic, medical and technical skills to become a plastic and reconstructive surgeon and in addition to being an accomplished physician… he is a painter, photographer, musician and published writer.

Dr. Kreithen currently lives in Sarasota, Florida with his beautiful wife, Melissa… who always serves as a source of inspiration and vision for his creative endeavors.

www.ingramcontent.com/pod-product-compliance
Lightning Source LLC
Chambersburg PA
CBHW060153260626
47160CB00001B/253